Stark Nakid

by Sean McGinnis

Deux Voiliers Publishing

Aylmer, Quebec

First Edition

Copyright © 2014 by Sean McGinnis

All rights reserved.

Published in Canada by Deux Voiliers Publishing, Aylmer, Quebec.

www.deuxvoilierspublishing.com

Library and Archives Canada Cataloguing in Publication

McGinnis, Sean, 1958-, author
        Stark Nakid / Sean McGinnis.

Issued in print and electronic formats.
ISBN 978-1-928049-11-1 (pbk.).--ISBN 978-1-928049-21-0 (Ingram pbk.).--ISBN 978-1-928049-13-5 (kindle).--ISBN 978-1-928049-16-6 (smashwords-epub)

        I. Title.

PS8625.G57S73 2014   C813'.6

                                                        C2014-908013-

                                                        C2014-908014-

Legal deposit – Bibliothèque et Archives nationales du Québec, 2014

Cover image by Ivan Kesic, used with permission.

Red Tuque Books distributes *Stark Nakid* in Canada. Please place your Canadian independent bookstore and library orders with RTB at www.redtuquebooks.ca. *Stark Nakid* is distributed in and outside of Canada by Ingram to wholesalers and bookstores under the ISBN 978-1-928049-20-3.

For Lori

I'm naked without you.

It is the dim haze of mystery that adds enchantment to pursuit.
—Antoine de Rivarol

Chapter One

On the ninth ring he sprang from the bed like a jungle cat, flung the covers clear across the room and lunged wildly for the phone. Grunting acknowledgement, he scrawled the address on a matchbook cover and slammed the receiver home. The game was afoot. After kicking a path through the empty Kokanee cans to the office window, he tore open the heavy velvet curtains and stumbled back as the bright sunlight hit his bloodshot eyes like a sack of wet cement. He struggled with the sill, yanked it free, stuck his head out and breathed in the city—narrowly avoiding the large neon letter *O* that hung ominously from the side of the building.

Ten minutes later he sat in his usual booth at the Mangy Moose Café, scoffing down the so-called special and washing it down with six cups of the best java this side of the Selkirks. The new waitress sauntered over and stood like a vision before him, her upper lip quivering with what he could only assume was unrequited lust. Her lips were full, painted a naughty shade of red and her teeth were as white as a bunny in a blizzard. A thick mane of shaggy blond hair fell wildly on her tropically tanned shoulders as the seam of her black stockings crept up to caress a perfect calf, pause briefly behind a much too sensuous knee, and kiss the hem of a red leather miniskirt that would have drawn stares in Rio. The rest of her uniform, some sort of spray-on black latex, revealed a cleavage that would make the Pope cry.

He managed to close his gaping mouth long enough to slyly wink at her. She rolled her eyes skyward, apparently thanking God for his presence, and tapped her pencil on the edge of the table. He leaned forward and whispered those three words women love to hear. She leaned in close and whispered two back. Had the second word been "me" instead of "you" it might have been the start of something big. He forced his gaze up to meet her sea-green eyes.

"What's your name, sweet cheeks?"

She had a voice so husky it could have pulled a sled.

"Get stuffed."

"I'm Nakid. Stark Nakid."

She frowned, dropped a business card on the table and vaguely gestured to the gent at the lunch counter before leaving. His dark blue suit appeared stretched to the limit, unsuccessfully attempting to house a Hulk-like body. He nodded toward Stark, flexing the side muscles in his enormous neck, which made the guillotine tattoo rise and fall.

Stark glanced down at the business card and spewed a mouthful of coffee on the window. He began to sweat, gasp and cough uncontrollably. The elderly woman in the next booth had to come over and slap him on the back to keep him from choking. He wheeled her back to her table and thanked her profusely. The Hulk got up and stomped swiftly out the door. Stark's hand trembled as he took the matchbook cover from his pocket and placed it next to the card on the table—the address matched. Bolting to his feet, Stark slammed a ten-spot on the table, raced out the door, hopped on a bus and headed toward destiny.

Chapter Two

The bus driver dropped Stark at a bench a few blocks shy of his destination in the high-rent district of the North Shore. He checked his hardware (some martial-arts throwing stars, a can of silly string and some pistachio nuts) and pulled up the collar of his black three-button suit jacket in a vain attempt to halt the annoying spray of a nearby lawn sprinkler. To avoid being followed he took the scenic route, scrambled over several hedges, set off two motion-sensor alarms and narrowly avoided the fangs of a pit bull. He emerged cautiously from a grove of bamboo and gazed up at the target residence.

The Dreadlock Mansion, a three-and-a-half storey, sixteen-thousand-square-foot Tudor-style behemoth, sat majestically on a thirteen-acre estate, overlooking Kootenay Lake with a hint of arrogance and a lot of bad taste. He spotted the Mexican gardener, a grizzled-looking old man with a nasty scar on his forehead, cutting a hedge into the shape of a chicken and decided to grill him for information. Stark's high school Spanish was a little rusty but good enough to discover that the gardener wasn't Mexican and spoke only a slurred dialect of English. Stark offered him a smoke and was reaching for his Zippo when the gardener pulled a wooden match from his tattered coveralls and struck it on the leathery skin of his neck. Stark winced. The gardener smoked like a man siphoning gas, then coughed, wretched and hacked hysterically before collapsing in a heap on the freshly mowed lawn.

Deciding to forego the rest of the interview, Stark made his way to the front door. An eerie rendition of "Mack the Knife" began when he pressed the horse head-shaped doorbell. The massive black door opened a crack, held by a man overdressed enough to serve royalty. He looked Stark up and down several times before advising him that deliveries were to be made in the rear.

"The name is Nakid."

Stark handed him a business card and gave him the sneer he reserved for old ladies with ten items in the nine-items-or-less line.

"Your boss is expecting me."

The butler led him down a hall as wide as the driveway and dramatically opened a set of twelve-foot-high double doors that led into what he referred to as the library. The room appeared much like a half-size version of the Sistine chapel, although the ceiling design was a little sacrilegious. The fresco looming two stories above appeared to be a combination of the famous paintings *The Last Supper* and *Dogs Playing Poker*. The walls were lined with floor-to-ceiling bookshelves, including a complex series of catwalks and ladders, while a fire the size of a Volkswagen blazed in the marble hearth. Glancing around in awe, Stark made a mental note to check his mailbox to see if he had made it into the final round of the Reader's Digest Sweepstakes.

The unmistakable sound of an impatient man clearing his throat broke Stark out of his reverie. Whirling around, he dropped low to the ground, right leg straight out, left hand held high in the classic Wu-style tai chi posture "Panther Tests the Water," before springing to his feet and finding himself nose to nose with the most famous beak in town. Anton Ratzlaff's ruthless reputation preceded him, as did his nose and nickname, the Rat.

"Glad you could make it, 'Kid."

The blue eyes were friendly but the voice held a menacing tone.

"Can I get you a drink?"

"I never drink on the job, thanks. I'll have a Flaming Blue Flamingo, or a beer if you're out of the little umbrellas."

Stark noticed for the first time that the Rat wore an Armani tux.

"You're probably wondering why I asked you here."

The Rat offered a cigarillo from a sleek gold case. Stark reached for three.

"No thanks. I don't smoke."

The Rat lit Stark's cigarillo, lit a cigar the size of a small dog for himself and handed Stark a beer before collapsing heavily into a forest green leather armchair that dwarfed his bulky frame. He motioned to the opposite chair with a puffy, ring-laden hand.

"I want you to find something for me."

He exhaled a mushroom cloud of cigar smoke.

"I want you to find some*one*."

"I am flattered, Mr. Ratzlaff, but if you follow the bankruptcy notices in the *Nelson Daily Crow*, you'll know I'm no longer employed in the criminal investigation industry."

The Rat ignored the comment and rudely shoved an eight-by-ten glossy an inch in front of Stark's nose.

"I'd like you to find this woman."

"She has all the right pieces in all the right places. Were those surgically enhanced?"

Stark studied the photo, took a large pull on his beer and silently acknowledged the contribution that spandex had made to the world.

"You're a funny man, Nakid. Probably not the first time you've heard that."

The Rat chortled, shot an evil glare and ground out his cigar in a chrome ashtray the size of a truck tire before continuing.

"Ordinarily I'd have one of my own boys do a job like this, but I need a man who is more discreet. A man of a thousand faces. A man whose liver I can rip out if he screws up."

"I'm your man then, Mr. Ratzlaff. I'm a man of a thousand voices and 'incognito' was my mother's maiden name."

The Rat raised one of his overly developed eyebrows and grunted.

"If you can find her I'll make you a rich man."

"You mean a rich*er* man."

The Rat snatched the photo from Stark's hand and fondled it in a disturbing manner. Stark took the opportunity to pound the remainder of his beer.

"Just my normal fee of two thousand a day plus expenses will suffice. I'm in this business for the good of mankind, not for the money."

"I happen to know your standard fee is two hundred a day and you eat your own expenses, but under the circumstances I'll meet your price."

He sighed loudly, sniffed and dramatically wiped a tear from his eye before continuing.

"I have my demons, 'Kid. I was raised by a mobster who drove my mother insane. Naturally I became one myself. My sister was disowned when she became a police officer instead of a criminal. She died in the line of duty many years ago. The woman in this photo is my daughter —although we've never met—and my only heir. My wife and I never had any children. I recently became aware that an affair I had two decades ago with one of our maids produced offspring. The mob business is not as honourable as you might think. I survived two assassination attempts in the past year alone. I may not be around much longer. I want you to find my daughter, Stark."

Stark couldn't tell how much truth the story held. He took the photo and let himself out. Near the end of the hundred foot long driveway stood a small Tudor-style servant's cottage that housed the last remaining descendent of Charles Dreadlock, the famous railroad tycoon. His grandson Damian Dreadlock, the crooked city councillor, was rumoured to prefer the modesty of the coach house to the grandeur of the mansion. The gardener continued snoozing on the lawn as Stark walked past him through the large wrought-iron gates. Away from the lifestyles of the rich and famous, back to the lifestyles of Joe and Jane Average.

Chapter Three

Watson arrived back at the lodgings at 221 Baker Street just before tea time and asked Mrs. Hudson, the housekeeper who lived on the ground floor, to add some shortbread cookies to the tray. Often finding the climb up the five flights of stairs with a full tray a challenge, Watson was not surprised to arrive in the penthouse suite without cookies or teacups on the tray. He arrived just in time to see Holmes entertaining a prospective client in the waiting room. Before Watson could set the tray down or make introductions, Holmes leaned back in the chair and launched into the usual spiel regarding the scope and breadth of their investigative skills. The client, who sat in the opposite wingback chair before the fire, leaned forward to listen closer, placing his bowler hat on his lap. Watson noticed the elbow patch on the left hand sleeve of his suit jacket appeared considerably more worn than the right, indicating that the man either had a poor sense of balance or drove a 1956 Nash Metropolitan. The Nash was famous for having an armrest made of something akin to steel wool. He himself had driven one in younger years, the amphibious model, which made a damn fine canoe as well. Watson fidgeted, preparing to slip in a question regarding the car, when Holmes noticed him standing at the doorway and signalled to keep silent by loudly clearing phlegm and hawking a large mass of it into the fire, then turning back to address the client.

"Mr. Ramsbottam, allow me to demonstrate the art of deductive reasoning. Your sloppy attire indicates that you left your fourth-floor hotel room this morning at 7:05, later than usual due to your ill-timed decision to 'polish the penguin.' The dribble stain on the front of your tweed trousers indicates a larger-than-average phallus, a fact that made you popular with your nannies and gym teachers but not with your father. The logo inside your hatband reveals your attendance at an exclusive, private boys school located near Tofino on Vancouver Island, Saint Cedric's School for the Endowed, which led to bouts of depression and general despair, no doubt caused by the constant buggering and ritual abuse administered by the Gregorian sect of brothers who served as your teachers. The bouts of depression resulted in years of facial reconstructive surgery, after a rather nasty band-saw accident in woodwork class caused by inattention and a poorly timed slap on the back of the head delivered by brother Siegfried, who later did some jail time. This ultimately led to your mother having an affair with the plastic surgeon, damaging her somewhat tenuous union with your father, to the point where he fled with his fortune to South America, only to die a year later in the arms of a young transvestite whom he met while pursuing his dream to perform on stage in the chorus of *La Cage aux Folles*. Your mother in turn married the surgeon due to his remarkable stamina between the sheets, but she has not yet revealed to you that your birth father was a gay porn star she met while in a drug rehab clinic."

The man seemed stunned, as he had been earlier that morning at the hotel when he located his wife under the front desk servicing the concierge. He covered his face with his hands and began to weep softly, then bolted to his feet and dashed out the door.

"There goes another client. Damn and blast, Holmes, must you continue to scrutinize every person you meet and make inappropriate comments regarding their personal habits or embarrassing episodes from their past?"

"Watson, you really don't see the bigger picture, do you? Everyone has a secret, old boy, even you. I merely shine a light into the dark. I lift the manhole cover to shed light on the sewer below. 'Stars hide your fires, let not light see my black and deep desires'—*Macbeth*, act one, scene three. You know my methods, Watson—do not challenge them."

Watson excused himself and left the room muttering. Holmes sat speaking on the telephone with both feet up on the desk when Watson returned in his loungewear.

"If I might quote Douglas Adams, madam, 'the word "impossible" is not in my dictionary. In fact, everything from "herring" to "marmalade" appears to be missing.' Alas, I am at present far too busy to take your case, interesting as it seems, given the circumstances of your daughter's disappearance. Perhaps I could suggest a colleague of mine to help you. He resides in this very building, down one floor, at the end of the hall. The name is N-A-K-I-D, pronounced nah-keed, but everyone calls him Stark. While his methods may be unusual, he is perhaps the most gifted student I ever instructed at the Vallican Hole School of Stealth, Detection and Hard Knocks."

"Are you giving away more of our business, Holmes? Perhaps we should ask Stark if he wishes to join us as an independent consultant."

Holmes slammed down the phone and leapt out of the chair. The pipe that had gone out sparked to life once more, lifting blue clouds of smoke toward the ceiling. Watson left the room to change the sign on their door from "Open" to "Closed" and returned to find an animated Holmes pacing before the fireplace.

"Damn it, Watson. I hope to God we are not already too late. If we are fleet of foot, old chum, we may yet be able to prevent a murder. 'Though this be madness, yet there is method in it'—*Hamlet*, act two, scene two. Let us blow like the wind, Watson, a harsh, hot, unpredictable Santa Ana wind. Do you have your revolver at hand?"

"I'm in my housecoat and pajamas, Holmes, as I always am after tea time. Why would I have my revolver on me?"

"Not on you, Watson. At hand. Damn and blast, man. At hand. Any fool can see you are wearing a housecoat and pajamas—the ones I gave you last Christmas, I believe, emerald green flannel with binoculars and magnifying glasses on them. Quite smart. They complement your figure and are both boyish and manly at the same time. The pajamas do clash with the brown bear-claw slippers you always seem to wear. Although I must say that your choice of housecoat, a vintage black smoking jacket, is a perfect match for the pajamas. I digress, Watson. Is or is not your revolver at hand?"

"It is in the desk there, as always, Holmes. Keep in mind it is a .32 calibre 1906 Webley Scott Bulldog loaded with blanks. We ran out of bullets for it years ago. I don't believe they make them anymore. We don't have a permit for it anyway, and handguns are illegal in Canada."

"Illegal. Preposterous. If you recall 'The Curious Case of Mr. Winky,' the murder weapon was a pistol."

"The man was an Olympic biathlete, Holmes. If you recall, he shot his training partner on the cross-country trail with his biathlon rifle."

"You are mistaken, Watson. That was 'The Adventure of the Baloney Pony.' It is of no consequence. Keep your revolver at the ready, old chum, and pray that we don't need it."

Chapter Four

Stark thought about it all the way back to the office and remained thinking about it when he stepped off of the bus in front of 221 Baker Street. The first three floors of the heritage building housed the Smoking Hound Bed and Beverage, a small inn offering budget accommodations complete with a complimentary morning cocktail. The Smoking Hound catered primarily to the hung-over skier and backpacker crowd as well as wealthier vagrants. Above it sat a floor of offices, with a rooftop deck and penthouse above that. The penthouse sat above Stark's office with the rooftop deck at the opposite end of the building. The tenants of the penthouse were two of his former instructors from the Vallican Hole School, who ran a consulting detective service on the side. It worked out well for Stark since he often got their spillover clients as well as those without a sense of direction.

Climbing the five flights of hardwood stairs two at a time, he arrived gasping and wheezing before totally collapsing against the stairway railing. After regaining his composure, he realized that he had once again climbed one flight too many, staggered back down and lurched toward the far end of the hall. He leaned against the door marked "Stark Investigations," below which the latest in a continuing series of bad mottos read "Walk Tall—Hire a Big Dick." As Stark searched for a key, his uncanny spidey-sense tingled, detecting the unmistakable sound of a diseased elk baying to the moon. Instinctively he dropped to the ground, placing his ear to the floor in the classic Chen-style tai chi posture "Monkey Listens for a Train," before leaping effortlessly to his feet again. Using his shoulder for a key, he discovered the sound to be the answering machine stuck in the rewind mode.

Since the office sat directly above the Hound Dog Honeymoon Suite, Stark kept a broom propped against the wall, always at the ready. The office consisted of an outer waiting room that housed a worn brown leather chesterfield opposite a large black one-way glass window. The wall next to the inner office door held a "Now Serving Number . . ." digital sign, as well as a number dispenser. A fifty-inch flat-screen television clung to the wall at the end of the room. A frosted-glass door led to the inner office, which was furnished with a large oak desk that sported a black dial telephone and a twenty-seven inch iMac. Two brown leather Queen Anne armchairs sat opposite the desk. The walls were lined with bookshelves filled with large dusty volumes inherited from previous tenants, some of Stark's favourite novels and his collection of obscure pop-up books. Two large mullioned windows framed the desk chair, providing a view of Baker Street below. A smaller room that could be accessed off the inner office housed a kitchenette and a small dining table. A Murphy bed hid ever hopeful in a curtained alcove at the far end of the room.

Stark sat at the desk, leaning far enough back in the chair to peek out the window at the street below. A tall dark figure in a trench coat stood illuminated by the streetlamp on the corner, smoking a cigarette. Stark pulled an envelope out of his coat pocket and placed it on the desk. According to the Rat, the mystery photo had arrived in the morning mail unaccompanied by a note. The envelope bore a local postmark and the address appeared to be written in a woman's hand. This would narrow the field of suspects to three or four thousand.

Stark took a closer look at the photo. She had long raven-black hair, almond-shaped deep-brown eyes, full sensuous lips and the good fortune of not having inherited her father's immense beak. The phone rang and the elk started baying again. He put the answering machine out of its misery with the heel of his shoe.

"Stark Investigations. You plug 'em, we plant 'em."

"Are you Nakid?"

The voice sounded so sexy he was afraid to stand.

"I was born Nakid."

His tone remained manly yet grovelling while he attempted to undress her with his ears.

"You met with the Rat today. I think we should talk. I'll meet you in front of the Snoring Elk Hotel at six tomorrow morning."

"Six in the morning? What are you, a rooster?"

"I work nights. Make sure you're not followed."

The line went dead.

When the alarm clock on the bedside table sounded at 5:00 a.m., Stark put a shot glass through it. He was startled awake at ten to six by the ear splitting sound of the back-up alarm, Barry Manilow's "Copacabana," blaring from the clock radio on his office desk. Throwing golf balls at it from the bucket next to the bed proved futile, as did throwing the bucket. Forced to get up, he shut it off with a nine iron. Stark dressed quickly in the clothes he had carefully laid out in a heap at the foot of the bed, raced out the door and ran the twelve blocks to his destination. As he ran by the Poodle Noodle, a hip local take-out joint where you could order anything you wanted as long as it looked like noodles and smelled like poodles, he caught a glimpse of his reflection in the smoked glass. He removed the several bits of Kleenex from his freshly shaven face.

While stopping to catch his breath in front of the Wasted Giraffe, one of twelve gourmet coffee shops within eyesight along Baker Street, he noticed a woman pacing on the sidewalk near the Ward Street entrance of the Snoring Elk Hotel. As Stark drew nearer he recognized her as the surgically enhanced subject in the photo and reflected that this could be just about the easiest two grand he had ever made. Halfway through the crosswalk a sudden movement from above startled him into action. He instinctively drew his feet into a cat stance, open hands above his head crossed at the wrist, forming the Yang-style tai chi posture "White Crane Soils his Nest." Stark froze in horror at the image above him. He tried to scream but when his voice froze he could only stare. The baby grand piano fell about four stories—in slow motion it seemed—and landed with a thunderous, sickening crash, smack on top of the woman in the photo. She would never play it again.

Chapter Five

Stark spent the next five hours as the honoured guest of the Nelson City Police Homicide Squad. Inspector Franco San Francisco was as happy as ever to see him.

"For Christ's sake, Nakid, you were holding her hand when we got there. You're telling me you were just walking by and thought she needed consoling?"

As usual the Inspector sweated like a moose.

"I thought she might be in need of medical attention—she appeared rather depressed."

Inspector Franco, a man who would make Mike Tyson look pretty, took a crumpled pack of Camels out of his sweat-soaked shirt pocket and crushed them in front of Stark's nose.

A few hours later, Stark thanked Detective Sergeant Harry Stuttgart for so kindly escorting him out of the police headquarters building and into a pile of rubbish and discarded boxes in the alley off of Stanley Street. Harry grunted savagely and slammed the door in Stark's face. As he picked stale Chinese food from his hair, Stark seriously considered taking Harry off his Christmas card list.

Since a five-hour grilling tends to make a throat dry, Stark meandered over to the Blushing Beaver Lounge at the Queen Bee Hotel on Baker Street to hoist a few to the memory of a certain exotic ex-piano player. He wandered in between shows and felt fortunate to find a vacant stool located along the polished oak counter just far enough from the stage to avoid discarded apparel or any chance of audience participation and just close enough to the bar to ensure fast beverage delivery. The waitress, a ravishing brunette with endless legs and muscular shoulders, sashayed over to take his order. She wore a bright peacock-blue Hawaiian dress that revealed a lack of tan lines, and she smelled delicious.

"Marry me, Breeze. I've got the certificate all filled out. You just have to say yes to make me the happiest man in the room, this far from the stage."

"In your dreams, Starkers."

She crinkled her baby-blue eyes and asked if the usual would suffice.

"The frostier the better, Breeze. You know in my dreams you wear a Catwoman suit and I wear those big Mickey Mouse gloves. Give it some thought."

She giggled and left for another patron. Stark stayed for three beers and two shows, including a spectacular tribute to Katy Perry's failed marriage and a medley of rude sailor songs played rather creatively on a clarinet, before leaving by the rear exit. He had his hand on the door when a photo in the "Coming Attractions" showcase caught his eye. Right beside a poster of this week's feature attraction, "Miss Nude Slocan City," sat an eight-by-ten photo of a beautiful bikini-clad woman, with long raven-black hair and almond-shaped, deep-brown eyes, who would definitely not be appearing next week.

Chapter Six

The headline said it all: "Piano Squashes Woman Like Bug." The journalistic integrity of the *Nelson Daily Crow* never failed to amaze. Stark quickly scanned down the page, past the full-colour photograph of a hand sticking out from underneath a crushed piano, to get to the meat of the story. Apparently the moving company involved, Two Small Men with Sore Backs, had gotten an early start moving the alleged musical murder weapon up to the rooftop lounge, in order to avoid the morning rush hour. The safety strap around the killer keyboard had suddenly come unbuckled and the instrument became airborne. The movers were now reportedly in the care of a professional grief counsellor. Information on the victim was sketchy, due to the usual search for the next of kin. The only identifying clue released indicated that the victim could be a female of about forty years of age. Stark froze and let the paper fall to the sidewalk.

By the time he bounded up the stairs to reach his office door Stark stood sweating like a sumo wrestler in a steam room. As he shoved the key into the lock, the door suddenly swung wide open and he fell heavily into the room. Instinctively rolling behind the brown leather chesterfield, he sprang up in a policeman's crouch, with both hands lifted high, palms forward, fingers clenched into claws, the left knee held high in the classic Chen-style tai chi posture "Tiger Steps on a Nail." Spotting a movement of light across the room, he covered the twelve feet in seconds, leapt skyward and levelled a savage kick at the inner office door, sending deadly shards of frosted glass and splinters of door frame hurtling into the room. After quickly panning the room while crouched down on one knee, right hand palm down and cupped over the eyebrows, left arm straight out, hand palm up in the Sun-style tai chi posture "Panda Seeks Spare Change," he instinctively rolled again, springing up near the beer fridge. Clothes, books, files and loose papers were scattered carelessly around the room. The place looked like Montreal after the '98 ice storm. Stark exhaled sharply.

"Thank God."

Everything was just as he'd left it.

Stark grabbed a fresh cold one from the fridge, lit up a Mehari's Sweet Orient cigarillo and began digging through the cluttered desk drawer in search of the big magnifying glass. He located it in less than half an hour, along with three Bic lighters, a pair of tickets to a Nelson Leafs hockey game, four bottle openers, a Captain Crunch decoder ring and an instruction manual for Windows 95 that had been missing for some time. He examined the front-page photo from the *Nelson Daily Crow* hoping to confirm a hunch. A detail in the photo suddenly hit him like a rock in the forehead. With the speed and dexterity of a disoriented kangaroo, he rifled through the desk drawer and placed the Rat's photo and the newspaper photo side by side on the desktop. In the newspaper photo, the hand sticking out from under the piano sported what appeared to be a modest wedding band, a ring that he recognized from holding the victim's hand, as a tattoo. In the Rat's photo, the lovely spandex model had no such marking.

Stark hid the evidence in the usual spot. He walked over to the bookcase and selected one of the larger volumes that had come with the office when he leased the premises a half-dozen years prior. The old book smelled of must but would provide enough space to discretely hide the photos. As he randomly opened volume one of the three-volume *Whatever Floats Your Boat: A Stern History of British Columbia Sternwheelers*, a letter fell out. The letter bore the address of a Mr. S. Nakid at Suite 4B, 221 Baker Street. The letter looked a little worse for wear and the postmark confirmed it had been mailed to Stark's address the year after his birth. The return address noted a Mr. Sanchez somewhere in Cuba. Stark placed the letter and the photos in the book and returned it to the bookshelf.

Stark stopped in at the Mangy Moose for the Monday night special —Spam meatloaf smothered in something that resembled mushroom gravy. Just like mother used to make—awful. The lust of his life appeared to be off shift, leaving him to gaze at the less than spectacular tattoo artwork of her replacement, Lonesome Bill LaRue, who doubled as the cook and the evening's musical entertainment. Stark washed down the special with several steaming cups of the house-blend coffee—rich, dark and with the kind of bite only a pit bull could deliver. He stayed for a tearful rendition of "Danny Boy" played on a comb-and-wax-paper harmonica that garnered a standing ovation from the sparse audience. He left Bill a sizeable tip and complimented him on the motorcycle-jumping-the-bus tattoo on his left forearm.

Chapter Seven

The next morning, when Stark stopped by the Mangy Moose for a quick coffee, his dream waitress sauntered over and handed him a note from Lonesome Bill LaRue. The note contained a name and an address. Elle Eldorado was the name of the murder victim—the same woman who had called his office earlier. She lived up the lake in Kaslo, where everyone knew her as L.L. She had managed the Sneaky Tiki Cocktail Lounge in the Cranky Bear Inn for the past decade. L.L. was a single mom whose daughter, Awesome, had left home for the bright lights of Nelson and the blackjack-dealer program at the Kootenay School of Darts after graduating high school.

Awesome Eldorado helped pay for her education by dancing part-time at the Blushing Beaver Lounge and lived in a condo on the right and the wrong side of the tracks. The building had begun as a diesel locomotive shop that serviced the powerful locomotive engines that pulled freight trains throughout the twisting mountain tracks of the Kootenays. The big steel-frame building closed in the early seventies and had sat rusting on the tracks for thirty-five years before being converted into apartment condominium units by an out-of-town developer who quickly turned the insolvent building into an insolvent investment. Once the bank foreclosed, the units were converted into a housing cooperative for low-income residents. The majority of the local population, who had chosen to live in Nelson for the lifestyle and not the income, welcomed the conversion.

Awesome had a nice apartment on the top floor of the four-storey building, complete with a lake view balcony. The developer bought the building for a dollar from the Grand Funk Railroad but went bankrupt before completing the deal to buy the land. The old diesel shop sat smack in the middle of the Nelson rail yard with only the main-line track still in use. The developers, Rail to Grail, had hoped that the sale of the condos would allow them to buy up the rest of the unused rail yard for pennies on the dollar. When sales were underwhelming, the land purchase dissolved, the main-line track diversion disappeared and plans for the rail yard's development did as well. As a result the housing co-op stood proudly in the middle of an abandoned rail yard, surrounded by tracks and without any nearby parking. The main-line trains rumbled through the ground floor lobby twice a day. Tenants noted that even though they were close enough to touch a train as it passed, the noise and intense vibrations went un-noticed after a few months. With no parking lot in place the tenants had to park up on Vernon Street and then walk down to the yard and step over several sets of tracks to get to the building. Stark would have to do the same.

Not a day went by that Stark did not utilize the skills gained from his stealth training at the Vallican Hole. Whether slipping unnoticed through a crowded shopping mall dressed in a foam rubber Gumby suit or infiltrating a secure government animal-testing lab dressed as a Labrador retriever, he felt as comfortable in his own skin as in any disguise. Stark decided to go with one of the oldest tricks in his playbook: pizza delivery. As a professional, Stark would not stoop to use a frozen pizza, nor would he use the same kind of pizza for every occasion. Stark custom-designed each pizza to suit the tastes of the intended recipient, even though they would never receive it. For Awesome, he chose an alligator pie, his own recipe of four cheeses with onion, mushrooms and fresh tomato on a bed of pesto and in the shape of an alligator. After pimping out the Lada with some spray-painted phone numbers and a large yellow foam cheese wedge that read "No Pants Pizza" for the roof, he felt ready to go. He dressed simply: a t-shirt and puffy winter jacket over some flattering Saxx underwear and some winter galoshes.

Under cover of darkness, Stark arrived at the building without issue, climbing the four flights to the top floor since he did not want to take a chance on riding up the elevator with a resident who might recognize him. The lock proved easy to pick using the lovely platinum set of lock picks he had received as a graduation present from Professor Holmes. Once inside the Awesome apartment Stark scanned the rooms for anything that stood out as unusual or out of place. Since the apartment consisted of only three rooms, one being a bathroom, the task did not take long. Stark came up empty after the cursory review and decided to delve deeper, which meant checking underneath drawers, under the mattress and behind paintings. The apartment consisted of a kitchen on one end, floor-to-ceiling windows on the living room end, and inside the small bedroom, a full wall bookcase that served as the headboard for the double bed.

Master Ho's words of advice came back to Stark: "If you cannot find what you seek, seek what you cannot find." Stark interpreted the saying to be along the lines of "if you can't see the obvious, look for the peculiar." Sure enough, the lack of personal photographs struck him as peculiar. The place had been professionally swept. He found a box of papers hidden in a secret compartment in the bookcase headboard and two small wallet photos hidden in a framed mirror, one of L.L. and one of a younger version of someone he would not recognize without a cigar the size of a small dog in his mouth.

Stark left the pizza on the counter and wiped down the bedroom to remove any prints. He placed the box of papers on the coffee table in the living room, lighting a candle beside it to avoid switching on the lights. Nature called and Stark dashed into the bathroom to syphon the python. Searching for a hand towel, Stark ripped the shower curtain open and gazed in shock at the body floating face down in the bathtub. He didn't need to turn over the tanned dark-haired woman in the Hawaiian dress to ID the victim. His body shuddered and tears welled

up in his eyes as he lifted the lifeless form of his friend from the tub
and into his arms for one last hug. Breezy sewed all the outfits for the
dancers at the Blushing Beaver to earn some extra cash. Stark new she
lived up the lake and would often stay in town with a friend if she had
a late night shift. She must have been mistaken for Awesome by the
killer. As he was thinking it through he heard a slight whoosh sound
come from the living room, a sound somewhat muffled by the water
sloshing out of the tub. As he dropped Breezy back in the tub, he heard
a louder whoosh.

Stark bolted into the living room in time to see a wall of flame leap
from a box of burning papers on the coffee table to the sheer curtains
lining the dining-room window. Acting on pure impulse and not a
modest amount of adrenaline, he frantically tore down the curtains and
beat the flames out with a leather Catwoman outfit he found draped
across the La-Z-Boy by adapting the classic Yang-style tai chi posture
"Elephant Finds Mouse in Soup." Stark raced into the kitchen, grabbed
what he assumed to be a pitcher of ice water and threw it onto the
burning coffee table. He felt certain he caught a whiff of gin and
vermouth just before the whoosh of flames singed his eyebrows and
shot up to the ceiling. Stark decided to abandon his firefighting efforts
about the time that the television exploded.

By the time he reached the hallway, the irritating sound of cheap
smoke alarms was almost deafening. He ran down the hall banging on
all the doors and yelling, "Fire!" "Sweet Jesus," "Free Beer!" and "Go
Canucks!" at the top of his lungs until satisfied that all but the
teetotalling, atheist, deaf Leafs fans would have escaped. The smoke
triggered the automatic sprinkler system. As if in some nightmarish car
wash, Stark sloshed down the stairs to alert the rest of the building. He
then beat a hasty retreat to the fire escape and down the cold iron
ladder to the tracks below. The flashing red and blue lights reflecting
neon glimmers off the wet rails and scattered pools of rainwater gave
the scene an eerie carnival-like atmosphere.

Stark hit the ground on a dead run and almost made a clean exit until he ran headfirst into Sergeant Harry Stuttgart, who seemed less than pleased to see him. He regained consciousness in Inspector San Francisco's office, where Stark found Sergeant Harry sitting in the inspector's chair with his size fourteen black oxfords propped on top of the desk. He grinned savagely at the effect his bear paws had made on Stark's delicate features. Stark tried to greet him in the standard manner, the Sun-style tai chi posture "Wild Boar Presses a Ham," but stopped shy when he spotted the security guard. Inspector San Francisco stormed into the office just in time to prevent Sergeant Stuttgart from slamming Stark's face into the water cooler. The inspector's neck glowed a French Cabernet red and the perspiration stain on his shirt ran from his underarms to his knees. He muttered through gritted teeth.

"You've gone too far this time, Nakid. Arson is a very serious offence."

"So is murder, Inspector."

"What the hell is that supposed to mean?"

"The body in the bathtub, she was a friend."

"What are you talking about, Nakid? Everyone got out. There was no body in a bathtub. The place was charred but the damage was contained. Lucky for you there were no casualties."

Stark began to put it together. The killer must have been nearby and returned to remove the body while Stark was alerting the other residents of the building. He watched the inspector slowly turn a darker shade of California Zinfandel before speaking.

"A prime minister's wife reportedly once said that some people are born great, others achieve greatness, and still others have greatness thrust into them. You and the Sergeant seem to fall into the latter category."

Stark could see the wheels turning in Sergeant Harry's head and figured it would be only a matter of hours before the light went on and the sergeant dismembered him. Just as the sergeant attempted to break Stark's left arm over a file cabinet, the phone rang. Inspector Franco answered gruffly, then straightened up to say, "Yes, sir," before quietly hanging up. His face slowly changed shades from a sugar-beet purple to a deep radish red.

"You got friends in high places, Nakid. You made bail."

Chapter Eight

She awoke gently, one nostril flaring slightly as she sniffed in the cool moist air that billowed from the humidifier next to the bed. She slowly elevated her goddess-like wrists, reaching with open palms toward the tall white bedposts, arching her back while stretching her sleek cat-like form to its full length on the black satin sheets. Her hand slipped through the white netting surrounding her bed and reached for the iPhone that lay beeping softly on the bedside table. As usual, the only party to share her bed was a life-sized stuffed penguin she had named Salty Bob. She gave her usual morning greeting: "Speak."

"Zuzu von Trapp, please."

"Go away."

"Could I talk to Bob, please?"

"Get stuffed, Nakid."

"I need your help, Zoo."

"Where are you?"

"I'm staying at the Whispering Owl Motel here in Nelson, under the name Julio Rodriguez."

"Good God, Nakid. Are you still doing that? Can you not for once stay in a hotel under your own name?"

"No."

"Not to mention you always choose some ridiculous ethnic disguise that you don't remotely resemble."

"I took the liberty of making you a reservation nearby at the

Laughing Cow Motor Inn, under the name Jasmine De Janeiro. Your choice of cover is that you are a discredited Tour de France cyclist, who has been forced into retirement after a nasty road-rage incident, or you are the new DJ for Elephant Mountain Radio, which has recently switched from an all weird-music format to an all weird-talk format."

"Why do I always have to have some hideous scar to cover up or be a retired pirate or just released from a mental institution? Why can't I just stay at the hotel and pretend I'm a tourist?"

"A tourist? A tourist? How lame is that? What kind of imagination does it take to come up with a tourist? What's next, no wheelchair?"

"No wheelchairs, Stark. Remember that year in Toronto when the elevator at the CN Tower broke down and you had to bounce me down ninety-eight flights of stairs? No wheelchairs, no fake legs, no false hands, no hooks and no eye patches."

"No hooks? No eye patches? Just what kind of disguise did you have in mind?"

"Did it ever occur to you that no one knows me in your weird little town? Why do I need a disguise at all?"

"Do you have any idea of the gravity of the situation here in Nelson? I myself have happened upon two corpses, which, I might add, also makes me the prime suspect."

"I have a job, you know. I can't just drop everything and jump every time you call. I have a life, Nakid. We are not an item anymore and that is not going to change. That ship has sailed."

"You cut me to the quick, Zuzu. This is not about us. As you said, that ship has sailed, that train has left the station, that Elvis has left the building. This is about saving the world as we know it. Have you ever looked into the eyes of a puppy that has just peed on the floor? It's about that. It's about puppies. And world peace. I need your special set of skills, Zoo."

"Nice tits and freckles are not a special set of skills."

"Don't count yourself short, Zoo. Not just anyone could pull off those freckles."

"I don't want to be a detective anymore, Stark. I have a real job in the real world. I can't just leave at the drop of a hat."

"I have taken the liberty of speaking with your employers, Inga and Wolfgang, at OMG Direct, as well as Blossom and Harmony at Bent Over Yoga, and explained the bobsled accident, the extent of your injuries and the expected length of your convalescence here in Nelson. Inga and Wolfgang sent a lovely fruit basket. Blossom and Harmony sent a bag of herbs and a water pipe."

"Fine. I'll take the DJ gig. When do you want me there?"

"I've booked a seat for you on the Silver Dog, leaving the Petro-Canada gas station on Lonsdale Avenue in North Vancouver at 0500 hours, arriving at WalrusMart in Nelson at 2200 hours. The ticket is in the name of Roxanna SleepyBear."

"I am definitely not spending fourteen hours on a Greyhound bus."

"Fifteen hours, actually, but if that is your wish I also booked a flight for you on Melting Glacier Air, primarily a freight carrier operating a pre-war Grumman G-111 Albatross that thunders off the water in Deep Cove like a pelican with a bowling ball in its pouch, and hopefully splashes down on Kootenay Lake much like Apollo 13 returning from an unsuccessful expedition to the moon. They are scheduled to transport a full cargo load of Birkenstocks for Camel Toes and Bare Paws, our two local shoe stores. They are looking forward to flying their first passenger. The ticket is in the name of Brigitta Hassenpheffer."

The flight to Nelson was uneventful, if one considers two near mid-air collisions upon takeoff and an emergency landing to refuel at Christina Lake uneventful. The owners of the Vicky Christina Barcelona Marina, Bud and Ethel Scheissen, appeared startled but took it all in stride, taking the opportunity to deplete their stocks of Eastern European army surplus items that had been dusting up the shelves since the end of the Second World War. As it turned out, the inflatable camouflage party raft came in handy getting to shore after a tricky splashdown in Kootenay Lake that involved brushing a wingtip on the underside of the creatively named Big Orange Bridge that links Nelson to the outside world. Yeti and Dmitri, the two Melting Glacier pilots, left the plane tied up at the wharf at the Thirsty Trout Lakeside Hotel and headed straight to the Grinning Gopher Lounge for shots of Stoli vodka. Zuzu declined to join them and stormed off to find her lodgings.

The Laughing Cow Motor Inn stood at the foot of Baker Street, at the natural boundary between the downtown core and a gritty industrial area highlighted by the decaying remains of the former Grand Funk Railway station. The Laughing Cow Motor Inn consisted of a quaint grouping of six black-and-white duplex cabins painted in a cow pattern surrounding a giant milk bottle. Once inside her room, Zuzu spied the cow-jumping-over-the-moon down quilt adorning the bed and noted the cutesy barnyard theme. The folk-art furnishings included a hay bale as the bedside table, a lamp resembling a stack of cow-pies, horn-and-antler coat hangers and a saddle complete with stirrups for an easy chair. Whether it was the white-knuckle flight or the forty-year-old saggy mattress, Zuzu fell into a deep sleep as soon as she laid her head on the pillow, and had the naked-Martha-Stewart-in-the-bathtub-full-of-chocolate dream again.

Chapter Nine

Rufus San Diego jogged up the winding flagstone path and bounded up the wide wooden stairs onto the wraparound porch. He seemed unusually tall. Words used to describe Rufus did not include stocky or big-boned. His lack of bulk and great height created an optical illusion that made him almost disappear when he turned sideways. His mother called him her little giraffe. His father often said, "The boy is tall enough to hunt geese with a rake." When he made a rare appearance representing a client in court in a suit and tie, he looked more the mortician than the judge.

Outside of court he wore his standard lawyer fare: blue jeans, flip-flops, a favourite black T-shirt with "Jesus Is Coming" on the front and "Look Busy" on the back. His perpetually tanned skin complemented his deep brown eyes and his Frank Zappa moustache and soul patch. For the past thirty-five years, since the age of eighteen, primarily to add some width and breadth to his silhouette, he had worn his dark brown shoulder-length hair in dreadlocks. Also at the age of eighteen he legally changed his name from Richard Santiago Junior to Rufus San Diego. When the locals had started calling his father "Big Dick Santiago" to differentiate papa from son, the writing was on the wall. Although the city may have been one Dick shy, Rufus had been confident it would survive as he strode to the train station on his eighteenth birthday with all of his meagre possessions in a backpack. Eight years later Rufus returned on the same train with the same backpack containing the same meagre possessions and a law degree from Gonzaga University. Go Zags.

Rufus stood in front of the undersized green door and placed his worn leather briefcase on the porch. He knocked softly. After a few moments he pressed the doorbell. He waited a few more moments and knocked again, a little louder, then waited, then pressed the doorbell again. He repeated the process several times, increasing the tempo of knocking and ringing until he stood pounding furiously on the door frame while keeping one finger pressed continuously on the doorbell, causing the frosted windows beside the door to rattle and shake with such intensity that a vase filled with old umbrellas vibrated off the porch and broke on the lawn. Maxwell Bolder threw open the upstairs window shutters, stuck his head out and screamed, "Stop it. Are you fucking insane? Stop banging on the fucking door. Nobody is home."

The shutters slammed closed. Rufus stopped pounding on the door and stood silently for a few moments. Then he resumed the door pounding and doorbell ringing. Ten minutes later, a defeated Max meekly opened the door. Leaving the door open, Max shuffled into the living room, tightened the belt on his blue plaid terrycloth bathrobe and sat down heavily in one of the two matching blue plaid armchairs that faced the blue plaid chesterfield. He put his feet up on the blue plaid ottoman, exposing a pair of plush white bunny slippers below the sky-blue flannel pajamas adorned with penguins and polar bears. Max ran his hands through his unwashed sandy-blond hair, leaving portions of it standing out above his ears, and rubbed the three-day-old stubble on his face. He had to admit that he felt like shit. Rufus sat in the opposite plaid chair, the briefcase on his lap, snapping the clasps open.

"You look like shit. Have you slept since the funeral?"

"Not a lot. I keep having these weird dreams."

"Sex dreams? Was I in them?"

"No and no. More like rocks and boats and storms and shit. It must be from sleeping in my old room again."

Rufus pulled a sheaf of papers from the briefcase, laid them on the ottoman, cleared his throat and spoke.

"Do you want the good news or the bad news first?"

Max pulled on his hair with both hands until it stuck out sideways like a circus clown.

"Let's just review here, Rufus. Monday night I get a call that my Dad is dead, discovered as the main ingredient in some homemade hot-tub soup. After which my wife, the alligator, informs me that not only is she not coming to the funeral but she is filing for divorce since she has been fucking some guy from her office for the past year and my bags will be on the lawn when I return. I fly home from Anaconda and find that my dad has had a stool with his name on it at the craps table of the Slim Chance Casino for the past ten years and owes money to almost everyone in town. The only people who showed up at the funeral either gave me debt markers or physically threatened me. This morning I get an email from my boss informing me that my wife was not fucking some guy from her office, she was fucking some guy from my office and that he was the guy. He also informed me that he has moved into my house and that I can consider myself no longer welcome and no longer employed. So, with all due respect, I don't think I want to hear any more bad news."

"Okay, look. I was kidding about the good news. How much do you know about your family history?"

"I have no family history, Rufus. I was born on a Friday in 1983, the same day all of my relatives died in a house-boating accident on Kootenay Lake while attending a reunion Due to my imminent arrival, my parents could not attend."

"Have you ever seen the movie *The Crypt Keeper*, Max? I'm kind of like the really old crypt-keeper guy. I knew your father for close to thirty years, since I opened my law practice here. Since then I have been burdened with the responsibility to keep the crypt sealed, so to speak, until certain conditions were met. Depending on how the circumstances played out, I would either seal the crypt forever or disclose some family secrets. The former circumstances include the one where your father dies of old age. Among the latter is the one where he's found cooked like dim sum in his hot tub."

The look of confusion on Max's face caused Rufus to stand and walk across the room to the fireplace, removing the centre candle from the menorah that sat on the mantle. A panel above the mantle slid open.

"Drink?"

He reached for a crystal decanter etched with the words "To the Max." He poured the amber liquid into two glasses and handed one to Max.

"Did you ever wonder, Max, how it came to be that a family named Bolder, with no living relatives, settles in Boulder, Colorado? Did you ever wonder how a blond-haired, blue-eyed boy could have such Asian-looking parents? Did you ever wonder where your father travelled to for several months a year?"

Max smoothed his hair and took a long pull on his glass.

"My father was a travelling fireworks salesman, Rufus, you know that. What are you trying to say?"

"The family history about all your relatives dying in a house-boat accident is true, by the way, except that it wasn't an accident and your parents were the only relatives you had on that boat. The rest of the people who died were members of a select group who were sent instructions to meet on the lake that night. Your mother, pulled from the lake just before giving birth to you, died of complications. The Bolders were not your birth parents, Max. The night of the tragedy on the lake, your parents' Vietnamese chauffeur fled with his wife and a very small baby to Boulder, Colorado, taking the name of the town they ran out of gas in, although spelling it incorrectly. I met your father Bill (Soon Fong) and your mother Raquel (Su Ling) a few days after I set up shop here. I helped them get settled and obtained some travel documents for them. My father, a Vietnam vet, had some contacts in the local survivalist community. Soon Fong was not a travelling fireworks salesman. He worked as an explosives expert, a government consultant and a freelance mercenary in his later years. Su Ling did not work as a schoolteacher, Max—she could barely speak English. When she drowned in the backyard pond I became executor of their estate."

Max drained his glass and slumped forward, holding his face in his hands.

"You are full of shit, Rufus. We had the best Fourth of July fireworks in the city. When I was eighteen, dad tried to talk me into selling roman candles door to door. Mom tutored me through freshman English. The last time I spoke with dad he told me about the big bonus cheque he had coming for selling a half-ton of ladyfingers for Chinese New Year."

"That's not all, Max. Those were not their only secrets. You were not an only child. The night your birth parents, Simon and Simone, were liquidated on Kootenay Lake, they left your brother, Nathaniel, sleeping in the car. They might land in prison for that now but in those days it was common to leave a kid alone sleeping in a car. People chain-smoked and drank cocktails while driving and didn't even wear seat belts. The plan involved a five-minute visit to the houseboat to make a quick appearance at the meeting and then head to the hospital for your birth. They rowed out to the houseboat but never made it back. The houseboat exploded just as they hopped into the rowboat to return to shore. Fate intervened in the form of a nearby coast-guard vessel, which had been practicing emergency manoeuvres, ensuring that you did not go down with the ship, so to speak. The bad guys had planned to detonate the car just in case Simon and Simone made it back from the boat. Nathaniel would have been kindling when the car blew up a few minutes after the boat did. Before that could happen a patrolling police officer saw your brother in the car and took him home, planning to drop him off at the station on her way. Once the details of the houseboat tragedy and the mysterious bombing of a car in the parking lot broke, she couldn't bring herself to turn your brother over to the authorities. Nathaniel became Stark when she took him to a local orphanage for safekeeping. She maintained close contact with him until she died in the line of duty some years ago when your brother was just eighteen."

Max's eyes were totally glazed over and bits of foam were coming from his nose.

"Your birth parents were also in the country illegally, as were their parents, who travelled to Canada to work for the Grand Funk Railway —following in the footsteps of your great-grandfather Jugo, and his brother Jorge, who both drowned in a storm on Kootenay Lake in 1898. Their surname was Nakid (pronounced nah-keed). The brothers were of Lebanese origin but had been living for decades in Cayo Largo, Cuba. Your grandparents travelled to Canada hidden in oak casks aboard a rum-runner that sailed through the Panama Canal and up the Pacific coast to the northern port of Prince Rupert, the terminus for the Grand Funk Railway. The casks were cracked opened a few days later by a disappointed gathering of Shriners in Nelson. Your birth parents, Simon and Simone, operated a private international school in Nelson, teaching English to foreign students from the Pacific Rim. They spent their spare time trying to solve the mysterious drowning of Jugo and Jorge. As you know, the police investigation of your adoptive mother's death five years ago was inconclusive. Your father, Soon Fong, left instructions for you to find your brother if anything should happen to him. He left this envelope with me to give to you. The other letter was slipped under your father's door a few days before he died. He left strict instructions to only open them in the presence of your brother. Stark knows little of the family history but he does have some knowledge and skills that you do not possess."

"Should you or any member of your team . . . This is bullshit Rufus. You made this all up."

Rufus refilled their glasses and handed Max a shoebox.

"These are Soon Fong's personal effects. I added the five thousand dollars for travelling expenses. I'll take care of his debts but this house and the contents will have to be sold to come up with the funds. He really was a terrible gambler. If we are to believe the information in that envelope, you may not be able to return here. If you need help in Nelson, I have an old friend there. A business card is in the envelope. Good luck and Godspeed, Max—or as your father might have said, may the dolphin of fortune swim up your alley."

"What, for the love of God, is that supposed to mean, Rufus?"

"Your father did not have a good command of the language, Max, but he meant well. I can't believe you never noticed that he was functionally illiterate."

"Functionally illiterate? He had a degree in pyrotechnic engineering from Juan De Fuca University in Bellingham, Washington. He spent every summer there as an intern before I started elementary school. He attended his twenty-five-year reunion just last year. His degree is on the wall there, beside all the family photos."

Rufus walked over to the sideboard to look more closely at the wall above it.

"Fuca U? Are you kidding me, Max? 'Pyrotechnic' and 'engineering' are both spelled wrong, as is your father's name. Did you ever think to ask a few background questions over the years? Did you ever actually see your mother leave the house to go teach at grammar school?"

"She worked steady nights, Rufus, so she could be there when I came home from school."

"School teachers don't work steady nights, Max."

Chapter Ten

Max lay down on the couch as soon as Rufus left. He had a lot to absorb. His father was dead. He was back in Boulder. The two letters lay unopened on the coffee table. One lay in a manila envelope, the other in standard office issue. The standard one, addressed to a Mr. S. Nakid in Nelson, British Columbia, appeared old and a little worse for wear. The letter in the manila envelope had been given to Rufus five years ago on the day they discovered his mother at the bottom of the backyard pond, weighed down with a plumber's tool belt. If he understood the gist of the conversation with Rufus, he had a lot to mull over. First and foremost, his parents were not who he thought they were. How could they not have mentioned his adoption? His mother, Su Ling Bolder, and his father, Soon Fong Bolder, were in fact Vietnamese refugees who had raised Max as their own since his birth parents died—or more properly, were murdered. His birth parents had died and with them every living relative except for one: a brother named Stark Nakid. How cruel fate could be.

Stark lived in Nelson, British Columbia, the same small Canadian mountain town, located halfway between Vancouver and Calgary, where Max had checked into the world and where his birth parents had checked out. Since beginning a new life in Boulder, Colorado, Max had not travelled much farther south than Albuquerque, New Mexico, much farther west than Salt Lake City, Utah, much farther east than Omaha, Nebraska, or much farther north than Casper, Wyoming. He had flown once, on a family vacation to Chicago, and filled several airsick bags. He and his parents had returned home on Amtrak. Once he had finished high school, Max had attended the only college that offered him a scholarship: Chief Dull Knife College in Lame Deer, Montana, a small Native American college in the heart of Cheyenne country.

Max had accepted a full-ride scholarship to play football, the only sport in which he showed any measure of talent. He had played quarterback on the ramshackle squad with mostly oversized indigenous youth taking the welding or the ranch management program as a condition of their parole. After the Wounded Knee uprising in the mid-seventies, where two FBI agents were shot on a reservation a few states away in South Dakota, Lame Deer had been fortunate to receive some of the windfall of government funding proffered to nearby states in an effort to circle the wagons. Lame Deer's location, less than an hour's drive from the site of the Battle of Little Bighorn, ensured it received a little more than its share of funding. With the infusion of cash, the relatively isolated ranching community became a college town. They even had enough cash to build a football stadium that could seat five thousand—the largest stadium east of Billings, Montana. Not bad for a town of two thousand.

In order to maintain the field for the football program, the college offered a degree in landscape architecture with a specialization in turf management, which is the program that Max received his scholarship in. After four years in Lame Deer, and two trips to the NAIA Frontier Division Semifinals, Max graduated and left for the big city—Anaconda, Montana, where he had been offered a job at the local school board to look after all of their fields and parks. Max was sad to leave his friends and teammates in Lame Deer but he did not go alone. His best friend, Freddy Broken Sky, a graduate of the same program, moved to Anaconda with Max to accept a job with Surf and Turf, the largest turf farm in the state.

When Max entered his late twenties, everything changed. He met the love of his life in a laundromat while folding socks. People referred to Sally as down-to-earth. Max recalled her telling him so the first time they had met.

"Stay away from me, Max. I'm nothing but a cheap slut."

Max had never met a girl like Sally. She wore her long auburn hair in pigtails and had plenty of freckles, which Max found irresistible. They were married after a four-month frenzy of dating that ended with Max realizing that "cheap" and "slut" were both qualities he admired in a woman. Things changed quickly after the wedding, as both aforementioned qualities seemed to vanish in a matter of months. Sally's wandering eye returned after a few years of marriage, taking the bloom off the rose and the lust off the table.

Max shook off the painful memories and rose slowly from the chesterfield to shuffle in his slippers to the den. The den hid in the back corner of the main floor, all pine tongue-and-groove panelling with a floor-to-ceiling corner window. Soon Fong had placed his desk diagonally just in front of the corner window so that when seated he could keep an eye on the back yard, as well as the points of entry to the house. The wall opposite the desk held a floor-to-ceiling bookcase filled primarily with the Vietnamese edition of the Encyclopaedia Britannica. Adorning the wall near the door were dozens of photos of his parents posing for their annual Christmas photo. Soon Fong had developed a wicked sense of humor, which Su Ling shared and encouraged. Each year the couple would hire a photographer and pose in some odd manner or odd costume to add to the wall of fame. Max could see all of his favourites from his perch behind the desk: the duck hunters (complete with plaid hats and shotguns), the James Bonds (white tuxes, guns pointed at the lens), the goat herders (real goats), the skiers, the figure skaters, the river dancers, the hockey players, the doctor and nurse, two of the Marx brothers, the cowboys, the Eskimos, the dog and cat, and several more. Max loved the framed triptych photos of his mother looking off to the right with binoculars, his father looking off to the left with binoculars and the middle photo of both of them looking at the photographer through binoculars. When Max left home his parents continued to send him a framed copy of the annual photo. Max still had trouble believing that his parents had lied to him, most likely for his own good. He had trouble believing he was adopted. He had trouble believing that both his parents and his birth parents were dead. He had trouble believing that he had a brother. Max just had trouble. He was about to have a whole lot more.

Chapter Eleven

Holmes tore open the French doors leading onto the rooftop deck of the penthouse suite. The man in the hot tub did not notice the intrusion, focused intently on the re-enactment of the battle of Trafalgar with the two-dozen replica British warships and another dozen random floating toys.

"Watson, I need to think. I believe we are all out of mind-altering substances. We must make do with fresh snow, fresh tracks and fresh mountain air to clear the mind. Windage and elevation, old chum. Grab your boards, man—we're off to taste the white water. I believe this is the last weekend of the season at the ski hill."

By the time they climbed the mountain highway to the city limits, snowflakes were beginning to fall. Within a few miles the snow began to swirl between the travelled lanes of the highway and to mount up along the shoulder. Watson gripped the wheel tightly, shifting the antique Land Rover into third gear for the slight hill before them. Six or seven other vehicles drove by them in the passing lane, sending swirls of snow across the windshield. The rear tires began to slide out on the icy surface before the tread caught and Watson regained control. Holmes slapped the back of the seat and laughed.

"Ha ha, Watson. Better shift old Betsy into four-wheel drive before we find ourselves in the ditch. We've been through tighter spots than this, as your proctologist likes to say. There's no time to spare, old chum—slam her into high gear. Pedal to the metal, as they say."

"Would you, for the love of God, Holmes, let me drive the damn car without your constant chatter and unwanted advice?"

Holmes sniffed and glanced out the passenger side window.

"If you recall, Watson, my driving skills got us out of a jam a few years back in 'The Adventure of the Twin Globes.' To say nothing of my snowmobile driving that saved our bacon in 'The Case of the Tattooed Barista.'"

Watson continued to drive the battered aluminum vehicle in a safe grandmotherly manner, some twenty kilometers under the speed limit. Several more vehicles swooped by with their horns blaring. He began to ease up as they approached the yellow flashing light that marked the turning lane off the highway to Whitewater Ski & Tree. As soon as he inched far enough to the left, the mounting traffic behind him blew by in a blur of snow and rude hand gestures.

"If you had not lost your driver's licence in 'The Problem of the Cheap Brazilian,' you might be in this seat now, Holmes—but keep in mind that Chief Inspector Francois Davide of the Nelson City Police has issued a warrant to keep you out of the front seat of any motorized vehicle in the West Kootenay."

"Chief Inspector Davide is a raving lunatic, Watson. It was a simple gas-and-brake-pedal error that anyone could have made. I believe his squad car was fully insured. Perhaps you will recall with fondness my chauffeur disguise in 'The Adventure of the Third Leg' and not be so quick to judge."

Holmes sniffed again and looked away.

"I do apologize, Holmes. You know I am still uncomfortable driving on the highway in winter conditions. It is all good, as we have left the Crowsnest Highway and have less than ten miles to go along Whitewater Road."

As they gained elevation the snow along the edge of the winding mountain road grew noticeably deeper, although the road itself appeared recently plowed and sanded. Crossing the bridge at Ymir Creek, Holmes quickly rolled down the window and made an inhuman bellowing sound.

"Moose, Watson. Did you see that? In the creek. The ever-elusive wildermoose of the Selkirks. I must make a note of it in my diary. How many points do you think were on his antlers?"

"Moose don't have pointy antlers, Holmes. It was an elk. Have you learned nothing from our years here in the mountains?"

"It is the human species that fascinates me. Much less furry, on the whole. Moose or mouse, they are all God's creatures—but they all taste the same on the plate, eh, Watson? 'The fool doth think he is wise, but the wise man knows himself to be a fool'—*As You Like It*, act five, scene one."

The road left the creek and climbed quickly through the towering cedar and ponderosa pine trees. The snow, which had stopped falling near the bridge, turned into fog and for the next few miles they were guided only by faint tracks in the snow on the road. They could not see further than a car length in any direction. Watson had slowed to a glacial pace, forcing a few ski enthusiasts behind them to make several dangerous and aborted attempts to pass. As they approached the next bend, the fog began to lift and within a few moments they broke through the clouds and were met with blue sky, bright sunshine and impressive snow-laden peaks. The four vehicles trailing them blew by in a rush of swirling snow and blaring horns.

"Do you know what Emily Carr, the famous turn-of-the-century British Columbian artist and writer, said about nature, Watson? 'It is wonderful to feel the grandness of Canada in the raw.' *In the raw*, she said Watson, *in the raw*. What balls she had. I admire a woman who can throw on a backpack, throw caution to the wind and go for a hike through the woods *in the raw*. Can you imagine carrying all her paints and canvasses and easels and stuff *in the raw*, Watson? The woman was a genius and a true visionary."

"I don't believe she meant it that way, Holmes. I think she was referring to the raw beauty of nature."

"Preposterous, Watson. Are you out of your mind, old chum? She said *in the raw*. Have you seen her painting *Blunden Harbour*—a bunch of giant nude carvings on a wharf? I rest my case, Watson. I might add that the few times I have ventured down to Red Sands Beach in Nelson I too have witnessed nature *in the raw*. Contrary to what you might believe, Watson, it is none too pretty."

Leaving their skis and poles in the rack nearest to the ticket window, they made their way inside the lodge and up the stairs, and found a seat at an empty bench near the coffee bar. Holmes removed the ski boots from the boot bag and made an elaborate display of dismantling them, setting the liners, buckles and assorted screws on the table. Shouting, "Ready," Holmes then reassembled the boots in what turned out to be a new personal best time, performing deep knee bends in the boots before Watson even had his ski socks on. While waiting for him to buckle his boots, Holmes took the opportunity to chat up the nose-ring sporting barista. A few moments later Holmes sat down beside Watson and handed him a non-fat decaf caramel mochaccino. Ten minutes later they were riding up the Silver King chairlift, gulping down a lungful of the crisp cool air and observing the magnificence of the surrounding peaks. Whitewater Ski & Tree was bowl shaped, with one chairlift on either side of a towering peak and a third chair down the back side. Ymir Peak soared two thousand feet higher than the top of the chairlift, infusing those who skied below it with a Zen vibe.

"I trust you brought your skins in your pack, Watson. We have quite a journey ahead of us if we are to make it out in daylight."

"I thought you just wanted to clear your head and get some runs in. Where are we headed?"

"I am writing a new monograph on forensic etymology in the granite and limestone caves of the West Kootenay. I believe I have discovered a new breed of maggot that can survive in the harsh environment of an abandoned mine shaft. It could revolutionize time-of-death analysis in northern climates. If you look to the left of Ymir Peak, above Goat Slide, you will notice a dark shape on the rock face above the ski slope. Take a look through this spyglass."

Watson noticed the dark shape and estimated at least a two-hour hike on skinned-up skis. Experienced backcountry skiers like Holmes and Watson used touring bindings that were hinged at the toe to allow the heel of the ski boot to lift. An adhesive skin, unfurled and applied to the bottom of the ski, rendered the ability to grip the snow when walking up the hill instead of skiing down. The extra width of their powder skis made for a larger surface on the snow and less effort to apply when hiking up the mountainside.

Holmes loved the ritual task of attaching the skins and removing them before skiing down an untracked slope. On any other day, the sunshine, light snow and crisp mountain air would have punched the ticket but Holmes had other goals in mind. After two hours of steady going along the top of the slope, they found themselves at the base of the rock face, staring at the entrance to the mine shaft above them. Holmes remained well in the lead and had time to enjoy a pipe while Watson caught up.

They paused on the saddle between Goat Slide and Ymir Peak. After changing from ski boots to rock climbing shoes, Holmes found some old pitons in the rock wall above them and attached some karabiners to the pitons before threading a climbing rope through them. Within a few minutes Holmes clung to the rock twenty feet above Watson, just below the lip of the mine shaft. A mine shaft is, for all intents and purposes, a cave, and Holmes lost no time scrambling over the lip and onto the smooth rock floor. The opening stood about ten feet in diameter, narrowing to just over four feet at the far end. The walls and floor were rough granite. A support frame made of large squared timbers stood at the entrance, and a rudimentary block and tackle lay on the floor of the cave. Once assured secure and safe, Holmes placed the block and tackle back on its hook in the ceiling timber and threw the rope down to Watson. Holmes safely towed Watson up to the lip of the cave before taking out a flashlight and exploring the furthest nooks and crannies of the mine shaft, returning satisfied with the inspection after ten minutes or so.

"Get your gear back on and take the skins off your skis, Watson. We must make it down before we lose the light."

"I am already exhausted, Holmes. Can we just rest awhile?"

"If you recall 'The Case of the Purple Nurple,' Watson, you will recognize the danger. That storm over Five Mile Basin is moving fast. If we do not make a run for it now, the rock bluff here could fill in with ice and snow and we may not get out for weeks."

"I believe you mean 'The Adventure of the One-Eyed Wonder,' Holmes. 'The Purple Nurple' involved breast-implant smuggling in Revelstoke."

"Blast, Watson. I know perfectly well what I mean but that's not the point. We must make haste. No time to lose. Did I ever tell you the story of how the French artist Toulouse-Lautrec got the nickname 'No Time Toulouse'? Not much of a lover, it seems, but I digress. There is no time to go back the way we came and the conditions are ripe for a class one avalanche. We have no choice but to traverse across the saddle, boot pack to the top and ski down the face of Ymir Peak."

"Saints preserve us, Holmes. I lack the skill to ski the peak. Perhaps you could come back for me in the summer."

"Man up, Watson. Let's go. Pick your balls up off the floor, old chum. Just follow behind me, and for the love of God, don't dally. Straight-line it if you must, Watson, but don't stop in the avalanche chute. Mind the debris field and skirt anything that appears nasty. Windage and elevation, Watson. Tips up. The mountain shall not best us today. By the twin moons of Venus, Watson, we shall taste Mrs. Hudson's sweet pie tonight."

To anyone looking up from the lodge down below, it would have seemed as if two ants were crawling down an ice cream cone. Every season a few daredevils and pros alike took a shot at the almost-vertical route down the ever-imposing Ymir Peak. Few succeeded. The ominous cornice at the top of the spectacular peak served as a warning to those without the stomach to tame the beast. In order to succeed, a skier needed to be fully on his or her game, commit to the twenty-foot free fall off the cornice and ski an almost-vertical face for two hundred yards before it began to level out. Once through the vertical section, the choice of routes was either over a small cliff onto another very steep face, or through a minefield-like, debris-filled avalanche chute. Holmes raced down the slope and headed for the cliff, the powdery snow thrown by the twin-tip skis billowing in clouds behind. Watson veered off to the left for the slightly less vertical terrain of the avalanche chute, a little unsteady but keeping the tips of his skis up to maintain stability and breakneck speed. Holmes caught up to Watson at the base of the cliff and skied alongside, shouting loudly.

"Take care, old chum. An avalanche can strike here without warning. I've triggered several here myself and have had to shovel out the poor bastards below who got the business end of it."

"Should you be shouting so loud then, Holmes?"

"Pshaw, Watson. It is an old wives' tale. As you well know, based on studies of sound waves derived primarily from shouting at mice in an enclosed space, the order of magnitude required to trigger a snow-slab avalanche would be massive. The human voice can register an amplitude of two megawatts. A jet flying overhead can register an amplitude of twenty megawatts, while a sonic boom can register an amplitude of two hundred megawatts. Explosives can register an amplitude of two thousand megawatts. That's why ski patrollers lob explosives to test slope stability instead of just yelling at the snow."

Watson glanced up to the top of Goat Slide where the surface-snow layer appeared to be shaking.

"It is said that the beating of a butterfly's wings can cause a tsunami halfway around the globe. Must be a very large butterfly indeed. In the mountains the added air pressure of a hummingbird's wings can trigger an avalanche, simply by adding a thousandth of an ounce of stress to a fractured, frozen snow layer. Ski like the wind, Watson, or mark my words, we shall be lucky to dig you or your hummingbird out in one piece."

As luck would have it, a hummingbird did not beat its wings on Ymir Peak when Holmes and Watson skied down. They made it safely to the lodge without incident, although both were covered from head to foot in a thin layer of ice and Watson may have lost control of his bladder once or twice.

"This calls for a hearty meal at the Fresh Tracks Café inside the lodge. Go clean yourself up, Watson. There is a change of clothes in my pack. I shall go up and order for us."

Watson cleaned up and dressed in black stretch stirrup pants with a green-and-white striped cardigan, returning to find Holmes sitting in front of a table filled with several yummy-looking items. Holmes spooned something out of a bowl while licking sauce off of a finger.

"You must try this, Watson. It is fabulous. I don't know why they don't write a cookbook and share the recipes for all of these great menu items. I would call it 'Fresh Track Crack' or 'Whitewater Cooks.' What do you think? With your waistline in mind I have bought you a Ymir Hippy Bowl and a Summit-Side Salad, while for myself a Terra Ratta Wrappa and some Bomb Blast Chili."

"Thank you, Holmes, I am a bit famished after all the fresh air and exercise. Why did you want to come here today? What the devil were you up to in that cave?"

"An experiment Watson, to lay a trap for the elusive maggot. I have accomplished my mission. Let us be off. I do hate to leave, though. There is a spirit to this place that warms my heart. Are you going to finish your hippy bowl?"

"All this talk of maggots has put me off my lunch. Please, be my guest, Holmes. I'll go get Betsy from the parking lot and meet you in front of the lodge."

Chapter Twelve

Stark looked up from the sidewalk, having wandered aimlessly for the past hour to sort things out. He found himself on Baker Street, in front of the Fussy Pack Rat, a second-hand store crammed so full of antique and garage sale items that clients had no room to fit inside. Instead clients could feed five dollar bills into an oversized arcade claw machine and try to manoeuvre the object they desired into a large bin where it would slide out a doggy door and land in a basket at their feet. As he had done each day for the past three weeks, Stark fed a fiver into the machine and once again tried to pick up the short black penguin statue. The claw found its mark and clamped onto the penguin's beak as Stark frantically worked the two joysticks. The rope grew taut, straining to lift the heavy object as the machine began to smoke and make grinding noises. Just as the statue began to lift off the floor, the rope broke and the bird settled back to its original position, the claw and broken rope still attached. Stark mimed his complaints to the manager, who sat chain-smoking in a rocking chair inside the front window. The man seemed to interpret the elaborate gestures correctly and agreed to have the statue delivered to Stark's office.

Stark turned to face the street and began jumping up and down waving his arms frantically above his head, hailing a rickshaw in the usual manner. When he stated his destination as the Kootenay Lake Hospital, the rickshaw driver groaned. Rickshaws had caught on in Nelson a few years back, when *Hockey Day in Canada* had selected

Nelson to host the nation in a *Hockey Night in Canada* broadcast, as well as an old-timers game and an embarrassing quiz show hosted by Don Cherry. The rickshaw idea began as a dogsled idea, since the event was held in January when the streets were covered in snow. Ferrying around all the celebrities from bar to bar in rickshaw carts on toboggan runners proved a big hit. When the event ended, the operator decided to start a year-round business to give Bad Dog Cabs and Eff Ewe Taxi a run for their money. He bought a shipping container full of vintage bamboo rickshaws on eBay. As an ergonomic engineer, he had the skills to modify the handlebars to reduce the coefficient of drag and he assumed that making it a little easier on the rickshaw pullers would keep them employed a little longer. Within a year the new service, Rolling Gazelles, put one of the local taxi companies out of business. Once ski season began, the number of available pullers dropped like a burlap-wrapped body off a bridge. Fortunately once the snow began to stick to the roads the sister service, Bobcat Dogsleds, required fewer mushers for the season.

The rickshaw puller took a long gulp of water from a bottle on her belt, grabbed onto the long bamboo handlebars and started to run up Silica Street toward the hospital. The Nelson town site was located in moderate-to-steeply sloped terrain. The downtown core, surveyed in the late eighteen hundreds, sat far enough above the lake to avoid an annual flood and far enough below the mountainside to keep the snow accumulation in feet to single digits. When residences, churches, hotels and other buildings were added, the city just adapted to the hills. While rickshaw pullers maintained a high level of fitness, they dreaded getting a call to head up the hill to the hospital or down the hill to the lake. Rickshaws shared the narrow roads of Nelson with cars and trucks, and were often on the receiving end of rude gestures or thrown food items from impatient drivers.

Although the puller's diminutive stature did not inspire confidence, she maintained a surprising pace, passing a bus and a leather-clad group of bikers at one point. As they began their ascent from the downtown core at the end of Vernon Street, another rickshaw pulled out of an alley and began to follow them. Stark recognized the Hulk as the passenger and ordered the puller to take evasive action by taking a hard right onto Cedar Street and doubling back down the alley to Hall Street. Their pursuers gained ground as they cranked a hard left onto Herridge Lane. A cacophony of popping sounds came a few turns later as they dashed up the steeply curving confines of Victoria Street, just a few blocks shy of the hospital. One of the bullets, much too close for comfort, shattered the windshield of a parked van as they scrambled past.

Near the top of the hill, Stark directed the puller onto the narrow bike path that led into Gecko Park and to the viewpoint overlooking downtown. The panicked rickshaw puller maintained a fifty-yard lead as they rounded the final turn in the path. Stark searched his pockets for a weapon and came up with a fistful of pistachio nuts that he dropped behind him onto the paved pathway. Stark's puller frantically ran around the edge of the circular viewpoint and onto the arched wooden bridge leading out of the park. Stark turned back to see his adversary level a pistol in his direction at the precise moment that the other rickshaw puller saw the pistachio nuts. As soon as the puller's foot hit the nuts he performed a surprisingly graceful double-high kick and soared soundlessly over the viewpoint barrier. His momentum caused the handlebars of the rickshaw to drop and catch on the concrete barrier, vaulting the Hulk and his gun up and over the edge of the cliff. After taking a quick peek over the edge for injuries and making a fast 911 call, Stark arrived in the rickshaw at the emergency room entrance of the hospital, his puller looking a little sweaty and shaken. He gave her an extra twenty, an energy bar and a business card for a local grief counsellor.

The Kootenay Lake Hospital had just completed a multi-million dollar emergency-room addition, which was clamped onto the side of the pre-war five-storey building like an outboard motor on a canoe. The latest in Leadership in Energy and Environmental Design technology, it resembled a glass bedpan with a retractable-lid roof. Due to the strict requirements of the LEED standards for energy self-sufficiency, the glass walls, roof, chairs, desks, beds and gurneys were all embedded with solar-power-generating chips. Glass and transparent materials were needed to generate enough solar power to supply not only the new wing but the entire hospital. To accomplish the task, shower curtains replaced bed curtains and no poster boards or art were permitted to adorn the walls. Even the paper and files used for doctor's orders and patient records were made of transparent cellophane.

The modern design resulted in an eye-popping emergency room that kept no secrets from any pedestrian glancing in from street level. No longer did loved ones need to call the hospital to check on a patient, since a quick drive by could provide the answer. More than a few nurses and switchboard operators had to be reminded of the benefits of wearing undergarments when sitting at their workstations. Doctors were forced to adjust their bedside manner, displaying more flamboyant gestures of care and attention to their patients when facing the street-side entrance. The staff would vote monthly on the best performance by a doctor or nurse, who would receive a gift card for coffee or adult novelties.

Able to slip past the guard at the emergency entrance by wrapping gauze around his head and faking an Achilles tendon injury, Stark hopped by the check-in desk and down the stairs to the basement level undetected in the classic Wu-style tai chi posture "Rabbit Loses Lucky Foot." At the end of the hall he returned to his natural stride and hurried through the red double doors to the morgue. He snuck into the locker room and slipped on a mask and gown just before the autopsy of the mystery piano victim began.

Doctor Svetlana Bon Voyage did not appear to notice Stark or his blood-stained scrubs and mask, recently retrieved from the laundry bin. With the green cloth mask covering his nose and mouth, along with the matching surgical head scarf, he felt confident of being totally unrecognizable. Dr. Bon Voyage looked up from arranging instruments on the tray and glanced his way.

"Evening, Nakid. Would you mind passing me that chainsaw by your foot?"

He winced and handed her the heavy yard tool.

"Feels like it may be out of gas. Would you pass me the gas can over there and the electric hedge trimmer over there?"

Stark had never actually seen an autopsy before and it appeared that Dr. Bon Voyage had not witnessed very many either. Word on the street was that the new emergency wing had caused some budget cutbacks, resulting in staffing reductions. The local pathologist became one of the casualties, so to speak. His twenty-four-seven contact number at the Bear Balls Lounge of the Granite Parrot Golf and Country Club did not help his performance review. Half of the rare autopsy requests in Nelson usually involved summertime mishaps from lighting a spliff off the gas barbeque. When the pink slip arrived, the local pathologist left in a huff with all of his surgical instruments, forcing his replacement, Dr. Bon Voyage, to improvise.

Svetlana Bon Voyage had arrived in Nelson as a locum. Locum doctors were recruited to fill a temporary absence of a family physician, usually when on holiday in warmer climes or when drying out at a rehab facility. Not unlike a sizeable number of physicians in Nelson, Dr. Bon Voyage came from South Africa. Her parents had emigrated from Belarus, defecting while bobsled training in the Drakensberg Mountains above the coastal city of Durban. Svetlana had attended the prestigious University of KwaZulu-Natal Medical School up the road in Pinewood. While in residency at the nearby Mahatma Gandhi Memorial Hospital, a nurse had discovered her in a broom closet with Bubu Vuba, the daughter of the president.

Svetlana had decided to finish her residency in Canada before having to discover what the business end of a dungeon looked like. Even with her parents' Belarusian embassy contacts, which landed her a new surname in the witness protection program, Svetlana could only get a residency position in Charlottetown at the University of Prince

Edward Island Medical Centre. Since she had listed her point of entry to Canada as Montreal, her options for a witness protection surname had included Bonhomme, like the Quebec winter carnival mascot, and Voyageur, like the early canoe-paddling fur traders. As a compromise she had chosen Bon Voyage. Upon arrival in Charlottetown, Svetlana had discovered her residency to be in the university veterinary hospital and she had spent three years providing medical advice primarily to sheep and sheep dogs. She graduated top of her class and developed a taste for lobster and ginger girls with long pigtails. Longing to return to the world of human medicine, she had moved to the wilds of Newfoundland after obtaining a surgical residency at Memorial University in St. John's. On the side, she had kept up her veterinary skills by triaging the exploding population of moose, one or two of which arrived at the hospital each day, strapped to the hood of an ambulance after having car parts removed from their antlers. After six years of cod tongues and seal-flipper pie, and without finding her Anne of Green Gables, Svetlana had accepted a locum in a small mountain town in British Columbia.

Dr. Bon Voyage loved Nelson and its low moose population. She arrived just in time to celebrate her thirtieth birthday. In her first five years in Nelson, Svetlana had not met the ginger girl of her dreams, but she did have a frantic affair with a gorgeous, neurotic French woman who had a thing for grapefruit. She also had an on-again, off-again relationship with a male colleague in the lab, after an incident in a broom closet late one night where she confirmed her status as a switch hitter. Stark had always found her Russian-South African accent to be on the erotic side of barely decipherable. He felt attracted to her but found her a bit grim and did not understand her Slavic sense of humour. She worked out like a demon at the gym and had an Eastern-European physique that had frightened him the one time he ran into her at Red Sands Beach. She seemed like the type of woman who would physically drain a man to the point of requiring a blood transfusion. Svetlana found Stark to be cute, in a lean, unmanly, clean-shaven kind of way, but also found him somewhat juvenile and did not understand his non-Slavic sense of humour.

Svetlana had met Stark soon after she arrived, when they both served on the Nelson Surgeon Rescue Team. The NSRT formed after an alarming number of local doctors wandered away from their posts in the hospital, remaining unseen for the rest of their shifts or for days on end. When the Nelson City Police formed the rescue squad they envisioned the team making perilous hikes up the treacherous peaks of the Selkirks or Valhallas, chasing serial killers and pediatricians with no sense of direction. The squad disbanded after a year when most of the AWOL physicians were discovered in the nurses' lounge or at a coffee shop downtown. Svetlana had enjoyed the Friday night Surgeon Rescue Team search parties, which involved games of hide and seek that lasted until dawn. Stark and Svetlana had decided years ago to be friends without benefits.

Anticipating Stark's arrival at the morgue for the autopsy results, Svetlana had strategically placed the chainsaw and electric hedge clippers in the room. Chuckling to herself, she winked at Stark, turned off the chainsaw, placed it on the floor and brought out a tray of surgical instruments to begin the autopsy. Stark noticed to his surprise that the body, after being hit with a piano from five floors up, did not look as pancake or cartoon flat as he had imagined. He managed to stay on his feet during the first major incisions but only made it through the removal of organs from the body cavity by trying to rate each one on a grossness scale of one to ten. He and Dr. Bon Voyage argued about whether the pancreas earned a six or an eight, but high-fived when both agreed on a ten for the lower intestine.

When the autopsy ended and all the organs had been weighed and bagged, Stark sat down with the doctor in her office to go over the details. Stark's lack of official status meant he could not be privy to the results of an autopsy, but since Svetlana despised the local police chief and his disparaging attitude, she readily gave Stark a summary of her findings. The victim, a female of about forty years of age, had sustained massive trauma. The back of the skull appeared crushed, as did sections of the pelvis, rib cage and lower spine. The trauma seemed consistent with a major impact event such as a high velocity car accident or a fall from a great height. Wood splinters were imbedded in the body, likely upon impact. No evidence of drugs or alcohol in the liver or blood.

"No surprises then, Dr. Bon Voyage. A textbook case of flatlining, so to speak. Nothing at all unusual."

"It is all very standard, Nakid. Nothing at all unusual—other than the rope burns and the cause of death, of course."

"What rope burns? What are you saying, Dr. Bon Voyage? The victim didn't die of airborne piano syndrome?"

"Water in the lungs, Nakid. She drowned. Based on the impact trauma and the rope burns I would guess that she died before being tied to the piano."

The door of the office burst open and a man in burgundy scrubs rushed in with a rack of test tubes in his hand. Stark stood up and spoke in a harsh whisper.

"Jesus McMurphy."

Chapter Thirteen

Zuzu rolled over to avoid the daylight streaming in through the half-open curtains. She yawned long and hard, noticed the bedside-table alarm clock flashing "M:00" and her iPhone gently vibrating beside it. She pressed the speakerphone icon.

"Miss De Janeiro? It's Bud at the front desk. You wanted a ten o'clock wake-up call."

"Thanks a million, Bud. Why does the clock say moo?"

"Oh right. It does that when we have a power failure. Miss De Janeiro? It's actually only 9:30 but there's a strange man here at the desk asking for you. He is wearing a sombrero and claims to be an associate of yours. Should I call the authorities?"

"No. That's OK, Bud. He has some serious identity issues. Just put away any sharp objects and I'll be right down."

She enjoyed a hot shower in the stall-themed bathroom, brushed her teeth in the oat bucket and dressed in black lululemon pants and a mandarin orange tank top. She considered calling the front desk for help with the spike-heeled, knee-length boots but managed to pull them up on the third try. A black zip-up hoodie completed her outfit. Her layered, espresso-brown hair needed no attention at all. A ginger as a child, she had left high school with hair to match Olivia Munn, and of course the freckles to boot. She put on a pair of Ray Ban Wayfarer glasses, the frames black on the outside and orange on the inside. The lenses were non-prescription as her vision was perfect.

Large-framed glasses brought out the almond shape of her green eyes and would fulfill the disguise requirements so rigidly held by Stark.

Zuzu arrived at the front desk to witness Julio Rodriquez having a spirited one-way conversation with Bud, the front desk clerk, in Spanish. Stark's false moustache had begun to droop on the left side and Bud's efforts to explain his lack of foreign language skills seemed to fall on deaf ears. Zuzu ushered Julio out the door, turning back to Bud as she closed it to make a gunshot-to-the-side-of-the-head gesture.

"You can lose the sombrero now, Stark."

"It's nice to see you too, Zoo. Let's go up the street and grab a bite."

"I'm not going anywhere with you dressed like that."

Stark reluctantly ditched the sombrero and poncho behind a recycling bin. Zuzu reached over and ripped the moustache from his upper lip. He winced. She handed him her glasses.

"Stop pouting, you can wear these."

Stark put on the glasses and smiled, happy to be back in disguise. Suddenly a loud but oddly familiar sound broke the morning silence. Stark reached into his jacket pocket to retrieve his cell phone. He had missed the call. Zuzu commented on the unusual ringtone. It rang again: "Ha ha ha, ho ho ho and a couple of tra-la-las . . ." Stark glanced at the incoming phone number and disconnected the call.

"Why didn't you answer that? People were beginning to stare."

"We don't stare in Nelson, Zoo. We look concerned, dazed, or confused. Occasionally we look surprised, and we may gaze off into space for extended periods, but we do not stare."

Stark punched a series of numbers into his phone and pressed send. Zuzu reached into her pocket and brought out her iPhone. "Ring, ring, ring, ring, ring, ring, ring, banana phone . . ." The text message read "Who doesn't love Raffi?"

"Ah, here we are. There, on the side street—the Awkward Turtle. Best eggs Benny in town. It's a used bookstore too, so you can browse the shelves as you scarf down your scrambled tofu wrap. No tables or chairs. It doesn't get much better than this."

They stood in line at the counter for about twenty minutes before the waitress finished helping the man in front of them find a copy of *Fifty Shades of Hay: An Erotic Exploration of George Orwell's* Animal Farm. Stark ordered the eggs Benny and a first edition of *The Patient English: An Oral History of the Queue.* Zuzu opted for a steak-and-egg omelette and a dog-eared paperback copy of *A Closer Walk with These: Breast Augmentation Amongst the Clergy.* Zuzu found it challenging but not impossible to balance her plate on a pile of dictionaries and eat her meal. It felt kind of nice to not just sit at a table and stare vacantly at the other patrons. Browsing amongst the stacks proved a little discouraging due to the amount of spilled food and the odd ketchup smear on some of the books. It seemed a little odd that they did not sell coffee or offer any beverage other than water. They left without their cloth bag of books and the waitress ran after them. Cute, short, dark and pixie-like with big blue eyes, she had each fingernail and toenail painted a different color. She gave Zuzu a big hug and a kiss on the lips.

"Welcome to Nelson. I'm Namaste. Come check out my yoga class and I'll give you a free massage. Each morning at seven, just two flights up."

She pointed to the sign on the wall and dashed back into the restaurant. The sign, small enough to miss and painted baby blue with a black-and-white Dalmatian doing a morning stretch, read "Dirty Dog Yoga—Namaste Santa Fe."

"The thing about the coffee is that they don't want to compete with the other coffee shops. It's the whole good-karma thing. It's big here. Come on, we'll grab one on the way. I want you to meet someone."

Stark led her down Baker for a few blocks, calling, "Hey," nodding hello or hugging almost everyone they passed. They stopped at the Toasted Tree Frog coffee kiosk that offered take-out service from a window on the corner. As they returned to the sidewalk, a woman in a business suit who was coming out of the adjacent bank bear-hugged Stark from behind and then gave him a light kiss on both cheeks. She spoke softly in French and made a gesture as if lifting up two grapefruits for inspection, then softly sucked on the knuckle of her baby finger as she winked at Zuzu. Then she threw her head back, laughed heartily and teetered off down the sidewalk on her stylish red Louboutins.

"What was that all about, Stark? What is it with this place? What is in the water?"

"Monique Percé, the Bank of Montreal manager. We just call her Moan. She likes you. She would like to get together just to feel you out and have a glass of wine, possibly a bite. Ah, this is the building. His office is two flights above the Pointy Bird Diner, best pad Thai and bubble tea in town."

Stark bounded up the stairs and down the hall to the left. One of the doors read Sun Bunny Travel and another across the hall, Porcupine Acupuncture.

"You have to meet Master Ho, my martial arts instructor from my days at the Hole."

Stark knocked on the door in a sequence of short and long, soft and hard knocks. The door opened a crack until they could see the chain pull taut. An eye appeared in the narrow opening. It looked up and down, taking stock of the visitors as if examining a diamond under a gem cutter's lens. Fingers suddenly shot out through the door opening and hung a small plastic sign against the glass. The fingers vanished as quickly as they had appeared and the door slammed shut. The sign on the door read "Back in twelve hours—take a seat." Stark began pounding on the door and after twenty or so heavy thuds it opened just a crack again. The eye looked them up and down. The door slammed shut. The sound of a chain rustling grew louder. Twice the door opened a crack and closed again. As they were about to leave, the door tore open, breaking the chain from the latch. Master Ho stood in the doorway and grinned. He invited them in.

"Knee-High. The years have treated you like a dog in a restaurant. Welcomed and loved, but for the right price, on the menu. Your technique has suffered without my training, Knee-High. You have brought a friend, I see. Is this the girl you spoke to me of the last time I saw you? The one who tore your heart out and stomped on it? The psycho bitch, I think you called her."

Stark shrugged at Zuzu and nodded to Master Ho. She studied the elderly man with the close-cropped dark hair. His features did not seem naturally Asian—rather it was the way he stood and moved that projected his Asian-ness.

"Master Ho, Zuzu. Zuzu, Master Ho Chi Minh."

Zuzu exchanged pleasantries with Master Ho and he apologized for the chaos of his Zen garden in the courtyard, which appeared through the glass to be impeccable and without a stone out of place. Stark clasped his hands together and bowed toward his teacher.

"Master Ho. It is so nice to see you again. It's been a long time. A day does not go by that I don't think fondly of your tai chi classes at the Vallican Hole School. Last I heard you were overseas on some secret assignment. How long have you been back in town?"

"Your memory is selective, Knee-High. You have put on weight. Do you not own a mirror? You have brought shame upon my art. It is good to see you nonetheless. I have only just arrived home to Nelson. A stranger in a strange land."

Stark turned to Zuzu to explain.

"When I attended the Hole School, Master Ho had nicknames for us all and since I reminded him of the old *Kung Fu* TV show character Grasshopper, I adopted the nickname 'Knee-High-to-a-Grasshopper.' Knee-High for short."

Stark knelt down to pick up a piece of the door frame and handed it to his teacher.

"Is it true that you were in prison for a spell in Montreal, Master Ho?"

"Your impertinence has grown, as has your waistline, Knee-High. I visited Montreal, two summers ago, on a special assignment. While walking to my hotel one evening on the Rue Saint-Denis, I was set upon by a roving gang of mimes. I managed to survive the encounter only due to my special training. Six of them came at me at once—chalk-white faces wearing evil grins while they set about the devil's work. I summoned all of my skills as the first two attacked me with the 'Man in a Box' pattern. I used a Chen-style *Chin-na* pressure point technique on the first, snapping his wrist like a twig, then performed the Sun-style tai chi posture 'Eagle Stretches His Talons' on the second, pulling the tendon from his left heel and tying it around his right ankle. While they lay screaming in pain on the sidewalk, the third and fourth mimes attempted the 'Climbing a Rope' pattern to escape but I countered with the Australian Wu-Hu–style tai chi posture 'Kangaroo Bitch-Slaps Koala'—a jumping spin kick to the forehead of the first—and 'Crocodile Whacks Gopher'—an iron hammer fist to the shoulder of the second. Both collapsed on the sidewalk like sacks of potatoes. The final two mimes attempted to divert my attention by throwing their wallets at me and raising their hands in the air. I recognized the pattern as 'Justin Bieber Comes to Town' and delivered the Sun-style tai chi posture 'Ground Squirrel Gathers Nuts'—a crushing bear paw to the groin of one—and 'Dragon Whips It Good'—a sweep kick and elbow smash to the nose of the other. By the time the authorities arrived, all six mimes were either unconscious or wishing they were. Unfortunately, my lack of skill in the Québécois dialect during my interrogation by the Sûreté du Québec resulted in a conviction for assault and reckless endangerment. I opted for a juried over a judged trial and regretted it when I noticed four of the jurors wearing team bowling jackets that matched those worn by the victims. Victory was not to be mine in court, as my lawyer arrived with a hangover, speaking neither official language, and pleaded guilty just to make the judge stop banging the gavel. My initial sentence of six months lengthened after an incident involving a dropped bar of soap in the showers that ended with four of my fellow inmates and two guards requiring medical attention and extensive physical therapy. Released on appeal after two years less a day's incarceration, I was ordered deported to British Columbia. On the plus side, the solitary confinement allowed me to perfect the Chen-style tai chi posture 'Creeping Leopard Rips Sleeping Dragon a New Asshole.' It is good to be back in your odd little town, Knee-High. I missed all the hugging. It is not taken with the same good spirit in the big house."

Zuzu had been studying the collection of what appeared to be voodoo dolls with acupuncture needles sticking in them that were displayed in a large glass china cabinet along one wall of the office. The one with the headphones looked a lot like her.

Chapter Fourteen

Stark arrived late for the piano victim's funeral. Nelson's Forest Floor Cemetery is located on a hillside off Creek Street about three miles east of downtown. For the first eight blocks of the journey, the Lada hummed along like a fine-tuned tribute to Eastern European engineering. The vast array of unrecognizable noises it emitted gradually increased until it finally ground to a shuddering halt six blocks shy of Stark's destination. When he abandoned the car on the side of the road, it stood billowing white smoke out of the engine compartment. Stark remembered his ex-mechanic's advice to only worry about blue smoke. Upon reflection, he also remembered that his ex-mechanic delivered pizza for a living.

The inside of the funeral home was decorated in subdued hues of burgundy and royal blue with an abundance of tacky red velvet accents. The foyer walls were filled with black-and-white photos of what appeared to be either the former presidents of the funeral home or the last twenty-seven stiffs in suits they had worked on—the difference seemed negligible. Stark straightened his tie and walked up to what appeared to be a hotel check-in desk. A bright-eyed and bushy-tailed attendant sat behind the counter reading the latest Stephen King novel. She wore her black hair in braids and sported a sombre black-and-red uniform with a short plaid skirt that made her look either like Wednesday from the Addams family or a hat-check girl in a Scottish restaurant. She seemed too engrossed in her book to notice Stark standing at the counter. His training at the Vallican Hole School had prepared him for such behaviour. In his mind's eye he reviewed the arsenal of responses open to him. The choice obvious, Stark began a feverish river dance on the hardwood floor until she looked up at him with her one good eye and continued reading with the other.

"May I help you?"

"Thank you kindly. I'm here for the Eldorado service. Could you tell me if she's been toasted or planted yet?"

She looked up at his comment and eyed him suspiciously.

"The interment service has just begun in the Gold Mountain section of the cemetery. Just follow Primrose Lane down to Easy Street and turn left."

She gestured vaguely to a map on the wall behind her and returned to her book.

Stark followed her directions to a T and found himself on a pristine lawn full of brightly painted wooden cut-out figures of the Flintstones and other cartoon characters. He retraced his steps back inside the cemetery grounds and noticed a large group of mourners surrounding a small blue-and-white-striped grave tent a couple of hundred feet below him near the edge of a clearing.

Stark slipped quietly behind a tree to put on his disguise—a pair of orange cloth coveralls with a City of Nelson logo stitched on the breast pocket. He strapped the leaf blower to his back, flipped the switch and began blowing piles of leaves toward the group of mourners. By the time he had covered the distance between them he had amassed a pile of leaves the size of a small car. Pretending to get a call on his cell phone, Stark subtly took photos of the group surrounding the grave to review in more detail later. He found the pastor to be somewhat grating, but took his suggestion to "stop blowing that fucking pile of leaves into the open grave, you fucking moron" to heart and decided to vamoose before he blew his cover. Before he left, while watching one of the mourners shovel the leaves back out of the hole, Stark overheard the thug nearest the pastor whisper, "Two down, two to go."

Stark vacated the cemetery without detection by posing as a homeless person. Once out of the orange coveralls, he did not even need to change his clothes to make the disguise complete. Weaving amongst the tombstones, he staggered out the front gate and down Creek Street. He covered the final ten blocks to the downtown core by using the Yellow Brick Road–skipping gait he had so deftly mastered at the Vallican Hole and decided to climb the extra flight to visit his mentors. Stark found Holmes sitting in the den, feet on the desk, lighting a pipe. After exhaling a plume of blue smoke, the pipe was proffered in his direction.

"No thanks. I gotta drive."

"How are you, my boy? We haven't seen you much around here. Not since 'The Strange Swelling at MacPherson's Knob.' I still have nightmares over that one. How can we be of service, lad? I hear you have brought your old flame to town for a visit. Is it love troubles? 'I will wear my heart upon my sleeve for daws to peck at'—*Othello*, act one, scene one. I too have felt the crushing blow of a broken heart—during 'The Case of the Belgian Whopper,' if I am not mistaken. If Watson had not been there for me, I don't think I would have made it."

Stark explained his unease to Holmes. It just didn't add up. He was telling Holmes about the funeral when Watson walked through the French doors into the den, and came over to give Stark a hug before sitting on the loveseat in the corner. He wore green pajamas with bear claw slippers. He motioned to Stark to continue the tale.

Stark told them about his family history, or lack thereof, and of the circumstances of his childhood upbringing. He told them about the letter he found in the bookcase, leaving a copy on the desk. He told them about the piano, the autopsy results, seeing Jesus McMurphy at the morgue, and finding Breezy in the bathtub. He rambled on, relating the tale of Zuzu and the incident in Japan and how upon return it felt like his heart had shattered like a wine glass on a dance floor. By the time Stark had finished, Holmes was softly weeping, while Watson was softly snoring. Holmes came over to give Stark a hug. Stark thought he felt his ass being squeezed but he hugged back and let it pass.

"Don't you let that girl go without showing her how you feel, my boy."

Holmes walked him out to the hall and assured him that the matter would be given the utmost attention. Inquiries would be made and contacts would be contacted.

Chapter Fifteen

Max felt a little dazed and bleary-eyed from the journey. After taking the red-eye flight from Boulder back to Anaconda, the next leg of the journey to Nelson, British Columbia, by rail was no mean feat. His 6:00 a.m. departure in a refurbished cattle car on the Butte, Anaconda & Pacific Railroad went fairly smoothly, although it took over two hours to cover the fifty-mile section, including a stop at every single siding to water and feed the trainload of cows in the fourteen boxcars behind him. The relentless mooing rang in his ears for hours after, as he completed the journey from Butte around the horn to Helena on Montana Rail. He enjoyed a four-and-a-half-hour layover waiting for the Drummond Bullet, which would cover the three hundred and fifty miles of track between Helena, Montana, and Sandpoint, Idaho, in just over seventeen hours. The speed that the aging locomotive managed to attain once up and through the Mullan Pass Tunnel seemed truly unsettling. Although children on bicycles appeared to be streaking by the windows, the rattling and shaking of the economy class railcar left an impression of rocket-like trajectory. Most of the other passengers seemed to be holding on to their arm supports as if they were clinging to a rope over a pit of alligators. At one point Max left his seat to grab a fast bite and three beers in the bar car and upon return noticed the train rocket past the same group of youngsters on their bikes.

Max arrived in Sandpoint near midnight and felt lucky to find a room at Sandy Sheets, a bed and breakfast near the train station whose owners were insomniacs who catered to late-night train traffic. Max walked back to the Sandpoint Railway Station in the morning, after a light meal of what looked an awful lot like porridge but tasted an awful lot like meatball gravy. The journey from Sandpoint to Kettle Falls proved slow and serpentine. Max had to bribe his way onto a freight train heading up the fifty-mile stretch along the Pend Oreille River to the Canadian border. After settling into a random boxcar, Max fell asleep as soon as he leaned his head back against a bale of hay.

Max opened his eyes, soaked with sweat and still shaky from the vivid dream of a ship sinking in a violent storm. He looked out through the open freight-car doorway and saw huge plumes of water charging over the spill gates of the Brilliant hydroelectric dam at Castlegar as the train left the Columbia River and chugged up the last fifty miles along the Kootenay River to Nelson.

Somewhere along the river Max realized he might not be the only passenger in the boxcar. The distinctive odour of skunk filled the air and seemed to be getting stronger since the door had slid shut. About ten miles from Nelson, Max completed searching every nook and cranny and determined that he did not share quarters with a family of skunks. The bales of hay that filled the boxcar were emitting the strong odour, since they were in fact bales of hemp. Max formulated a plan to jump out when the train slowed down just outside the Nelson rail yard. By exiting the train before it arrived, he could hopefully avoid being arrested for smuggling weed and for being in the country illegally without the passport he had left in his glove compartment in Anaconda, Montana. The problem with Max's plan became apparent when the train didn't slow down before it arrived in the Nelson yard. Max forced the door open and could see the dilapidated Grand Funk Railway station building getting closer. Rather than slow to a gradual halt, the engineer chose to crank on the brakes and let two powerful blasts of the whistle go as they screeched to a halt alongside the aging station platform. Max had arrived at his destination.

Max worried about arriving in Nelson in a freight car full of pot, expecting at any moment to be arrested by the railway police or by Canada customs agents or by the local constabulary. When he did emerge sheepishly from the freight car, stepping gingerly on the railway platform, he felt a little surprised to be embraced by the station master who gave him a good long hug.

"Welcome to Nelson."

The station master, a portly Latin-featured man dressed in a khaki uniform, did not seem remotely surprised that someone had arrived in the back of a freight car filled with hemp bales. He walked by Max and pulled a length of stalk from one of the bales, put the end between his teeth and returned to stand beside him.

"Bags?"

Max pointed to the backpack slung over his shoulder. The station master nodded, provided directions to the Dancing Bare Inn and slipped a few dollars in Max's pocket while giving him a hug goodbye.

Chapter Sixteen

Max left the Grand Funk Railway Station at the foot of Baker Street with some trepidation. He had travelled five hundred miles to reach his destination. Having rarely travelled outside his home state, he now found himself outside his home country. The scenery reminded him of home—a river valley surrounded by rounded hills with mountain peaks in the distance. Anaconda, Montana, did not have a lake to swim in like Nelson did. Although the valley bottom was narrower in Nelson, the hills appeared to be the same size. Anaconda, located between Glacier and Yellowstone National Parks, was renowned for its hiking trails, while Nelson was the gateway to both Kokanee Glacier and Jumbo Glacier, only an hour's drive away from the stunning peaks of the Valhalla mountain range. Outside of Anaconda, Max felt more at home in Nelson than he had on the flat plains of Lame Deer or in the metropolis of Boulder.

After the first block, Max realized that as opposed to the unfamiliar terrain, the residents caused his unease. To say the locals were a bit odd was to say that the Tea Party was a little right of center. Before arriving at the train station, Max could only remember being hugged when he was six, by a girl who had traded lunches with him in first grade. His parents loved him but were not physical due to their cultural backgrounds. Displays of public affection were not welcomed in the home villages of Soon Fong and Su Ling. Blending in with the residents of Boulder, Colorado, proved easy since the mostly redneck population was not keen on gestures of affection that did not involve fists, sleeper holds or thrown beer cans. In contrast, the local residents of Nelson appeared to be on the Muppet side of friendly.

In the five blocks from the railway station to the hostel a group of people whose car he helped push-start hugged Max, as did a woman he held a shop door open for and a busker playing Yo Yo Ma songs on a ukulele, who also offered a place to crash for the night. Max made his way to the Dancing Bare Inn, located on the top two floors of a lovely granite-block building on the corner of Josephine and Victoria. The inn was directly across the street from the Kootenay School of Darts, housed in a similar granite-block building that had been at various times the city jail and the city power plant. The school's enrollment had exploded with the growth of the casino industry and remained the only accredited gaming institution in British Columbia to fill the void. The school trained blackjack and poker dealers, as well as casino management staff for the hospitality industry. The school also catered to those seeking to become professional card players, as well as those focused on professional careers in billiards and darts. Had Max been awake on his journey from the Canadian border to Nelson, he would have noticed the three casinos they had chugged past, including the newly constructed facility beside the Castlegar Airport called Cash and Burn. The revolving sign out front compared and contrasted, with hourly updates, the odds of dying in a plane crash and the odds of winning at the roulette table.

The check-in counter of the Dancing Bare Inn stood on the ground floor, accessed off the alley. Once inside the grand foyer a sweeping staircase appeared, more suited to a *Gone with the Wind*–era mansion, about twelve feet wide with plush red carpet and gold-leaf gilded banisters on either side. A *Phantom of the Opera*–style chandelier ten feet in diameter hung down two stories from a coved plaster ceiling. The remainder of the building's main floor was occupied by Scandihoovian, a less-than-profitable Ikea-style furniture store that only carried zoo-themed items from Norway, all of which required assembly. The store's owners didn't mind having a hotel above them, since they had such little foot traffic that most days the only customers they had were lost hotel guests. The hotel guests, occupying rooms ranging from a very basic shared hostel variety to hip boutique-style suites, had access to a rooftop patio with a lap pool that overlooked the downtown core. Max made his way to the check-in desk, which was a jade sculpture of a polar bear on his back holding a glass tabletop up with his paws. The desk clerk had a cancellation and upgraded Max to the Yogi Bear Suite on the top floor.

The bellhop took Max's pack and led him up to his room. Max, short on change, gave the bellhop a big hug, which seemed to more than make up for the lack of a tip. The large room appeared sparsely furnished, with each item built from logs, in keeping with the theme, including the picnic table complete with a checkered tablecloth and wicker picnic basket. Full-sized Yogi and Boo-Boo wax figures waved from their log perch in the corner. Although the room smelled like a campfire, Max fell asleep quickly once tucked into the fluffy cotton sleeping bag set up on a bed of fake leaves on the floor. He had the same strange dream with the boat and the storm. He woke up in a cold sweat after a disturbing image of a large rock falling off a cliff, smashing the small boat below it to smithereens.

Chapter Seventeen

Kootenay Lake—1898

The morning after the storm Captain Lars von Trapp awoke to the sound of gently lapping waves. When he opened his eyes, he found himself lying on top of a large wooden crate floating in the middle of Kootenay Lake. The crate that held his exhausted frame drifted with a sense of loneliness, without another crate, vessel or any sign of life joining its journey south past the gloomy rocks and trees that lined the lakeshore. The storm had forced warmer air into the valley as the rain ceased during the night. The weather had been unseasonably warm all month. As an experienced ship pilot, Lars knew such weather could produce the fiercest of storms. He shivered in his wet clothes, thankful for the wool jacket that stayed warm when wet. Scanning the blurry peaks above the lake brought him no closer to identifying his location, but he sensed the sound of a waterfall nearby along the shore and got the odd whiff of smouldering pine, no doubt from woodstoves in the small group of cabins across the lake at Sanca. He could barely move his left arm. His shoulder appeared to be swollen, possibly dislocated. The large wooden crate he found himself on drifted low in the water with barely a foot floating above the surface. He seemed to be drifting toward shore and a small waterfall—possibly Midge Creek, if he was right about the smoke from Sanca. He lay back and tried to link together the events of the previous night. He remembered the storm and the sense of panic as the ship began to capsize. The captain should go down with the ship, yet he had not. What of his crew? He would later learn that eight men had died. Nine reported lost, including Lars. Eight bodies recovered, one missing. Captain Lars let his head rest back down on the crate as the lapping sound of the waves brought back the painful memory of how it had all begun.

The sternwheeler left the wharf in Nelson around noon, her bright orange paddlewheel churning hesitantly. Not much fanfare, just a few ropes untied, and a few winks and waves from a trio of streetwalkers and a gay longshoreman. The crew lined the foredeck, excited to have SS *City of Ainsworth* back in action. Captain Lars left Tank, his faithful canine companion, tied to the rail and climbed up the service ladder to stand on top of the wheelhouse, grinning down at his men. As the paddlewheel clunked into high gear and the eighty-foot-long ship slipped away from the dock, Captain Lars unzipped his trousers, pulled out his Johnson and, maintaining tradition when leaving port, peed over the side into the lake below, over the heads of several passengers on the men's saloon foredeck. The crew followed suit and also peed over the side, reminding Lars why so few members of the general public came to see the ships off. The *Ainsworth* had been in dry dock since it sank the previous fall while tied up at the wharf in Kaslo. Loaded to the gunwales with ore from the Bluebell mine, she had lacked the strength to fight the gale that blew into the sheltered bay from the east shore. After floundering in the bay for a week, a tug righted and towed her into the shipyard at Nelson. The *Ainsworth*'s young, newlywed shipbuilder had originally designed the ship to mirror his bride's hourglass figure. Due to the bride's impressive rack, the second floor of the vessel had more deck space than the main floor. The unusual design gave the ship a tendency to list when fully laden. Due to the ship's floundering in Kaslo Bay the previous spring, the design was considered a failure and some modifications had been made to improve her stability. Two months before the *Ainsworth*'s scheduled return to service, SS *Kaslo*, the largest freight vessel on the lake, was abruptly taken out of service for repairs. With few options available to the steamship company to pick up the slack, Captain Lars had gotten the nod to test out the hastily refurbished vessel.

Captain Lars had been working odd jobs in the shipyard since the Ainsworth had first been brought into dry dock. When the formal investigation determined the *Ainsworth* had been overloaded and declared her design suspect, Lars breathed a sigh of relief. Only he knew that his fading eyesight had contributed to the problem. Captain Lars had accidentally backed the ship into the steel loading platform in Kaslo, causing the vessel to list into the stormy swells and flounder in the bay. Lars's affliction had started slowly—a little blurred vision and a few floating spots—but over the course of a year, when he had one of his spells, he couldn't tell shit from Shinola and only recognized crew members by their peculiar grunts and smells. The doctor called it episodic blindness and explained that though unrelated, the symptoms were similar to narcolepsy, the disorder that caused a sudden, unpredictable lapse into sleep. Lars hid his affliction from others by always wearing sunglasses, whirling frequently to shout orders in all directions and relying on his trusty dog Tank to guide him through the spells. Lars went everywhere with the mangy black crossbreed, who resembled a black German shepherd, with one pointy ear and one droopy one. Kept on a short leash, Tank negotiated his master through the streets, docks and rough waterfront bars in Nelson, barking directions that only Lars seemed to decipher.

Captain Lars's crew, thrown together on short notice, had more than enough experience for the short journey up the lake to Kaslo, across to the Bluebell mine, south to the smelter at Pilot Bay then down the lake and over the border to meet the main Grand Funk Railway line at Bonner's Ferry, Idaho. The wind on the west arm of the lake remained steady but light. The clouds, a mix of light and dark, thick and thin cumulus, were beginning to swirl. The thick dark ones looked full and heavy, drifting off the lake to collide with the tree-lined hills above the rocky shore. A few hours up the lake the *Ainsworth* pulled into the narrows to stock up on a few cords of wood for the boiler. They took on the birch, greener than expected, and after an hour pulled into Sunshine Bay for a few cords of drier jack pine. The drier the wood, the quicker the burn, resulting in a hotter boiler and more steam power at hand to churn the massive paddlewheel.

The air on deck was foul as they chugged up the lake on that Tuesday afternoon. Deck hands Yuri and Yori, the Jasper brothers, had spent the morning judging a chili cook-off at the Hume Hotel and were paying for it with alternating visits to the crew toilet on the aft deck. Thankfully the rain that had begun as light drizzle just an hour before had thickened and the wind, just a breeze when they had left Nelson, had picked up enough strength to clear the foul emissions that clung to the main deck like a giant squid.

SS *City of Ainsworth*, considered a relatively small sternwheeler for Kootenay Lake, had a licence to carry 50 to 80 passengers and had a small dining room, six small staterooms, a men's saloon at the bow and a ladies' saloon at the stern. The main deck held the freight area, the firebox and boilers and gears for the paddlewheel. Above the main deck, both fore and aft, large covered deck areas adjoined the saloons to enable passengers to take in some fresh air or heave their lunch over the side along their journey. The men's saloon could house forty men, cramped but without spilling a drink, with the ladies' saloon being about half the size. The six small staterooms provided a bunk to rest on during the long passage from Nelson to Bonner's Ferry, Idaho. Prior to the retrofit, the owner had planned to convert the vessel into a floating brothel to service the more remote mines up the lake, but his wife caught on and put the kibosh on the idea.

The modifications made the big boat resemble a cartoon tugboat but she felt much more stable leaving the wharf. Once four cords of wood were piled on the bow she started wobbling like a Jell-O salad. Captain Lars remained skeptical that the modifications would make any difference at all. His thoughts were more focused on his affliction, as the spells were becoming more frequent—several times a day now, lasting between two to thirty minutes. Tank stood by his side and seemed to sense the sudden loss of his master's sight, tugging on the leash to drag him around obstacles and keep some distance from the deck railing and any open deck hatches. By the time the *Ainsworth* tied up to the wharf at Kaslo, the wind was swirling violently and the swells had doubled in size. The *Ainsworth* was at half-capacity with ten crew members, twenty-five passengers and little freight. She had no trouble crossing the lake to Riondel. Loaded up with ore from the Bluebell mine, she attempted to hug the shoreline south toward Pilot Bay. With the heavier load and growing swells, the *Ainsworth* bobbed and weaved in the driving rain like a punch-drunk boxer. She listed from port to starboard and back to port with wild abandon. By slowing the pace and hugging the shore the *Ainsworth* made it safely to Pilot Bay without incident, and without the contents of most of the stomachs on board.

Just a few years prior, Pilot Bay had been a thriving community of a thousand souls with four hotels, three brothels and a bowling alley. When a bigger smelter had opened in Nelson in 1895, the owners mothballed the Pilot Bay smelter, forcing most of its residents to leave for greener pastures. The smelter remained mostly boarded up, except for the occasional week in the winter when overflow ore from the Bluebell mine was brought in by ship or rail to prevent heavily laden vessels from having to make the journey to Nelson in rough winter waters. With only two longshoremen at the wharf, it took half an hour to unload the ore off the *Ainsworth* and load up the two crates of freight. The *Ainsworth* had been hurried back into service not only to ferry passengers around but also to ferry this custom load of freight from Pilot Bay to the main-line rail terminal at Bonner's Ferry, Idaho. Luke, the first mate, had arranged a bonus of fifty dollars for himself, twenty for the crew and a hundred for the captain if the freight made it on time. Lars thought it odd that his first mate had set up the delivery, rather than the company steward, but applauded his ingenuity.

Pilot Bay seemed more vacant than usual. A tall red-brick cone chimney puffing away gently was the only sign of life around the deserted company wharf. The early evening sky darkened quickly as the rain turned to sleet and seemed to come from an increasingly horizontal direction. When Captain Lars asked why such a small crew was loading the cargo, he was told that that everyone else had wandered down to the hall for a wedding. The second crate fell heavily on the deck as the block and tackle used to lower it broke free. Sandy Bollocks, the fireman on the crew, jumped onto the dock with his kit bag on his shoulder.

"Lay up here for the night, Lars, I'm begging ya. The wind is gale force now. The swells are over six feet. That wood we took on is crap, too green to get enough heat in the boiler. She won't make it down the lake with all that weight on the bow. She's packed to the gunwales. Come down to the hall and we'll drain a few jars. You can leave at first light."

Lars saw nothing, experiencing another spell. He misjudged the source of the words and turned to yell in the opposite direction.

"Get back on board, Sandy. I'll double your pay. We shove off in a few minutes. We need to get to Bonner's tonight or we lose the bonus."

"Go without me then, you daft bastard. I'll not risk my life for a few coins. Think of your men. Would you risk losing them, Lars? What of your wife and young lad? How would they survive without you? This is a bad one. Drag that mangy hound with you and come have a few jars till it blows over."

The crew had assembled on the foredeck and overheard the loud conversation. Lucky Jim limped forward and yelled.

"Sod off, Bollocks. We don't need the likes of you. The rest of us want the bonus. Grab your balls out of your kit bag. It's just another storm."

Yuri and Yori joined in the jeering, as did Luke and Billy, the cabin boy. They all stepped up to the side of the deck, turned around and dropped their trousers to moon Sandy Bollocks.

"You're all daft pricks. A pox upon the lot of you."

Sandy turned and strode off down the wharf toward the hall, leaving Lars without a fireman for the journey. Sandy's words rang in his ears. No one knew his marriage existed in name only, and had for years. Had he lost his hearing rather than his sight it might have been a bonus. He spent most of his time on the water rather than dealing with his wife's lack of interest and her unpleasant family.

As Lars's vision returned, he noticed the old hag at the end of the short slip below the main wharf loading sacks of flour and other supplies into a small ketch. She glared up at him and spat as he walked by. The Wicked Witch of the East Shore had gotten her moniker when her two sons had drowned off Cape Horn a half-dozen years before. The bodies that had washed up on shore near the Tipi Camp on Cape Horn were discovered after having ripened for a few weeks. Afterward she moved to a shack near the point and lived a hermit's existence. Mad as a hatter when she did come into town, she swore, spat and cursed at those who ran afoul of her.

Captain Lars was standing at the top of the ramp leading down to the lower float when something heavy and wet hit the side of his neck. A dead water rat fell on the dock. The old bat glared up at him and yelled into the driving rain.

"Go not onto the water tonight, Captain, or you will live to regret it."

Lars left Tank on the wharf, picked up the rat and ran down the ramp toward the old woman. He stopped a foot from her withered face, threw the rat at her feet and clenched his fists in rage.

"Piss off, you old hag."

Another dead rat slapped the side of his face and landed on his shoulder. Lars lost it. He shoved her roughly off the dock and into the icy water. She floundered in the churning waves before going under. Tank scrambled down the ramp and began barking incessantly at the water. Her shrill voice came from under the dock.

"A curse upon you, Captain. He who takes a life in vain shall be forced to live one. Until you right your wrongs, I will haunt your dreams. Die as you live, Captain. Atone for your sins, or those souls who perish will not rest. Each generation will feel your pain. See you in hell, Captain Lars."

Her final words were cut off by the waves that overtook her. Lars dove into the icy water where the churning waves had swallowed her and swam under the dock. He searched frantically but could find no trace of the Wicked Witch of the East Shore. Lars managed to scramble up onto the dock and lay on his back gasping for breath. The quick dip in the bitter cold water had sucked the air from his lungs. Tank stopped barking and licked his face. Silence filled the night air. He stood warily, made his way up to the wharf and thought about heading down to the hall for help, when a young man carrying a duffle bag and violin case ran up the gangplank toward him.

"Are you the captain? I saw Sandy. He's my uncle. He said you were heading down the lake tonight. I'm Caleb. Can I hitch a ride along as far as Kuskanook? I've another wedding to play tomorrow night."

Captain Lars turned and stared back down into the water by the dock and saw nothing but surging waves. He glanced back toward the sternwheeler and turned to face away from Caleb.

"You're welcome to join us if you can fill in for your uncle for the trip down to Bonner's. We'll return to Kuskanook afterward. Have you ever worked on a sternwheeler?"

"Are you talking to me, Captain? I'm over here. I worked on SS *International* last summer with Uncle Sandy. He taught me the trade in case the music doesn't pan out."

The wharf at the Pilot Bay townsite, built beside the smelter and facing the open lake, sat protected from the elements by large rock outcrops along the south side of the bay. Pilot Bay itself was on the opposite side of Pilot Point Peninsula, considered to be the most protected harbour on Kootenay Lake. As the *Ainsworth* left the wharf and headed out into the lake to chart a course around Pilot Point Peninsula, the awesome force of the gale became evident. Captain Lars, wet and cold from his dip in the lake, could feel another spell coming on and gave the command to shove off. Lucky Jim looked a little spooked and made the sign of the cross several times before scurrying back to serve drinks in the men's saloon. Once out in the open water the weight of the two crates, combined with the several cords of wood stacked on the bow, caused a noticeable rise in the waterline. By the time the ship passed the lighthouse on Pilot Point, the swells were swirling as high as six feet. Twenty-pound trout, tossed up like salad by rogue waves, flopped about on the foredeck before skidding across and back into the lake on the other side. The icy water broke over the bow and rode up the stockpile of cordwood. As if summoned from the inky depths, a knee-deep blanket of fog appeared and crept slowly over the deck. The foghorns at the lighthouse sounded as the *Ainsworth* neared the rock bluffs that formed the western edge of Pilot Point.

Chapter Eighteen

Holmes appeared noticeably elated and visibly agitated after showing Stark out the door, returning to shout down the stairwell.

"Mrs. Hudson. Put the kettle on."

Waking suddenly and finding himself alone, Watson wandered to the window, gazing absently from his perch upon a typical Baker Street afternoon. Watson noticed Mrs. Hudson, the housekeeper, struggling with an armload of parcels. Her ample bottom was perfectly framed in the tight black yoga pants she wore, though most women of her age might think twice about the choice. He found himself becoming slightly aroused as she bent over to recapture an escaping parcel. He stepped closer to the window and was unfastening his robe when Holmes burst into the room.

"Put that thing away, Watson. Good Lord, man, just give it a rest. The game's afoot."

Holmes strode forcefully to the desk, sat down and rummaged about in the side drawer, pulling out a bottle of expensive single-malt scotch and two glasses, and pouring a healthy shot of scotch into each glass before handing one to Watson.

"Did you catch much of the story Stark related to us, before you collapsed into a snore-filled stupor? Do you have any idea of the gravity of the situation here, Watson?"

Watson took the glass and drained it.

"It is of no consequence. I fear young Stark and his companions could be in mortal danger. We must act quickly. 'So wise so young, they say do never live long'—*King Richard the Third*, act three, scene one. If I am not mistaken, after perusing the letter Stark provided, it is of the utmost importance that we find out what maritime mishap occurred on Kootenay Lake in the late eighteen hundreds. Pounce like a wounded cougar to your laptop, Watson."

Watson sat down gingerly at the desk and fired up the MacBook.

"Good God, Holmes. Listen to this. On November 29, 1898, during a fierce winter storm, a steam-powered sternwheeler, SS *City of Ainsworth*, sank off of Cape Horn, on the east shore of Kootenay Lake. Nine lives were lost, making it, at the time, the worst inland maritime disaster in Canadian history."

"'O villain, villain, smiling damn villain'—*Hamlet*, act one, scene five. Get a list of the victims, passengers and crew, Watson. I fear we are treading on very thin ice with very dull skates."

Within moments of obtaining the list, Holmes had speed-read a local historian's book, *The Story of SS* City of Ainsworth, and had deduced that the passengers were inconsequential pawns in the tragic events of that fateful night. Watson and Holmes then went through the ship's manifest and discovered that the crew was a ragtag group of ne'er-do-wells that had been thrown together at the last minute. The captain, experienced but a bit of an oddball, had a reputation for dressing unusually and for falling off wharfs. Watson found a diary, kept by Nelson's first postmistress and published in 1900, that contained an entry regarding Captain Lars von Trapp. From the description, Holmes deduced that the captain was either an eccentrically dressed dog-lover or he was blind as a bat. Whatever the case, the decision to proceed through the wild swells and gale-force wind was that of a madman.

The true secrets of the voyage lay below four hundred feet of water and because of this an expedition to find and explore the wreck did not occur for a hundred years. Commissioned by the Archaeological Society of British Columbia, divers had taken a few fuzzy photos and determined the pilothouse was missing and the upper deck was smashed to bits. After another decade and a half and having finally received some grant funds, a follow-up search had only recently occurred, with substantially better results. Improvements in underwater photography equipment and developments in submersible technology contributed to the strength of the findings. During the first expedition the divers had had to spend hours decompressing from the four-hundred-foot depth and could not spend much time at the wreck site. During the follow-up expedition a submersible robot explored the intact hull and paddlewheel as well as the pilothouse, which was lying on a deeper shelf a hundred feet away. The submersible found the ship's safe as well as a few other items from the pilothouse.

"I fear we are getting closer to our adversary, Watson. Perhaps you could confirm some details at the museum and find out the contents of the safe. Have you your revolver at hand?"

"Let's not get started with that again, Holmes."

Holmes was standing in the shower singing a medley of off-Broadway hits when Watson returned from his unsuccessful trip to the closed museum archives. Mrs. Hudson had left a tea tray on the desk in the sitting room a few minutes before five o'clock. Watson added a flower to it, picked up the tray and took it into the bedroom. The bathroom door opened and Watson noticed Holmes, draped in a fluffy white towel, getting out of the shower. After all the years that had passed since they first met, the sight still took his breath away. Holmes saw the flower on the tray and walked over to where Watson stood by the bed. She dropped her towel, cupped her breasts in her hands and winked. Holmes leaned in and kissed Watson softly on the lips as she reached into his robe to guide him toward the bed by his hardness.

"Really, Watson. You are incorrigible."

Chapter Nineteen

Watson had first met Holmes at Whitman College in Walla Walla, Washington, upon discovering a mutual interest in the literature of Sir Arthur Conan Doyle at a campus book club meeting. Holmes had gone on to complete a master's degree in English literature with a focus on Conan Doyle, and a doctorate in philosophy with a focus on deductive reasoning. Watson had pursued his master's in molecular biology until his research into Conan Doyle's military career and his stint as a doctor in South Africa had led Watson to transfer into medical school, specializing in forensic pathology.

Holmes and Watson had hit it off and remained friends after college while settling in different cities. They would get together every other year in Edinburgh, Scotland, at the West Port Book Festival's Conan Doyle Week. They both loved the tour of Conan Doyle's old haunts and always wound up the night in Rutherford's Bar on Drummond Street, which had been the author's favourite watering hole, as it was for Robert Louis Stevenson in his student days. They would pound down rounds of Dead Poets, the house signature drink—a shot of absinthe in a pint of Guinness. Holmes and Watson had helped each other through the joys and sorrows of life including a marriage for each of them—Holmes's ending in divorce and Watson's in widower-hood, after the tragic death of his wife Mary, the consummate multi-tasker, as she ironed in the bath.

When Holmes's divorce became final, she left her post at the

Institute of Behavioral Science at the University of Colorado, wrapped up her weekly radio call-in program *Holmes on Holmes* and moved to the small Canadian mountain town she had visited on occasion with her ex-husband. By accepting tenure at the Vallican Hole School of Stealth, Detection and Hard Knocks, she could bring the passion she held for deductive reasoning to an audience that could unleash its full potential. Watson had completed his second tour of duty in Darfur as chief forensic surgeon for Médecins Sans Frontières when the offer to join the Vallican Hole School came from his fondest chum. He could resist neither the offer nor his good friend's charms.

Chapter Twenty

Henderson Cairo, the director of the school, stood up from his chair and stretched, arching his back and extending his limbs like a cat rising from a nap. He yawned fiercely, ending with an extended shriek, and walked around his desk to face the young man who sat on the daybed sofa that guests were forced to either sit uncomfortably on or lay embarrassingly on. The director took a pencil from the glass on his desk and, just for effect, snapped it in two.

"As you may be aware, Mr. Germaine, our school does not advertise its location. In fact, we change the location of our campus each year, causing ourselves no end of grief but at the same time providing a ready method to streamline the application process. Entrance to the program is contingent upon locating our campus. Oddly enough, aside from an enormous tuition fee, it is the only entrance requirement. We are rethinking the strategy at this time since we could not operate the program last year when no one found us. The Vallican Hole School of Stealth, Detection and Hard Knocks prides itself on maintaining a contributory presence in the academic community. The school fully supports the Hoffman and Hofmann theory that given enough monkeys and typewriters in a room, perhaps smartphones in the modern context, a work of William Shakespeare would eventually be reproduced. We were forced to abandon our efforts to recreate this effect when a number of the monkeys refused to work with our first-year students."

The director returned to his desk, sat down and leaned back in his vintage oak chair, placing his hands behind his head and his feet on the desk. A soft rap on the outer door caused him to vault forward in the chair, throwing with deadly accuracy the pencil he had hidden behind an oversized ear. The door opened and a young woman dressed in ninja attire entered, ducking swiftly, causing the pencil to sail harmlessly over her before impaling itself within a grouping of several dozen other pencils in the wall opposite the door.

"Moneypenny. Could you not just once use the bell before entering the room? You could have lost an eye."

The director accepted the pile of mail she offered and motioned for her to leave with a shooing gesture. With blinding speed she produced a knife concealed in a sheath on her upper calf and cut the shoelaces off of the director's loafers. He glared at her as she backed out of the office, making the two-fingered "I'm watching you" gesture before bumping into an oddly dressed man coming in through the same door. The director gestured toward the man as he spoke to Mr. Germaine.

"Ah, allow me to introduce you to Friar Horace Mogadishu, who leads the spiritual and language arts training at the school."

The short, rotund fellow, dressed in a Franciscan robe complete with rope belt and roman sandals, held out his hand. His hairline, greying and thinning, formed the traditional bowl shape of a monk, complemented by a trimmed short beard. His nose appeared large enough to have belonged to two men—wide and flat but well suited to the wide, flat face on which it sat.

"A pleasure. Please call me Brother Mo."

"Brother Mo is new to our staff this year, replacing Master Ho, who is on sabbatical. Brother Mo, born just up the valley, only recently returned from an extended journey to the Far East."

"Near East, actually. Newfoundland and Labrador. I spent some time at a spiritual retreat for the optimistically challenged in a place called Happy Valley. I have reviewed the academic calendar and noticed that the term starts the first of August—the feast day of St.

Ethelwold of Winchester, known as the 'Father of Monks,' owing to his peculiar habit of patting the other monks on the head and using the phrase 'my child' a lot. Ordained by St. Alphege the Bald in 943, he died in 984 in the arms of a man he cured of blindness through prayer and by turning his balaclava around. The term ends on December 20, feast day of St. Ammon of Thebes, who as you must know was beheaded in Egypt in the year 250 after suggesting to the guards of the prison, during a vigorous torture session, that they hear the call and become converts. The guards thought he said something about having the balls to become convicts and handed him his entrails on a plate."

"Brother Mo has no religious affiliations but does possess a great knowledge of religious holidays and all things monkish. He is a veritable encyclopedia of feast days. He also speaks six languages and plays a mean hand of canasta. Brother Mo is also chairman of the board of the Nelson chapter of the Foreign Legion."

The director handed Mr. Germaine a colourful brochure and explained that it contained a wealth of information on the school not covered on his short tour. He recognized the brochure's cover as a photograph of Nelson's Big Orange Bridge. Upon closer inspection, there appeared to be something suspended by a rope a little ways below the bridge. A magnifying glass revealed the staff of the school inside a large wooden crate, dangling from the bridge on a cable and waving excitedly to the photographer. Inside the brochure appeared to be blank. Mr. Germaine turned it over and opened and closed it several times before looking, somewhat baffled, in the direction of the director, who handed him half a lemon.

"You need to squeeze a little lemon juice on it and then hold it over an open flame."

Mr. Germaine rubbed the lemon on the blank brochure and took the proffered lit candle from the director. As he moved the paper over the candle, writing began to appear—just before it burst into flames. The director handed him another brochure. He repeated the process with greater success and read the text that magically appeared before his eyes:

The Vallican Hole School of Stealth, Detection and Hard Knocks offers a three-year training program in stealth, detection and deductive reasoning, based primarily on ancient martial arts manuscripts and the investigative methods penned by Douglas Adams and Sir Arthur Conan Doyle. The Hole School received its charter in 2003, due in large part to a typographical error, with a staff of six and a student population of eight. Ten short years later the staff and student populations have more than doubled. The school is fully accredited in British Columbia as a technical institute. Graduates of the program have found such varied careers as security systems analysts, investigative journalists, police officers, private investigators, bartenders, hotel security personnel, front desk clerks, convenience store front-line staff, and vagrants.

The staff of the school includes:
➢ Henderson Cairo—Director of Operations
➢ Holmes Barcelona—Professor of Deductive Reasoning
➢ Dr. Watson Amalfi—Professor of Forensic Analysis
➢ Namaste Santa Fe—Yoga, Dance and Seductive Arts Instructor
➢ Moneypenny Constantinople—Stealth and Combative Arts Instructor
➢ Friar Horace Mogadishu—Language and Spiritual Arts Instructor

The director had been sitting at his desk looking at his watch while Mr. Germaine read the brochure. He suddenly leapt to his feet, reached over and tore the brochure out of the hands of a startled Mr. Germaine. As he threw the brochure into the large metal wastebasket beside his desk, it burst into flames.

"All a part of our national security clearance, I'm afraid. The brochures self-destruct after ninety seconds. I'm sure I don't need to explain to you the number of lawsuits we've had from slow readers. Shall we continue with the tour of the facilities, Mr. Germaine? Might

I call you Heinrich? Perhaps Susan? No. Very well, Mr. Germaine, please come this way."

The director led his client through a maze of hallways, offices and staircases, eventually arriving on a rooftop deck overlooking Baker Street with the lake in the distance. The rooftop included two main sectioned-off areas. The largest consisted of a wooden dance floor with a yin-yang symbol in the centre and some shooting-range targets set up against the far wall. A row of lockers and an open-air shower sat in the corner. The director walked past the target area, through an oval wooden gate and into a walled-off area consisting of a Zen garden surrounded by low wooden benches. One section of the garden was covered with yoga mats and another was set up with stools, easels and painting supplies. He led Mr. Germaine to one of the benches and sat down. The entire rooftop, while open to the elements on the sides, stood covered with a new type of self-heating Plexiglas using embedded solar chips to prevent snow accumulation during the winter. Nelson typically received several feet of dry Kootenay powder snow during the winter months.

"As you have discovered, Mr. Germaine, the school has relocated to the top two floors of the four-story Burns building, which has been anchoring this block of Baker Street since 1899. Built by the cattle baron Patrick Burns, it once housed the largest butcher shop between Vancouver and Winnipeg. The butcher shop closed in the thirties and the building now houses two retail stores on the main floor, a zoo-themed wallpaper store called the Flattened Zebra and a marriage counselling and adult specialty shop called Leave It to Beaver. The second floor is home to City Mouse, a government-funded sustainable-harvest venture dedicated to providing space for free range chickens in under-utilized office buildings. The school occupies the rest of the building and since it is one of the tallest buildings in the downtown core, the rooftop training area is virtually invisible."

The director stood up quickly and walked over to the edge of the rooftop, peering over the wall to the alley below. He picked up a small potted plant and dropped it over the edge. A tempered crash and concerned meow could be heard from below.

"Damn cats."

Chapter Twenty-One

Elephant Mountain Radio, located at the corner of Baker and Hall, sat on the top floor of a three-storey brick heritage building complete with turrets and wrought-iron balconies. The building owners operated a combination lingerie shop and pet store on the ground floor called Pet These Puppies. Elevators were rare in Nelson, having been banned decades before to promote fitness and to encourage heritage-building restoration. Zuzu's twice-weekly workouts on the StairMaster were not in vain, as she made it up the four flights only slightly ruffled, parched and a little sweaty. There were three offices along the narrow hallway. Two of the offices, whose frosted glass doors read "Dog Gone Investments" and "Ponzi Possums," appeared vacant. The door to the third office appeared broken. A *Baywatch* poster had replaced the glass. Pamela Anderson's impressive cleavage appeared most inviting, as someone had written "Elephant Mtn" on her left breast and "Radio" on her right. Zuzu knocked softly on the wall beside the door. Nothing happened. She knocked again, louder.

"Entrée! Bienvenue. Hola. Olly olly oxen free."

Zuzu opened the door and walked into the smallest office she had ever seen. The room could not have been more than eight feet wide by about ten feet long. A large oak desk consumed most of the available space, leaving just enough room to stand on one side and just enough room to sit on the other side. Sitting behind the desk, a peculiar looking older gentleman with a large white moustache and tufts of white hair peeked out from beneath the pith helmet he wore. He wore a khaki-coloured, military-style shirt with what appeared to be a hedgehog embroidered in red on the pocket.

"Jasmine De Janeiro, I presume? I'm Commodore Gerald Foxington Oddfellow, owner of the station."

"Nice to meet you. Just call me Jazz, everyone else does."

"Righty-oh then. Feel free to call me Commodore."

"Righty-roo, Commodore."

"Spot on. Please have a seat or stand at ease. I have your resume before me. You graduated with honours from Juan de Fuca University in Asian Art History and you have a post-graduate diploma in criminology, specializing in art theft, from Simon Fraser University. I assume Jasmine De Janeiro is a nom de plume."

"Yes. My given name is Zuzu von Trapp."

The Commodore fell back in his chair, knocking the pith helmet off his head and sending askew his thinning white hair.

"Good Lord. Not *The Sound of Music* von Trapps?"

"Yes. My father Christoph was the youngest of three children Maria and the Captain produced after their escape from Salzburg. I hardly knew my grandmother. The constant singing drove my father crazy and some bad blood existed between them. I can still remember the last time she visited, her spinning around on the front lawn singing 'The Hills Are Alive' just to aggravate him. My father used to bring out grandfather's naval whistle and blow it when he felt upset. The final showdown was something to see—the two of them facing each other a foot apart, Maria belting out 'Climb Every Mountain' while my dad blew his whistle. I was only six when Maria died from a cerebral hemorrhage while performing 'The Lonely Goatherd' at the mall. My grandfather died decades before I was born. I use a stage name to avoid retelling the story."

"Your resume mentions some radio experience?"

"I had my own show, *The Trapp Door*, on Fuca U Radio while I attended college. More recently I worked for a small gallery in

Vancouver and travelled frequently to Japan. Some underworld figures owned one of the collections we were interested in. They also managed the Megalopolis Radio Network, which broadcasts a limited number of English language programs throughout Japan. Long story short, my boyfriend was kidnapped and beaten like a rug by the *yakuza* for pretending to be some sort of private dick and I was blackmailed into hosting a live radio call-in program to basically advise ex-pats not to fuck with the yakuza. After four episodes they cancelled *Yakity-Yak* and my boyfriend was released. We moved back to the Coast but drifted apart, and he moved back to Nelson while I stayed in Vancouver. While attending SFU, I worked as a DJ in a private strip club, half of which consisted of a glassed-in cigar lounge. You may have heard of it—Butts and Sluts. That's pretty much it in a nutshell. I need a job and there aren't any openings at any of the Asian art galleries in town. The Blushing Beaver seems to be the only strip club in town, except for that clothing-optional dentist's office, Grin and Bear It, and the clothing optional day spa and tanning salon, Red Red Robin—none of which are taking resumes. You weren't the first on my job-hunting list but you did make the top fifteen."

The Commodore, stunned by her candidness but clearly impressed by her cleavage and revealing yoga apparel, mopped his sweaty brow with a handkerchief and directed her to get out of his office and go to the sound booth. The sound studio, fully encased in floor-to-ceiling glass panels, seemed only marginally larger than the Commodore's office. Inside the booth sat a glass desk, a glass chair, and two clear, plastic, high-backed bar stools. A microphone stood on the desk beside a small soundboard with a large red button and a large green button in the centre. As Zuzu passed back through the Commodore's office on her way out, he handed her a schedule. She would be on the air at midnight.

When Zuzu returned at eleven thirty, she almost knocked over a young woman in an F. M. Rogers High School uniform. The fact that Nelson should have its only high school named after the soft-spoken, cardigan-wearing host of the *Mister Rogers* children's television program said a lot about the population. Zuzu had driven by a construction site earlier in the day and had noticed the Ernie Coombs Memorial School sign being erected in honour of *Mr. Dressup*, the iconic Canadian children's television show. The cute, pig-tailed, mini-kilt sporting young lady who backed out of the office mouthed, "Thanks for having me," in reply to the Commodore's "Thanks for dropping by." The Commodore attempted to smooth his rumpled hair as Zuzu squeezed by his desk.

Ned the technician sat before a large panel of complicated-looking switches and knobs, which he appeared to adjust randomly without ever removing the smouldering cigarette from his hand. He sat separated from the studio by a large glass panel, which captured most of the smoke billowing from his lungs. He would have been a dead ringer for Tom Selleck, if he were taller by a foot or two, and handsome. His shoulder-length hair was greying and tied back into a ponytail. He wore large, black, horn-rimmed glasses that predated the type that had recently come back into fashion. His trimmed moustache and goatee seemed at odds with the contours of his face but lent an air of sophistication he neither invited nor deserved.

Zuzu glanced into the sound studio and immediately recognized the man with the headphones seated behind the glass desk. He had aged and looked a little more rotund but his signature shaved head and soul patch betrayed his true identity. Famous for his commando-style talk shows, Jack MacLeod was a legend in the Vancouver radio scene. After reducing politicians and celebrities to tears for decades with his frank and direct approach, he had retired to a small cabin on Kootenay Lake. After a few years of relative seclusion, Jack had approached Elephant Mountain Radio with an offer to resume his show, *Hey Ewe Get Off MacLeod*. He settled into a routine two-hour slot every Tuesday and Thursday night. Zuzu observed the master at work for the last half of the open-line portion of the show. He looked up and nodded toward her as he took a drink from his glass, moved the microphone closer and bellowed into it.

"MacLeod. Line one. You're on the air."

"Hi, Jack. Love the show. I'm Len from Balfour, first-time caller . . ."

Jack slammed his fist down on the large red button beside the microphone.

"Too much information. Next caller. MacLeod. Line two, you're on the air."

"Hey, Jack. Bob, from Blewett. What do you think of the NHL lockout?"

Jack slammed the button down again.

"We don't do sports here, lad. Tell you what though, Bob-from-Blewett, why don't you get off your fat ass, take that wee prick of yours down to the rink, grab a beer, sit in the stands and watch some youngsters play some real hockey, ya daft sot. Ah, I see line three flashing and Ned has just informed me that we have a special caller."

Jack raised a tall half-full glass of what appeared to be rum and coke and drained it.

"MacLeod. Line three, you're on the air."

"Hi Jack. It's Betty from Procter."

"Ah Betty. Now here's a lady who knows the ropes, knows how to share an opinion. Welcome back, Betty. We haven't heard from you for a while. Are you keeping well, luv?"

"Oh, thank you, Jack. Yes, I'm well—oh, the usual problem with my hip, and I can't seem to find my glasses, and my daughter-in-law, Judith, don't get me started there, but . . ."

Jack slammed his fist on the red button.

"Too much information, dear. Keep it brief, keep it clean, and GET TO THE FUCKING POINT. Next caller. MacLeod. Line one, you're on the air."

With five minutes to go, Zuzu went back to the green room and used the facilities, grabbed her bag and listened to Jack's theme music, the Rolling Stones' "Get Off of My Cloud," play him out. Coming out of the sound booth, Jack greeted her with a soft hug and an air kiss on each cheek. She seemed a little surprised by his warmth.

"Sorry about that, lass. I've been in this flipping town too long. I would've punched you if we were still in Vancouver. Break a leg with your show and don't take any shit from the deadbeat callers."

Ned tapped softly on the smoke-filled side of the glass booth and pointed at the red light flashing above the sound studio door. Zuzu rushed in and took a seat behind the glass desk. The light above the door turned green. Zuzu von Trapp had left the building. Jazz De Janeiro was on the air.

"Good evening. Welcome to CFUC at ninety-three point five on your radio dial. You're listening to Elephant Mountain Radio, where we never hide the elephant in the room. Welcome to *Jazzercise*, my new show that will run twice a week, following *Get Off MacLeod* and preceding the late-late-night call-in show, *What the CFUC?*, with host and technical wizard Ned Nimrod. I'm your host, Jasmine De Janeiro, but you can call me Jazz. I've come to your beautiful city from the coast and I'd like to let you all know how lucky you are to live in Nelson and the stunning West Kootenay. Let me tell you a little about myself. I grew up in a small town in Montana that was named after a snake. I can appreciate cold beer on a hot day and hot rum on a cold day. I love the sound of a cello. I love *ukiyo-e* woodblock prints. My favourite film is Ridley Scott's *A Good Year* and my favourite book is *The English Patient* by Michael Ondaatje. Now let me tell you a little about the show. To all you music fans out there, this show is not about jazz. This show is about you and me, and about puppies and world peace. Over the next few weeks I hope we can get to know each other. I will have an open-line segment and special guests. Let's start the show with a call from a local DJ, Sweet Pickle, who is releasing a new track from his latest EP, *Big Pickle in a Little Jar*."

The sound of soft sobbing could be heard when she hit the green button.

"You had me at cold beer, Jazz. You had me at cold beer."

More sobbing ensued until Jazz uploaded the track and pressed the large red button on the console. The studio filled with electronic house music. Ned gave her the thumbs up and lit another smoke. He picked up the microphone from the desk in front of him.

"Your first interview has arrived. Should I send him in?"

Jazz nodded and moved the two chairs to face each other. She placed a headset on the opposite chair. An elderly man dressed in a vicar's garb walked into the studio. His white Van Gogh beard complemented the closely cropped white hair. On his head he wore some sort of religious beanie that resembled a Scottish Regimental cap. He shuffled into the room looking somewhat dazed. Jazz offered him a glass of water, which he gulped down noisily. She gave him a headset and told him just to speak in a natural tone. She had asked for a sample of locals to interview on the air without any regard for age, sex, or occupation. Judging from the first arrival, perhaps she should have been a little more specific. Ned slowly faded the music volume down to almost nothing and gave her the five-four-three-two-one signal with his free hand. She made out only the five and the three through the smoke.

"Welcome back to *Jazzercise*. To those of you still with us, I'm with Vicar Vladimir Vladivostok of St. Sebastion's Anglican Church here in Nelson. Welcome, Padre. I understand St. Sebastion's is celebrating a milestone this year."

"Da. Thank you, Jazz. I do not have mild stone but I have big balls at the church this year."

"Wrecking balls, Pastor Vlad? I understand that you are building a new wing on the church, the first addition to the building since it was built in 1898. There are so many lovely stone buildings here in Nelson."

"St. Sebastion's is stoned too, Jazz, much like my home in the gulag. Many stone buildings built near end of century. I come from Russky Island off coast of Vladivostok. First school in Vladivostok built in 1899. It is very much like Nelson, without all the hugging."

Through the smoke, Jazz could see Ned make a circular motion with his hand to speed up the interview.

"The new wing is under construction now, Your Homeliness—sorry, Holiness?"

"Da. We have to demolish the rectum and dig up the cemetery to install the new baptism pool."

"Do you mean the rectory, Your Worship? When do you expect it will be complete? Where are services being held during the construction?"

"Da. We have service up the road at Casbah of Merry Virgin. Not on Sunday. Bastards. We have service on Tuesday. Infidels."

"You mean the Cathedral of Mary Immaculate? It's nice that you can share facilities with the other churches."

"We appreciate the infidels very much."

Ned frantically mimicked the slice-across-the-throat signal with his right hand while making a hanging-from-a-noose gesture with his left hand.

"I see we've run out of time, Vicar. Thanks so much for coming in to tell about all the exciting things happening at St. Sebastion's. Next time we will have to discuss the two bestselling books you have written —*Jesus H. Christ: The Man, the Myth, the Legend,* and of course the new one, *Oh My, Jesus: Scantily Clad Parishioners in the Pews*. Have a safe walk home, Your Bishopness."

Jazz hit the mike-off button and opened the door to let the shuffling Russian out of the sound booth. Ned seemed happy to get him out of the building before everyone had shut off their radios. He pointed to the microphone on the desk and mouthed the words, "On the air."

"Welcome back to *Jazzercise*. That's about all the time we have for our first show. Thank you all so much for being a part of it. Stay tuned for the Ned Nimrod open-line show, *What the CFUC?* The number is 250-352-CFUC, that's 250-352-2382. The lines are open."

Zuzu saw the red light over the door go out. She sighed audibly, gathered up her things and walked numbly out of the sound booth. She couldn't make out Ned's face through the thick smoke inside the sound booth but she waved in case he could see her. She could hear Ned's first caller as she walked past the booth.

"*What the CFUC?* Line one."

"What the fuck, Ned?"

"I hear you, dude, I hear you."

Chapter Twenty-Two

On her way back to the Laughing Cow Motor Inn Zuzu bumped into Monique. She had stopped briefly to buy some coconut water at the Kootenay Kangaroo Co-op and ran straight into Monique near the bulk section. Zuzu helped her up off the floor and they exchanged a big hug. Zuzu was pretty sure that Monique squeezed her ass when they were hugging but she didn't let on. She agreed to join Monique for a nightcap at the Vocal Varmint, a spoken-word jazz bar located above Bee Hive Hair, in a cool old three-storey building with sixteen-foot coved ceilings and period furnishings. They shared a double-sized wingback chair, the only seat left in the crowded room. Zuzu ordered a Barking Spider, Monique a Flaming Giraffe. They were just in time for the headliner, Vinny Boombah, who did a spoken-word performance of the take-out menu from So Su Mi Sushi. When he finished his act four minutes later, half the audience gave him a standing ovation while the other half appeared to be applauding but were just trying to flag down a waitress for last call.

Monique enjoyed squeezing into the tight chair and took the opportunity to run her hand up Zuzu's thigh. When Zuzu turned to protest, Monique kissed her softly on the lips. Stark chose that moment to walk across the room with a round of drinks in coconut husks, with straws and little umbrellas, for the three of them. He snuggled between them in the chair, much to the dismay of Monique. She rattled off a long string of strong-sounding French and made the grapefruit gesture again, while motioning with her eyebrows toward Zuzu. She stood up, tut-tutted, stomped her foot, grabbed her coconut drink and stormed off across the room. Stark handed the other drink to Zuzu.

"She's a little miffed that she forgot to pick up some melons today and thanks you for the lovely time."

"You don't even speak French, Stark."

"They speak with their hands, Zoo."

Zuzu settled into the seat and sipped her drink, which looked and tasted a lot like a Hawaiian Punch Slurpee but with fresh coconut, fresh mint and six ounces of rum in it.

"Is everyone in this town gay, Stark?"

"If by gay you mean overly affectionate, full of joie de vivre, with the wonder of a child and a similar attention span, then yes, everyone here is gay."

"That's not what I meant, Stark."

"OK then, it's about fifty-fifty. Can I get you another Cuban Missile Crisis?"

"No, thanks. I think I should drink some water. Did you go to see your old teachers?"

"Holmes and Watson? Yes, I did. They think the letter is linked to a maritime event that happened here at the turn of the century."

"I heard Nelson was the biggest city between Vancouver and Winnipeg at the turn of the century. It may not have been as weird back then. What happened?"

"From what I can gather it has something to do with a sternwheeler sinking in a storm. It may also be tied into the legend of the gold boulder."

"What's the legend of the gold boulder?"

"There is a plaque about it over at Gray Creek on the east shore of the lake. To give you just the highlights, some local rubes were out searching for cows when they stopped for lunch and found this big moss-covered rock that turned out to be solid gold. It wasn't really all that big but it weighed about a tonne. They tried to lower it into a boat but the rope broke and the gold boulder went straight through the bottom of the boat to the bottom of the lake, which was about four hundred feet deep. Wham, bam, thank you, ma'am. End of story."

"Wow. That's kind of weird. Ever since I arrived here I've been having these dreams about boats sinking and storms and stuff. Seems like a strange coincidence."

"Master Ho would say there are no strange coincidences, only strange incidents. Fate leaves breadcrumbs on the trail but destiny eats them. He talks like that a lot. It's difficult to figure out just what he is getting at but he means well."

A woman in a red tank top with black leggings and spike-heeled Jimmy Choo boots who had been standing near their chair came over to join them. Zuzu stood up and gave Namaste a tight hug. She took Stark's place in the chair as he went to the bar to launch another missile.

Chapter Twenty-Three

Stark sat down on the wooden stool set before the fire. He rubbed his hands together for warmth and to dispel the nervous energy surging through him. Holmes sat observing the pair from across the room while reclining on a leather chaise longue. Zuzu took Starks hands in hers and looked deep into his soft grey eyes.

"Are you good with this, Stark? I don't have to hypnotize you if you don't want me to."

Zuzu had learned the skill as a child, at the knee of her Aunt Macy, who had been a fortune teller in a travelling circus. She had used her talents on a few of the early cases she had worked on with Stark. Zuzu considered the spinning-watch method of hypnosis to be cheap theatrics, employing instead the click-clack method that utilized a popular children's toy. Two glass orbs, each suspended by a short length of string or cord joined to a handle, when swung together would describe opposite arcs before colliding and making a click-clack sound. Who could have predicted that two glass balls colliding with a tremendous G-force directly in front of a child's face could be dangerous? After several lawsuits and a sudden surge of interest in pirate eye patches, the manufacturer pulled click-clacks off the market and went back to making lawn darts. Zuzu discovered quite by accident that when the device swung softly at a steady cadence, it had a mesmerizing effect.

"We need to find out what happened. I'm good with it, Zoo. I trust you with my life."

The steady cadence of the click-clacks had already begun to take effect, slurring Stark's speech so that the word "life" came out "wife." Zuzu continued a soft click-clack rhythm until Stark fell into a deep sleep and his head slumped forward.

"Listen only to the rhythm of my voice. Notice how it sounds like the click-clack of the balls. Let the sound of my voice soothe you. Let my voice wash over you like waves on a beach. When I count backward from eight you will be completely under my command. Do you understand?"

"Yes."

"Four . . . three . . . two . . . one. Let's go back a few days to when you got a phone call from a woman who asked you to meet her at the Snoring Elk Hotel early in the morning. You woke up late, dressed and ran down to the hotel. You saw her pacing on the sidewalk in front of the hotel. You were crossing the street to meet her. Tell me what you see."

Stark's voice came slow and heavy, as if he were speaking in slow motion.

"I . . . am . . . cross . . . ing . . . the . . ."

"You can speak in your normal voice now."

Stark's regular voice returned.

"I see the woman on the sidewalk in front of the hotel. I am crossing the street. The crosswalk timer on the corner is counting down: ten, nine, eight, seven, six, five . . . at four I hear a cracking sound from above. I look up and draw into a defensive stance. I see something falling—large, black, tumbling in the air . . . a piano."

"Stop there. Freeze the frame. You will see the rest in slow motion, one frame at a time."

Stark's voice returned to slow motion.

"I . . . see . . . some . . . thing . . . fall . . . ing."

"You can speak in your normal voice now, just see it in slow motion."

"Something black falling. A piano . . . tumbling . . . something on one side . . . gone now . . . piano falling . . . spinning . . . something tied to one side . . . gone now . . . piano . . . turning . . . getting closer . . . thirty feet . . . body tied to one side . . . look at sidewalk . . . woman gone . . . piano tumbling . . . piano hits ground . . . splat . . . run to help . . . woman under piano . . . hand sticking up . . . take hand to check for pulse . . . nothing . . . funny tattoo . . . police."

Stark began shaking and sweating, fidgeting in his chair, swatting imaginary flies. Zuzu bent down and took his hand in hers, leading him to his feet. She hugged him and rubbed his back.

"It's OK now. You're safe. It's over. When I count backward from ten, you will slowly regain your focus. When I say three, you will feel relaxed. When I say two, you will tell me exactly what happened in Japan. When I say one, you will address me as honey bunny. When I snap my fingers, you will awaken. You will feel refreshed and alive. You will feel a great weight lifted off your shoulders. When I snap my fingers again, you will no longer be under my command."

A short while later Stark heard a sound like a finger snap. His eyes shot open. He felt refreshed and alive. Holmes had left. Zuzu sat across from him with a big smile on her face. She looked beautiful. Stark leaned over and kissed her. Then he noticed that he wore a set of bunny ears and Zuzu's bra and panties. He fondled the bra cups and looked quizzically at Zuzu.

"Honey bunny?"

"Opportunities like this don't knock every day. You can't blame a girl for having a little fun."

Zuzu snapped her fingers again.

Chapter Twenty-Four

Japan - 2008

When Zuzu offered Stark the chance to accompany her to Japan, he jumped at it, hoping to take their relationship to the next level. Just before they left, he received a message from Master Ho asking him to retrieve a copy of a manuscript from a rare school of *ninjutsu* while he was in Japan. Air Canada's direct flight from Vancouver to Kyoto included stops in Honolulu, Taipei, Seoul, Shanghai and Tokyo. Stark would not admit to being afraid to fly, but held Zuzu's hand tightly enough to leave marks until the plane left the tarmac. Once airborne, in an effort to keep his mind off of the flight, Stark led the passengers in a singalong of every Broadway musical hit known to man, as well as sixty-two verses of "Barnacle Bill the Sailor," including the fourteen rude ones in guttural Japanese.

Once safely on the ground in Kyoto, Stark and Zuzu caught a bus for the hour-long drive into the northern mountains to the rural village of Ohara. They were booked to stay in Ohara No Sato, a small traditional inn located close to the Sanzen-in Temple, which dated back to the year 985. Stark wanted to visit the ancient Buddhist temple before heading to Zuzu's appointment at the Jotenkaku Museum within the nearby Shokokuji Temple grounds. While Stark wandered around the grounds in amazement, Zuzu successfully arranged her Vancouver gallery's showing of the museum's collection of prints by

Tokuriki Tomikichiro, who helped re-establish Kyoto as a centre for print making in the pre-war and post-war periods. Since no visit to the Shokokuji Temple is complete without a dip in the public baths, Stark and Zuzu jumped in to frolic in the buff with a tour bus full of wide-eyed seminary students from Kansas City. Early the next morning, Stark and Zuzu continued on their way to Kobe. Stark noted how the lush green hills in the countryside whizzing past the train window were similar to those up the Slocan valley back home.

Zuzu arranged to meet some members of the Yamaguchi-Gumi family of yakuza who had offered up a collection of original prints by Kawase Hasui, who had been possibly the finest artist of his generation in the early twentieth century. The gallery she worked for did not ordinarily deal with underworld figures but such an extraordinary opportunity demanded an exception. After a short walk from the train station, they found the Negiya Ryofukaku, a small traditional inn, surrounded by a lush forest, with a spectacular Zen garden and its own outdoor hot-spring–fed public bath. Stark wasted no time disrobing and plunging into the scorching water. Zuzu joined him and had a pleasant conversation in broken Japanese with another couple who had just arrived from Osaka for the weekend. The meeting with the Yamaguchi-Gumi was set for four o'clock the next afternoon.

While Zuzu prepared for her meeting, Stark decided to take the bullet train to Yokohama, the port city just south of Tokyo, to meet with Master Ho's contact and pick up the manuscript. Stark left at five in the morning, joining the throngs of salary men taking the same leg north to Osaka, before boarding the Tokaido Shinkansen bullet train, which covered the three-hundred-mile journey to Yokahama in just under two and a half hours at speeds of up to one hundred and seventy miles per hour. Once in Yokohama, Stark made his way to Yamashita Park for a scheduled meeting with his contact, a few blocks from the largest Chinese community in Japan. Stark made his way to the third bench from the left, facing the pond and beneath the massive camphor tree, as per Master Ho's instructions. After waiting almost an hour past the appointed time, Stark was preparing to leave when a rope dropped down from the tree above him and dangled unsteadily in his face. Stark glanced around to ensure he remained unobserved before grabbing onto the knots tied into the thick rope and gaining a foothold in the loop at the end. He found himself being slowly hoisted into the canopy of leaves above him. Once secured on a thick branch, he noticed the man whom Master Ho had described dangling upside down and hogtied to the trunk of the tree. For a second Stark thought he glimpsed the face of Jesus McMurphy, his arch-enemy, through the leaves. As a protective measure he dove forward, lay flat on the branch and entwined his limbs in a death grip around it, performing the Wu-style tai chi posture "Python Takes a Knee." He felt the presence of the three ninjas before he saw them or the smoke bomb that exploded just before he lost consciousness.

Stark awoke in a darkened room, tied to a chair. A large Japanese man with close cropped hair and no neck stood guard by the door, shirtless and covered in colourful tattoos depicting the fifty-three stations of the Tokaido, the infamous shogun-era route between Kyoto and Edo. The man noticed Stark lift his head and walked over to his chair to deliver a backhand across the face. The force of the blow sent Stark over backward. As he went over his right foot shot up, connecting forcefully with the groin of the large no-necked man in the classic Sun-style tai chi posture "Startled Horse Loses a Shoe." When the oversized thug regained the ability to stand upright he grabbed Stark by the throat and throttled him with a cantaloupe-sized fist. Stark saw it coming and quickly threw his head back, narrowly avoiding a trip to the morgue. For the next several hours the thug beat Stark senseless in what Master Ho had once referred to as "a long walk off a short pier."

When Stark regained consciousness he started babbling incoherently, the obvious result of the spent syringe that lay on the table next to him. The no-neck thug was nowhere in sight, having been replaced by a stern fellow in a white lab coat sporting black horn-rimmed glasses. He asked Stark a series of questions that Stark later had no recollection of answering. By the end of the hour he had given up his computer passwords, his ATM PIN codes, his connection to Master Ho, his locker combination at the Nelson Rec Centre, his involvement with Zuzu and the nature of her negotiations for the paintings with the Yamaguchi-Gumi in Kobe.

Stark felt a hand shake him awake some time later. Strapped again to the chair in the first room, a man in a black business suit sat opposite him. He took a long pull on his cigarette, grinned and blew the smoke in Stark's face. He spoke in halting English.

"You have been a naughty boy, Mr. Stark. I am Takumi Moto, head of the Kansai branch of our organization. You have dishonoured us by attempting to steal an item of great historic value. The brotherhood of Banke Shinobinoden Kensyujyo ninjutsu is strong. The Takumi-Gumi clan of the yakuza has its roots in the warrior class of assassins who practice this art. Attempting to steal our founder's original manuscript was unwise. Your girlfriend's insulting offer to the Yamaguchi-Gumi for the rare works of art was also unwise. You can thank your former acquaintance Mr. McMurphy, one of our lab consultants, for suggesting that she host a radio show for us to make up for her poor judgement. Had your sensei Master Ho not proposed an acceptable deal we would have killed you both. He has managed to obtain and return the original manuscript to our hands. He explained to us that the theft resulted from an untrustworthy contact. The man you saw in the tree will not see another sunrise. In order to show our appreciation to Master Ho, we have arranged for you to be entertained by one of our geishas."

Stark began to protest but stopped when Mr. Moto held up a hand and spoke again.

"Should you refuse our hospitality we would be forced to show your girlfriend the business end of a shallow grave."

"I would be pleased to accept your hospitality, Moto-san. Zuzu and I aren't really that close. She is more of a sister to me than a girlfriend.

Perhaps more like a stepsister or a distant cousin."

Mr. Moto stood up and struck Stark a glancing blow across the head with a wooden kendo sword. The room went black. Stark regained consciousness some time later lying on a futon in a hotel room enclosed by rice paper screens. Sitting at a desk across the room, a woman dressed in a traditional Japanese kimono, with a large bow on her back, carefully removed the white face paint of a geisha. She turned and nodded to Stark before returning to the mirror to complete her task. She introduced herself in broken English as Miko-san. She stood up and removed her clothing before lying down on the quilt-covered tatami mat in the centre of the room. Stark got up and stood before her, shrugging the black silk kimono he was wearing off his shoulders before speaking.

"Miko-san, you are the most beautiful geisha I have ever seen. Your twin peaks of delight, impressive in both size and uniformity, beg to be climbed and conquered. Your forest of love, trimmed like a bonsai, reveals the beauty of your jade gate, as inviting as a cherry blossom to a bee. You can clearly see how your beauty has transformed my little warrior into a samurai. I can see you are startled by its dimensions. I admit that it frightens me at times. I want you to know before we begin that I respect your body, your intelligence and your geisha skills. You are a priceless Ming vase, Miko-san, even if you are forced by your underworld masters to do unspeakable things with your vessel of love. If we must lie together tonight to honour the Takumi-Gumi, let us not do so in vain. Show me the way. Teach me how to pleasure a woman until her toes curl, and how to achieve my life's ambition—a standing ovation from the woman I love. I will devote myself fully to your needs and desires. I will lick the love sweat from your hidden folds and secret passages should you so command. I ask only that you tell your criminal bosses that I have fulfilled their request. Should I scream out the term 'Holy Mother of God' several times, do not be alarmed, as I shall only be praying for a swift resolution to our dilemma."

The young geisha got comfy on the quilt, wet her lips and pointed to his inflated manhood.

"Kondo-san?"

Stark picked his jacket off the chair and pulled a box out of the pocket, holding it up.

"Right. Got the party pack."

Chapter Twenty-Five

After undergoing hypnosis, Stark felt flummoxed. When the instructors at the Vallican Hole School of Stealth, Detection and Hard Knocks were flummoxed, they relied on chaos theory to create order from disorder. Stark picked up his phone and punched in a number. It was time for a meeting of the board. He called the Vallican Hole School and asked Henderson Cairo to send over a quorum for the meeting and to bring the board. While he waited for them to arrive, he recalled the director delivering a motivational speech from his graduation year.

"I want you all to know that I have been in the very same shoes you find yourselves in now. I also want you to know that in the past I have been inebriated and incarcerated, and I have been committed to an institution for the mentally unsound. During those stressful times I developed the philosophy of this school. The philosophy focuses on three areas. First: stealth, for which we train in theoretical physics, soft shoe dance routines and ninja camouflage skills. Second: detection, for which we train in deductive reasoning, forensic analysis and water witching. Third: hard knocks, for which we train in the combative arts. After three years of intensive study, most of you will graduate without lasting injuries or recurring nightmares. You may be assured that your time here has not been wasted—although you, Johnson, have been wasted almost constantly. Aside from reaching the type of peak physical condition normally found in circus performers or air-traffic controllers, you have attained the level of skill necessary to slip through the world undetected and solve the most baffling conundrums. Always remember that if you follow the random path in life, chance and destiny will be your constant companions. If I may paraphrase Douglas Adams, 'You may not have gone where you intended to go but I think you have ended up where you needed to be.' Welcome to our world. Go forth and prosper."

Stark snapped out of his reverie when the group arrived, bustling and laughing in his outer waiting room. He welcomed Namaste, Brother Mo, Moneypenny and Henderson Cairo into his office. Zuzu arrived and received a big hug and kiss on the lips from Namaste. Stark completed the round of hugs and spoke to Henderson.

"Did you bring the board?"

The director held up a well-worn board-game box marked *Cluedo* and replied.

"The original British version created to pass time in air-raid shelters during the Blitz."

Moneypenny quickly assumed control of the game and the room, moving furniture to set up the board on the large carpet in front of Stark's desk and handing out game pieces to the group. She kept Mrs. White, gave Colonel Mustard to Henderson, Miss Scarlett to Zuzu, Mrs. Peacock to Namaste, Reverend Green to Brother Mo and Professor Plum to Stark. The cards were quickly shuffled and three cards were placed in the solution envelope: a character, a weapon and a room. The remaining cards were dealt to the players, the dice was rolled and the game began. Within moments Stark, Henderson and Moneypenny were all shouting suggestions to narrow the field of suspects. Brother Mo piped up to change the subject and reign in the keeners.

"Holmes mentioned that this was all connected to the sinking of some ship in 1898. Would you happen to know the date of the incident, Stark?"

"November 29."

"Ah. Feast day of St. Brendan of Birr, not to be confused with St. Brendan the Voyager, so called because he had his own oxcart. A disciple of St. Columba, St. Brendan of Birr died in 572 after falling into a vat of grapes while preparing the sacramental wine. St. Columba had a vision of angels carrying away St. Brendan's soul but later recanted after cleaning his glasses."

The director leapt to his feet and shouted at Namaste, who appeared to be doing a back handspring as she demonstrated the *urdhva dhanurasana* yoga pose to Zuzu.

"Namaste. Get your head in the game, girl."

As usual, the game deteriorated quickly into a shouting match of suggestions and accusations. Moneypenny made the decision to call it a day and left to deliver the game report and solution envelope upstairs to Holmes. Zuzu and Namaste left to grab a coffee, holding hands and giggling, and randomly stopping to perform more yoga poses as they went. Henderson and Brother Mo left to return to the Vallican Hole. Stark sat at his desk when they left and waited for the call. As he had predicted, the results were inconclusive, resulting in a tie between Colonel Mustard in the library with a lead pipe and Miss Scarlett in the lounge with a rope. Stark thought a better solution might be a rat in a hotel with a piano. He wondered if the board game reflected the influence of destiny and fate in life. Considering recent events, he realized that one cannot escape one's destiny nor change one's fate, but one could change the path toward that destiny and help shape that fate. The woman who had called after his meeting with the Rat had helped shape her own fate by stepping into her daughter's shoes. Perhaps her fate was always to save her daughter's life by losing hers. She couldn't have known that if destiny drops a piano, fate might not catch it.

Chapter Twenty-Six

Moneypenny Constantinople, the daughter of Canadian diplomats, spent her childhood in several countries around the globe as her mother and father were posted from one embassy to the next. The longest stretch had begun in her twelfth year. Her parents were posted to the Canadian consulate in Nagoya, Japan. The consulate sat two blocks north of the Higashi Betsuin Temple, built in 1602 by the Tokugawa shogun as one of two temples of the pure-land sect of Shin Buddhism. Behind the temple, hidden near the garden wall, stood a small thatched-roof building that housed the Niten Ichi Ryu *kendo dojo*. Niten Ichi Ryu (two heavens as one school) traced its ancestry back to Japan's most famous swordsman, Miyamoto Musashi. Moneypenny kept a dog-eared copy of Eiji Yoshikawa's nine-hundred-page epic *Musashi* under her pillow.

Moneypenny lived with her parents in an apartment above the consulate. When not attending class at the international school she spent all of her free time on the temple grounds. She loved the Zen garden and the giant golden Buddha in the main temple hall. She became fast friends with Tamiko, whose father, a ninth-generation *ueki-ya* (professional gardener), was sensei of the dojo. After six months of mopping floors and trimming shrubs, Moneypenny was accepted as a student and became Tamiko's training partner at the dojo. Moneypenny was drawn to the style in part because Musashi was so confident of his aggressive two-sword system that he replaced his steel swords with wooden *bokken* (hardwood sword) in his final years.

After three years of twice daily workouts, she achieved *shodan* (first-degree black belt) at the age of fifteen. At the age of eighteen, when her parents were transferred to the Canadian embassy in Christchurch, New Zealand, Moneypenny had earned her *sandan* (third-degree black belt) and had become the first foreigner to win the All Japan Junior Kendo Open Championships. Four years later she earned a degree in landscape architecture from the University of Canterbury, before spending three years at Oxford on a Rhodes scholarship in oriental studies. Her brilliant thesis—creating a Zen garden based on Miyamoto Musashi's *Book of Five Rings* and Benjamin Hoff's *The Tao of Pooh*—won her a master of letters degree and an invitation to join the faculty of several prestigious colleges in Europe and North America.

Moneypenny spent the next five years teaching in the graduate-level Landscape Architecture program at the Rhode Island School of Design. Throughout her college years and afterward, she continued her kendo training, achieving the rank of *renshi* (sixth-degree black belt) at the age of thirty. When the department shifted focus to less intensive courses to lessen the failure rate for their pretentious students—whose Tea Party parents were shelling out fifty thousand dollars per year— she agreed to teach a course called "Zen for Men." While at a martial arts conference in Vancouver, Moneypenny met a tai chi master from a small mountain town in British Columbia who invited her to come and visit a small private college called the Vallican Hole School of Stealth, Detection and Hard Knocks. She fell in love with the school, the eccentric staff and the town of Nelson. When she received an invitation to join the faculty, Moneypenny jumped at the chance to return home to Canada for the hockey, the coffee and the hugs. Within a few months of her arrival, she had opened her own Niten Ichi Ryu kendo dojo and taught senior and junior classes of about a dozen *kendoka* (students) each, in addition to her duties at the Vallican Hole School.

Moneypenny stood at the edge of the rooftop, gazing down at a busy Baker Street afternoon. She turned and walked silently through the row of kendoka engaged in *suburi* (striking exercises) with the *shinai* (bamboo sword). She paused occasionally to correct a posture, sword grip or strike. Each kendoka wore a navy blue *kiekogi* (jacket) and matching *hakama* (wide-leg pants). Moneypenny wore a white keikogi with the black hakama and weathered black belt of a sensei. Looped into the belt were two short bokken. As she strode across the tatami mat into the centre of the dojo, she addressed the group.

"Today I am going to demonstrate the concept of *suki*—to create an opening. Today I will teach you what my sensei taught me on the day I achieved shodan. He taught me that to understand suki, you must understand the first rule of combat."

Moneypenny whirled around swiftly, drawing the bokken from her belt as she spun, and walloped the nearest student in the back of the head, causing him to summersault into a heap on the mat. He rolled over and looked up with glazed eyes, rubbing the back of his head.

"The first rule of combat is to always expect the unexpected. Class dismissed."

Moneypenny tucked the bokken back in her belt and walked casually past the row of stunned students and into the waiting elevator.

Chapter Twenty-Seven

Captain Lars ducked into the small locker room and changed into the dry clothes that Tank dragged off a chair, then made his way up to the wheelhouse. The crew on the bridge had begun to panic over the strengthening storm and did not notice that their captain had dressed as a head waiter. For the most part the passengers were kept amused with free drinks and rousing, bawdy choruses of sailors' ballads, led by a chaplain from Queen's Bay. The Italian passengers took turns singing excerpts from Rossini and Puccini operas. The two youngest were in their early twenties and could hold the long notes until the crystal glasses on the bar began to shake.

Captain Lars transferred command to Luke, who seemed otherwise occupied and did not comment on the captain's strange dress. Lars climbed down the spiral staircase from the wheelhouse into the boiler room. Caleb, black with soot and drenched with sweat, madly threw freshly split birch into the firebox. Waves were breaking on the bow faster than the tilting of the vessel could drain the deck as the water began to slosh about his feet. Spray from the waves smashing on the large crates on the foredeck blew into the open doorway, making the boiler sing as cold spray met hot steel. Caleb focused on the job at hand and did not notice the captain enter the close quarters. Captain Lars shouted over the din of the wind, the hissing of the boiler and the sizzle of the burning wet wood. Caleb glanced up to see the Captain shouting at the boiler.

"Caleb. I need more steam to power her through the storm. Can you get the boiler much hotter?"

"Sorry, Captain. I didn't see you. I'm over here. This wood is shit. It's mostly green and what isn't green is wet. It's all I can do just to keep it burning. Maybe we should accept the shelter of Pilot Bay until the worst of it blows over."

"We need to push on, Caleb. Just do your best. I'll get Yuri and Yori to jettison a few cords of wood if the swells get any higher. I don't know why she's riding so low in the water. They must not have unloaded all the ore at the smelter. Can we still make it to Kuskanook with half the wood on deck?"

"We should still have enough. Just don't get rid of the dry logs, if there are any."

Caleb turned back to split more wood and cram what he could into the firebox. Luke's loud voice bounced down the staircase.

"Captain. You'd better get up here. Looks like the back of my nuts out there."

Lars scrambled back up the stairs, regaining his sight just in time to witness the cause of Luke's panic. The wind had shifted direction and increased in intensity. The bow had drifted several feet away from the waves and toward the shore. If they could not bring the bow around to face the wind, they would find themselves crossways to the swells, and with the extra weight in the bow, they would scarcely avoid capsizing.

"Bring her around, Luke. Bring her around or we're done like chicken. Yuri, Yori, toss all the wood over the side. Faster, you Bolshevik bastards. Billy, get down to the passenger lounge and tell Lucky Jim to ready the lifeboats. Get those damn Italians to stop singing and give you a hand. Luke, give me the wheel and go help ready the passengers. Caleb, more steam."

The situation rapidly became a crisis. Captain Lars could not bring the big boat around in time. The heavy swells began to slap the side of the ship like a spurned lover. She listed to port so far at one point that the smokestack took on water. Luke prepared the passengers to abandon ship, discovering too late that the deck-side bin marked "Life Jackets" contained nothing but children's alligator-shaped float toys. As soon as the first lifeboat launched, the group stampeded and swamped it. Only three of the five aboard were rescued from the lake. Two more went in from the second boat but managed to grab onto a hastily inflated alligator. Luke brought out a flare gun and fired one round into the air and a second directly at the group of panicked passengers, singeing the eyebrows of several. The group settled down. The other two lifeboats were soon ferrying the passengers to the shore. The ship had listed very sharply away from the wind, trapping Lucky Jim under the overturned bar as the saloon became submerged. In the boiler room young Caleb managed to narrowly avoid the driveshaft that sheared away from the boiler under the force of the waves and crashed down toward him. He wasn't as lucky with the boiler itself.

Captain Lars had another spell while abandoning the wheelhouse and clung to Tank's collar as he scrambled over fallen obstacles, making his way through the nearly capsized vessel. Tank began barking furiously as they passed through the engine room but Lars failed to see Caleb crushed under the rubble of the boiler. Tank growled and moved toward the foredeck where Luke struggled to cut the ropes, trying to pry the large crate free from where it was lodged behind the main mast. Lars struggled to get a foothold on the deck, feeling the driving force of the rain like needles on his skin. He shouted through the wind.

"Luke. What the devil are you doing out here? Did the passengers all get away?"

"A few crew and a few passengers unaccounted for, but most are safe. The last boat is just returning. There it is now."

Lars turned but did not see the oar coming. He lay dazed against the wooden crate, noting a yelp and a splash before he lost consciousness to the sound of breaking glass as the pilothouse rained down on the deck around him.

Chapter Twenty-Eight

Holmes stopped pacing in front of the fireplace, placed her empty glass on the mantle and turned to face Watson. She stooped to pick up the vacuum cleaner that Mrs. Hudson had neglected to put away. While bent down, she noticed a small white shape on the rock-climbing shoes she had left in the corner. She stood and held out a finger to Watson.

"Maggot!"

Watson pointed back and countered, "Hose bag!"

"I beg your pardon, Watson?"

He pointed again.

"There, on the floor—you forgot to move that hose bag from the vacuum cleaner out of the way. You will trip on it as sure as blazes."

"What did you just say?"

"I said you forgot to move that hose bag."

"No, before I found the maggot on my shoe."

Holmes placed the specimen in an empty pill bottle as Watson responded.

"I said, 'It's a pity we can't see how it really played out.'"

"By God, that's it, Watson. We can act it all out. 'The play's the thing, wherein I'll catch the conscience of the King'—*Hamlet*, act two, scene two. Perhaps your theatre friend, the odd chap who does all those historical plays, could help us out. If I am not mistaken, there is a performance of the off-Broadway musical *Reefer Madness* tomorrow evening at the Alley Cat Theatre. If we could entice our underworld friends, Anton Ratzlaff and Damian Dreadlock to join the audience, we could force one of them to reveal their cards. Leap like a gazelle to your phone, old boy. There is no time to lose. Pour us a couple of stiff belts first, old chum, for as you often say when becoming aroused, 'This could be a long one.'"

Holmes sat in the armchair by the window, moving the curtains just enough to glance down at a lonely Baker Street below. A tall figure in a trench coat leaned against a street lamp and sparked a cigarette. Filling a pipe from a small Chinese box on the side table and sparking it to life with one of the long fireplace matches kept in a vase beside the chair, Holmes felt at peace. Puffing madly, she held the sweet smoke in her lungs for a moment before expelling a huge blue cloud into the room.

"This could be a job for the Baker Street Irregulars. I believe most of them are out-of-work actors. We haven't made use of them since 'The Incident at Brokeback Mountain' last summer. They are keen, mostly unemployable and well suited to this dangerous business."

"I think you mean 'The Adventure of the Well-Hung Jury,' when we took Betsy over the Kootenay Pass to Cranbrook."

"Did I ever share with you the story I heard when we worked on 'The Case of the Abandoned Shaft'? Some years back we had a francophone prime minister. As the story goes, he was preparing to depart on a tour of western Canada. He had scheduled stops in Edmonton, Calgary and Cranbrook. The prime minister had thinning hair and always wore a hat when outdoors. In the process of packing for his trip he asked his wife to advise him on the many options laid out on the bed. Their conversation went as follows (please excuse my attempt at a French accent): 'I wear the toque in Edmonton and the cowboy hat in Calgary, but what should I wear in Cranbrook?' She looked at him quizzically. 'Cranbrook? Where de fox 'at?'"

"You have told that one before, Holmes. But I love the way you tell it. Would you like to come to see my friend at the rehearsal? I believe it begins in about an hour."

"That should give me just enough time to write a little addendum to the play."

Holmes sat at the desk and typed at a furious pace on the laptop for about fifteen minutes before printing off a few pages and handing them to Watson.

"Make some copies and hand them out to the actors as daily rewrites. They won't notice the script change until they get to scene eight, where Mary is shot. I have changed the scene to have Mary drowned in a bathtub before being tied to a piano and thrown out the window. Have a read through, Watson. I believe it is quite a smooth transition. 'Brevity is the soul of wit'—*Hamlet*, act two, scene two. We will have to bring in a piano and bathtub and leave them backstage. I will call the Irregulars and get them moving on it. Off you go to your meeting, Watson. I shall hold the fort here."

"But Holmes, you can't just add a scene that fundamentally changes the play. They have rehearsed it for months. To throw this rewrite in the night before it opens just seems wrong."

"Do you know the history of the musical *Reefer Madness*, Watson? It had the misfortune of opening off Broadway just four days after 9/11. The production was doomed from the start with its unfortunate timing —it never recovered and closed within the week. Catchy tune, though: 'Reefer madness . . . ree-fer-mad-ness.' Doomed from the start, Watson. No one will notice the script change."

"Holmes. I know the theatre. I once played Captain Jack Sparrow to a packed house at an open-air theatre in Darfur. Three local critics referred to my performance as 'pure genius,' 'astounding' and 'a snore-fest.' I can assure you that they will notice a change in the script from a character that is shot after a short struggle with a gun to a character that drowns in a bathtub, is tied to a piano, and is then thrown out a window."

"Perhaps you are right, old boy. I have it. I shall have the Irregulars replace the entire cast. Send the leader, that Cooper chap, up here on your way out. He can play the lead. The boy is pure magic on the stage, Watson."

The Irregulars managed to smuggle a lead box containing a radioactive isotope used for medical treatments into the dressing room backstage by disguising it as complimentary takeout from So Su Mi Sushi. When the starving actors opened the box, they were exposed to low-level radiation, as well as an invisible paint that blew out of the lid as a mist. The invisible paint glowed blue in the presence of a black light, which one of the Irregulars, who was dressed as a janitor, turned on in the hallway. The entire cast panicked at the sight of the blue paint glowing under the light and went into voluntary quarantine in the isolation ward of Kootenay Lake Hospital.

With opening night just a day away, the Irregulars managed to take over the play and had a full twenty-four hours to memorize their lines. The stage manager and director had been over at the Blushing Beaver for a liquid lunch and returned to find an entirely new cast, crew and script. The stage manager accepted the rewrite as a challenge and quickly set about building a set to accommodate a bathtub drowning and a falling piano.

The next evening saw Holmes and Watson disguised as two Russian babushkas, wearing head scarves and long black dresses, sitting in the row behind Anton Ratzlaff and his wife, Minnie. Locally they were known as the Rat and the Mouse. Sitting beside them were Damian Dreadlock, known locally as Dread-Head, and his life-partner, Silas. Holmes had made arrangements with Jack MacLeod to phone up Silas and the Mouse and offer them a pair of tickets to the musical for guessing correctly what Jack wore beneath his kilt. Silas responded more descriptively than necessary, while the Mouse needed a second shot at the question. The calls resulted in the presence of the Ratzlaffs and the Dreadlocks at the Alley Cat Theatre on opening night.

Holmes and Watson sat unobserved behind the power couple, close enough to witness any reaction to the play within a play but far enough to avoid being overheard in conversation. At intermission the Irregulars received a standing ovation. Deciding to stay true to the original production and use genuine marijuana cigarettes instead of props throughout the play helped. The audience sat bathed in blue smoke up to the lower balcony by the end of intermission. Three-quarters of the way through the final act, the script change approached and Holmes watched the Rat intently to gauge his reaction. When the murder scene unfolded—Mary drowned in the hotel bathtub, her lifeless body tied with rope to a piano before being thrown out the window to crash on the sidewalk below—the Rat giggled while Dread-Head began shaking and making gurgling noises in his throat. He kept trying to get up to leave the theatre but a disguised Holmes shoed him back down with angry Russian words and gestures. When the play ended—after three encores—Holmes overheard Dread-Head giving directions to one of his henchmen near the exit to liquefy their assets.

Chapter Twenty-Nine

At exactly 6:52 a.m. Stark pulled into the parking lot of the Granite Parrot Golf and Country Club. Golfing this early in the spring was a major victory in itself. The Nelson tourism brochures advertised that you could ski and golf on the same day. Although occasionally true, most years this meant that three feet of snow covered the golf course and an extra bucket of balls and snowshoes were in order. Stark's black-and-rust-coloured 1985 Lada Signet sedan, purchased from Yugo Girl Iron Curtain Auto Emporium in Castlegar, backfired loudly while spewing a huge cloud of blue smoke when he attempted to turn off the ignition. Stark regularly abandoned the vehicle several times a month as one breakdown or another occurred. A uniformed parking attendant kissed the pavement as the Russian race car blew off another cannonading backfire before shaking and sputtering itself into silence. Stark turned to the attendant.

"Lighten up—it's a Lada."

The angry-looking young man in the imitation RCMP red serge uniform rose warily from the asphalt and brushed himself off. Stark was trying to open the nasty-looking trunk latch when the key snapped off. Attempting to remain inconspicuous, he retrieved a bear flare from the back seat and shot a hole in the lock. The parking attendant whirled around with an angry glare as he strode up the steps into the clubhouse, shaking his head as he disappeared inside. Hastily Stark grabbed his bag of Sam Sneed–autographed clubs that dated back to sometime before the invention of string and dragged them toward the pro shop.

The mayor of Nelson, Jim "Dawg" Germaine, was an easy man to spot on a golf course. He wore green and orange plaid polyester slacks with a white belt to match his white Footjoy golf shoes. The neon-green golf shirt he had chosen for the occasion complemented the orange golf cap emblazoned with the City of Nelson logo. Had he added a red rubber nose he could have had a career under the big top. Practicing putts on the green beside the clubhouse, he looked up and nodded as Stark passed.

Stark found Anton Ratzlaff, dressed in red-plaid, plus-two golf slacks and an apple-red golf shirt, warming up impatiently at the first tee box, using what appeared to be a sand wedge to drive great divots of earth and soggy grass toward the row of gleaming white golf carts that stood stoically along the red brick pathway. He stopped to glare at Stark, who was wearing conservative khaki slacks and a tan golf shirt with the little alligator on the pocket, then drove another clump of grass toward the roof of cart number three, which had begun to resemble a pygmy hut, as depicted on *Mutual of Omaha's Wild Kingdom*. The Rat grunted and snorted at Stark, spitting out words through gritted teeth.

"Glad you could make it, 'Kid. We tee off in two minutes."

Ignoring the Rat's obviously pissed-off demeanour, Stark propped his Sam Sneeds against the railing and removed the Bullwinkle J. Moose–head cover from the one-wood, which he referred to as the Antichrist. Stark would, under normal circumstances, prefer to pluck out his own eyes than use a one-wood on the first tee but due to an unfortunate infestation of rodents on the rooftop deck above his office, the rest of his clubs, with the exception of a putter and a nine iron, were broken or eaten. Stark fished around in his tattered red-plaid golf bag and came up with a Titleist that looked like it might still have a few whacks left in it.

"Two minutes is fine with me. I warmed up in the car."

Stark knelt down to cinch up the buckles of his Birkenstocks and noticed two gentlemen step out of the pro shop. Stark recognized the plump older fellow in the yellow jogging suit as Damian Dreadlock, the outspoken city councillor while the other was Mayor Dawg. Rumour had it that Dread-Head had used his underworld contacts to turn a small plumbing business into the largest building contractor in the Kootenays. Their voices rose in anger as the mayor shoved Dread-Head harshly off the cart path and onto the grass. He jumped back to his feet and lunged at the mayor, stopping short when another golfer approached on the path. Dread-Head glared at the mayor and strode off in a huff towards the lounge. The figure that stepped between them, dressed in white slacks and a blue Hawaiian shirt, needed no introduction. Stark knew her from his high school days when they had both worked for the campus rag. After graduating she had become a big shot reporter for the Toronto Star. She had recently returned to town to manage the *Nelson Daily Crow*. Stark waved and grinned at her.

The Rat had asked Stark and Marcia "Badger" Casablanca to join him and the mayor for a match to see if they could sniff out any underworld ties to the piano incident involving his daughter. The mayor had a reputation as a man who always had his hand out, looking for a payoff. He wasn't known as Dirty Dawg for nothing.

Aside from a ridiculously stringent dress code, the Granite Parrot Golf and Country Club also had a mandatory golf cart rule. Stark won the coin toss and the privilege of sharing a cart with the Dawg, leaving Badger and the Rat in the other cart. From the outset the Dawg made it clear that Stark would not be taking command of the vehicle. As usual, the early morning start brought out the best in Stark's game. On the par-five first hole he miraculously managed to make the green in six, then two putted, for a respectable eight. The Dawg, who earned a six even though he landed in both sand traps, remained stubbornly silent until they reached the second tee box. Stark tried to pump him for information on the piano incident but golf appeared to be as sacred to the Dawg as donuts are to policemen. When Stark casually mentioned the name "Awesome Eldorado" as they were driving toward the woods to find his second tee shot, the Dawg careened the cart off a slippery elm tree.

After five-putting the green, Stark managed to keep his score in the single digits on the challenging par four. The Dawg managed a birdie after driving two shots into the creek. When Stark questioned the validity of his calculations, the Dawg suggested they switch cart partners for the next hole. Stark opted to ride with Badger over the Rat, since he knew that, like him, she had a natural slice, and unlike him, she would still have beer left in her cooler. Badger hadn't changed much in appearance over the past decade. Still cute, still a little on the plus side and still smoking hot, like a dormant volcano. As they were approaching the final green, Stark asked her to pull over so he could "walk the iguana." He tried to discreetly write his name at the edge of the sand trap but as usual he had trouble with the *k*. The unscheduled stop put them well behind the other cart. As they raced to catch up, the Rat and the Dawg crested the hill toward the hidden green.

Stark's ears were ringing as he and Badger found themselves flung out of their cart and onto the ground by the force of the explosion. A small mushroom cloud of flame and fire rose from over the crest of the hill. They raced up the slope together and were stunned at the sight before them. What remained of the golf cart was partially submerged in the pond beside the green, as were the larger pieces of the Rat and the Dawg. The weeping willow tree next to the green appeared to be weeping blood. Bits and pieces of the Rat and the Dawg were hanging from branches and scattered over the green and fairway. Badger stopped to lose her breakfast by the edge of the pond. Stark noticed a dismembered hand, still holding a golf ball, lying next to the cup. The deceased appeared to have missed a hole-in-one by just a few inches. Stark wondered if a penalty stroke would apply. He noticed Dread-Head get into a black Escalade and beat a hasty retreat from the parking lot. Stark realised that he had just switched carts with the mayor, and that he and Badger would have been alongside the Rat and the Dawg had Stark not stopped to drain the lizard. Stark was still shaking on the way back to Baker Street—still a little uncertain as to whom the intended targets really were.

Chapter Thirty

When the Ranger Smith alarm clock rang at seven-thirty the next morning, Max was already wide awake. He had a quick shower and—dressed all in khaki, much like the railway station master—went to find a coffee. Hidden in the trees at the end of the block sat a small coffee shop called the Roasted Rooster. The barista, a beautiful dark-haired young woman with striking blue eyes behind provocative black horn-rimmed glasses, wore a black cardigan over a black tank top with a wine-coloured bra visible above the low neckline. Max ordered a triple-shot red-eye Canadiano with a twist, assuming it would be comparable to a double-double at Tim Hortons. The barista gave him a kiss on both cheeks with his change. The tattoo above her impressive cleavage was a Chinese character that read "travel south," if he was not mistaken.

Max sat, somewhat flustered, at the counter by the window and retrieved the address that Rufus had scribbled on a napkin: 221 Baker Street. The address rang a bell but he couldn't place it. He reached into one of the two envelopes he had in his inside pocket and brought out the business card that Rufus had given him. It bore the same address. Max finished his coffee and let the rush of caffeine waft over him as he wandered the six or eight blocks down Baker toward the train station. He passed several ladies' clothing shops, a few shoe stores and seven or eight outdoor specialty stores. The complexity of the window displays astounded Max. He was more used to the sublime tastes of old-school shopkeepers in Anaconda, Montana, whose idea of a window display was a sign that read "Open." The outdoor shops of Nelson seemed to be locked in a serious competition to create the most elaborate window display in town. Rivers, Oceans, Lakes, Creeks, Streams, Ponds and Puddles had a remarkable live-action window design that included one of the staff paddling a full-sized kayak madly up a waterfall, while the cashier attempted to knock him off the display with a fly-fishing rod. Customers could shoot rubber arrows at him with a crossbow.

Not to be outdone, the window display in Snow Bro, Snow Ho included a huge snow-covered ramp where customers could test out the demo skis at full speed, landing in a swimming pool filled with Jell-O. Both stores were full of customers but had little action at the till. Max continued on his way down the street, receiving hugs from two or three random street people who just appeared to be lonely. Before he knew it he stood in front of 221 Baker Street.

Max stopped to read the names between the door buzzers and the mailboxes near the building's side entrance. Stark Investigations occupied 4B on the fourth floor, located opposite 4A—an office shared by Dr. Bob Smiley, a freelance mortician, and a Dr. Betty Giggles, the city coroner. After climbing up the four flights, Max rapped softly on the recently repaired frosted-glass door. When he got no response he twisted the doorknob and found it unlocked. From the look of the waiting room, the office had been vacated some years before, although the sofa looked as if someone had only recently risen from it. Max could not see through the large black tinted-glass window and ignored the "Take a Number" box, which read three hundred and ten, even though the "Now Serving Number . . ." sign read six. He approached the frosted-glass door marked "Private" and slowly twisted the knob. He had taken half a step through the open door when he became airborne, knocked to the floor from behind by what he sensed was a large raccoon. He found himself pinned to the floor, powerless to stop his hands and feet from being duct-taped to the legs of an armchair and a desk. When he tried to voice a protest, another piece of duct tape covered his mouth. The raccoon spoke.

"Ha ha! Not today, Mr. Nelson Hydro, not today. A week overdue and you send one of your goons to collect. Well, you can go back to your masters, Mr. Nelson Hydro, and you can tell them that they will get their blood money in due course. Do not poke Mama Bear, Mr. Nelson Hydro, unless you are prepared to be poked in return. I have acquaintances in the mayor's office. Janitorial staff primarily, but I am not afraid to call in a few markers. I could have you reassigned to bylaw enforcement, although that might be a step up—certainly a wage increase. Nevertheless, minion of the city works yard, you will not make your quota today. Admit that I have outfoxed you and you may be on your way."

Max tried to speak through the duct tape.

"Mmmph noddd nnnnesonnn hiroph."

The raccoon turned out to be a man wearing a full-length fur coat and a faux-fur Russian winter hat. Stark took off his coat to reveal a set of black long johns embroidered with gold ninja weapons.

"What? Where? Oh very well, I'll remove the tape."

Stark ripped the tape from the man's mouth in one jerk.

"Ouch. Shit. Is this how you treat all your clients, Mr. Stark? Assault them and take them prisoner? How do you sleep at night?"

"A mild sedative in a glass of cocoa. You are not from the power company? How do you explain your khakiness? You do look familiar. I must apologize. Did Holmes send you down? Perhaps we should start again. I am the proprietor of Stark Investigations. Mr. Stark Nakid, at your service. Let me help you up. Would you like a cup of tea? Biscuit?"

Max got up from the floor, brushing several layers of dust from his clothes. He looked pensively at his quarry. While the reflection staring back seemed closer to what he might see in a sideshow mirror as opposed to a real one, there did appear to be a resemblance. They had a similar look about the eyes. Far-away eyes, his mother Su Ling used to say. She would play the famous Rolling Stones' song and laugh in that way of hers, which usually ended with a coughing spasm and Max slapping her on the back. Stark walked to the window to peek out of the curtains at the sidewalk below. His thick, unruly dark hair contrasted with Max's short-cropped mane but they shared a similar Roman nose. Stark stood taller, about six-foot-two to Max's five-foot-ten. Both had a similarly lean frame. Mostly it was the grey eyes and the mannerisms—the way Stark arched the one eyebrow and the way his eyes scanned the room without moving his head. Stark suddenly turned and dropped to the floor, rolling across to his desk in the classic Wu-style tai chi posture "Snakes Get Them Off Get Them Off" before springing to his feet and taking a seat in his chair. He opened a drawer and rummaged within it, gesturing with a package of Zig-Zag cigarette papers to the chair opposite. Max sat down heavily in the brown leather Queen Anne chair before exhaling noisily.

"Mr. Stark, I have come here to share something troubling with you."

"Mr. Nakid. Or Stark. Not Mr. Stark. Might I call you Max?"

"I don't believe I introduced myself, Mr. Stark. I came here to tell you—"

"I am not without resources, Max. You came here to tell me that you are my brother."

Chapter Thirty-One

Max almost fainted with the news that Stark knew they were brothers. A glass of water helped clear his head while he tried to determine how he had tipped his hand. Stark explained the series of steps he had taken to discover not only Max's presence in town but his motives as well. The clothing, his conversations with station masters, desk clerks and others, all added up to his startling conclusion. Max felt impressed, then confused and finally baffled, before suddenly opening his eyes wide.

"You spoke to Rufus."

"I may have. He wanted to make sure you arrived safely. He said to tell you to take your medication. He also said you had a letter to share with me."

"How much do you know about your birth parents?"

"Rufus gave me the rundown on your history, Max, just as he did for you about mine. He told me about Soon Fong and Su Ling, and Boulder, Colorado. He told me about the houseboat and how Trixie found me. Rufus didn't know that before she died, Trixie told me the whole story of Simon and Simone and their untimely demise. She didn't know anything about you but she did know a little about our family history."

Stark told Max the story Trixie had related to him a few weeks before she died, when he was just eighteen. Trixie had found Stark all alone in the station wagon in the parking lot the night of the explosion.

She had broken a window in the locked car and pulled out Stark in his car seat and strapped him into her squad car. She told Stark that her initial plan was not to rescue him but to hold him for ransom. Once she had gotten Stark home and taken care of him for the night, she had opted for plan B—to raise him as her own. Plan B had lasted for a week. Trixie was a Ratzlaff, although she was estranged from her father, the famous mob boss, who had disowned her when she joined the force. As Nelson's first female police officer, she could not suddenly acquire a child out of nowhere without arousing suspicion. She couldn't formally adopt Stark without raising attention and perhaps putting the little guy's life in danger. Trixie had known that eyes were upon her and that there was only one place where Stark would be safe from those who had murdered his parents. She had a friend who had recently become a nun at the Sisters of the Precious Brood Orphanage. She had taken Stark to see Vicar Vladimir Vladivostok, of St. Sebastion's Church.

Vladimir had driven Stark up the hill to the orphanage, which was a beautiful, lush, green three-acre estate almost hidden from the mostly suburban homes in the area. A tall Japanese box hedge formed the perimeter of the estate. The entrance held an eight-foot-tall set of double wrought-iron gates that led onto a winding paved driveway, bordered on each side by alternating plum and cherry trees. The driveway led to an ivy-covered manse, connected on one side to a courtyard and surrounded on each side by long, modest, two-storey ivy-covered buildings that housed the dormitories, classrooms, and chapel. Above the main gate a sign read "Sisters of the Precious Brood Orphanage—You Breed, We Brood." Vicar Vladivostok took the boy to see Trixie's friend, the young novice Sister Moonbeam. With the help of some creative paperwork and the odd forged document, Nathaniel had become Stark Nakid, orphan at large.

Stark reached into his jacket pocket and brought out a silver flask. He unscrewed the lid, took a deep draw on it and passed it to Max, who hesitated before tipping it back. He immediately spewed a mouthful of the dark liquid throughout the room. He recognized the taste as Jägermeister. Stark took the flask back, took another short swig and returned it to his pocket. Max reached into his jacket pocket and brought out the letter. He placed the worn envelope on the desk.

"My father received this letter last week, a few days before he died. It's addressed to Mr. S. Nakid. The return address is Cayo Largo, Cuba."

Stark reached into his other jacket pocket and brought out a similar yellowed envelope.

"I have one too. It's addressed to Mr. S. Nakid at this address. Same return address. It was mailed in 1983 and I found it hidden in the bookcase."

Stark suggested that they seek counsel before proceeding further. He reached into his jacket pocket once more and brought out his cell phone. Punching numbers seemingly at random into the phone resulted in the blinking of a green light in another building, a finger pointing toward a glass partition and a button being pressed on a microphone.

"Line two, welcome to *Jazzercise*—you are on the air."

"Hi Jazz, this is Leo from Four Mile. First time caller, big fan. Do you think dogs fall in love? Do you believe in love at first sniff?"

"I'm working, Stark. Call back later."

"Interesting development, Zoo. I need you."

"You've said that before, Leo."

"The Blueberry Blowfish after your shift. Come alone."

"I always do. Next caller—line three, you're on the air."

Zuzu could hear soft sobbing and sniffing in the background.

"Sweet Pickle, is that you? I caught your webcast, *Live From the Pickle Jar*, last night. Awesome."

"You had me at 'Is that you?' I want to have your children. Not any children you already have, of course—that would be weird. I mean new children that the two of us could get together over a mocha cappuccino and create. I know what you're thinking. OK, not really—that would be weird. I imagine what you might be thinking. No heart, no headaches—but you need to be open to love. My father would often say, 'Time for you to pack your bags and hit the road.' I took that to mean it was time for me to pack up my troubles in my old kit bag and seek life's path with an open heart. I discovered only later, when I returned to find my packed suitcases on the front porch, that his simple saying had much depth. Just throwing it out there, Jazz. Breathe like you mean it. Namaste."

"Just met her the other day, Sweet Pickle. Get some rest. Next caller."

Chapter Thirty-Two

Prior to the start of her show, Zuzu had watched Jack MacLeod in action again. He had blown her a kiss from behind the glass as he hit the green button beside the microphone.

"MacLeod. Line one, you're on the air."

"Hi Jack. Hey, I guess you never want to say that in an airport. I'm Jo—"

Jack slammed down the red button.

"MacLeod. Line two. You're on the air."

"Hey, Jack. Love the show. I'm Erik, from Proctor. Just wondered what you thought of this whole keep-the-beat thing these kids do at the park to raise money. How long do they have to keep the beat?"

"Let me ask you something, Erik-from-Proctor. Would you say you know me?"

"I don't know, Jack."

"That's exactly right, Erik."

"What's exactly right?"

"You don't know Jack."

His fist pounded down on the red button.

"Look. Let's try a different approach tonight. I ask the questions. You give the answers. Next caller. MacLeod. Line two, you're on the air."

No response came.

"Good. You're listening. Now, what is your name?"

"My name is Raoul, from Queen's Bay."

"What is your quest?"

"Quest? What's my quest?"

Jack pounded the red button.

"Look, you daft bastards. These are not difficult questions. Next caller. MacLeod. Line three, you're on the air. What is your name?"

"My name is Max, from Anaconda."

Jazz almost fell out of her chair when she heard the name of the town where she was born. She managed to regain her composure and sat up to hear the rest of the call.

"What is your quest, Max?"

"Well, Jack, I guess my quest is a search for knowledge and adventure, like most great quests are. I'm searching for some long-lost stuff. Some of the stuff is people and some is just stuff."

"Now we're logging, Max. Are you silly buggers listening out there? This is a man with a quest. Every God-fearing son of a bitch out there needs a quest. If you don't have one, get one. Time's up for the show. Get off MacLeod. Sod off."

The first part of Zuzu's show went without incident. Several of the callers vented over the show's phone-in topic, urban legends and spiteful gossip, which Zuzu had chosen to stir up some local dirt. Most of it was spiteful and not at all interesting, but there were a few calls that hinted at a connection between Damian Dreadlock, organized crime and the late Mayor Dawg. She took the call from Stark just before the break.

After the break, Zuzu sat in the glass sound booth across from her interview guest. The woman was dressed conservatively in a blue skirt and matching jacket and appeared to be in the forty-something range. Her blond hair, cut shoulder length in a fluffy bob, would have looked more at home on a poodle. She held the aroma of someone who had just finished chain-smoking an entire package of Virginia Slims, two at a time. The red light above the door began blinking and Ned waved frantically through the thick smoke that filled his control room. Zuzu pressed the large green button on the desktop console.

"Welcome back to *Jazzercise*. I have a special guest with me here in the studio. Bonnie Lyzover is the owner of a much-loved pet-therapy practice on Front Street called Release the Hounds. She is the author of *Hose It Down*, the book that Oprah described as 'Eckhart Tolle with a garden hose.' Welcome to the show, Bonnie."

"Thanks, Jazz. I'm honoured to be here. It has been a real whirlwind the past few months since the book came out. Who knew it would catch on like it did. Oprah practically peed herself when we met."

"Perhaps you could explain to us how you came up with the whole 'hose it down' philosophy."

"It just came to me one day as I started cleaning up the studio after a day of pet-therapy sessions—where clients come in and basically roll around with the dogs. There was dog hair everywhere and I felt really tired, so as I surveyed the mess and filled up the water bowls with a hose, I thought, 'Why not just hose it down?' So I did. Then I mopped it up and I felt great. When I got home and began to have the daily after-school argument with my daughter, I thought, 'Why not just hose her down?' So I brought the garden hose into the kitchen and let her have it full blast. Again, I felt great. When my husband got home from work and started complaining that his dinner wasn't ready and saying stuff like 'What the fuck is that hose doing in the living room?' I thought, 'Why not just hose him down?' So I did, and let me tell you something, Jazz—it was a life altering moment for me. As I stood there with the hose in my hand and he stood there dripping wet from head to foot, I felt a power shift in our relationship. That's when I came up with the slogan 'When life fucks up, hose it down.'"

"That's beautiful, Bonnie. Words of wisdom coming from a true visionary. I'm sure at some point we've all been tempted to hose someone down. Not many people would have the fortitude to bring out the hose as you did, though. I understand the trend is catching on following your Oprah appearance. I read something about it having an effect on homeowner insurance."

"Yes. Even some law enforcement agencies are replacing their Tasers with high-powered squirt guns. The Nelson City Police have agreed to outfit their patrol cars with water cannons to see if it lowers the crime statistics. Who knows where it will go."

The light over the door began blinking again and Zuzu could make out an arm wave through the smoke in Ned's enclosure.

"Well, that's about all the time we have for the show today. I want to thank my guest, Bonnie Lyzover. Perhaps you could hose down the Commodore on your way out. Just kidding. Till next time, homies. Keep it real. Peace. Out."

Chapter Thirty-Three

Stark stood in front of his desk, one arm around the shoulder of his newly discovered brother, and gestured to the woman walking into the room.

"Max Bolder, let me introduce you to Marcia Casablanca, of the *Nelson Daily Crow*. She has been working on a story about the recent rash of suspicious deaths and she witnessed the golfing tragedy with me."

Marcia "Badger" Casablanca watched Max the way a wolf watches a flock of sheep passing below a hidden vantage point. Max appeared equally enthralled with Marcia, who was a plus-sized girl with curves in all the right places. She had shoulder-length, dark-brown hair and bright-blue doe eyes. She had a creamy milk-chocolate skin tone. Growing up as one of the few non-pasty kids in town, Marcia had developed a quick wit to bring the hecklers and the token racists to their knees. She wasn't afraid to show a little cleavage and nothing slipped by her intellect. She did have one tiny little eccentricity. When she felt attracted to a member of the opposite sex she could not contain the sexual innuendo in her speech.

"Hi, Marcia. Nice to meet you. I was hoping you might clear up a few details about the murders. Are you familiar with my background?"

"I'll bet you would like to get familiar with my background, Max. You haven't stopped staring at my tits since we met. My eyes are up here."

"Sorry, Marcia. Please forgive me. I am not used to women who are beautiful and not afraid to show it. My ex-wife thought only hos showed cleavage, and she ceased to be one soon after the wedding. After we were married the only F-word she used was "forget it," which she used a lot. Do you know anything about the circumstances of my arrival in Nelson?"

"I'm sure it was a lot like when I first came. Only louder."

Stark stepped in to relate the circumstances of the mutual discovery of their brotherhood and the houseboat tragedy that had taken their parents. Marcia opened her briefcase and brought out a sheaf of papers from the dead-letter department of the newspaper.

"I went through some of the microfiche in the records room after you called, Stark. I found a few articles about the houseboat explosion and the twelve victims, marking it as the worst maritime disaster on Kootenay Lake. They considered it odd that none of the victims knew each other, but the police investigation went nowhere. The elderly Mr. Ratzlaff was implicated in the bombing when some unexploded charges were found with his name scratched in pencil on them but the investigation hushed up on orders from the mayor's office."

Max leafed through some of the reports while looking directly at the tattoo of a bumblebee on Marcia's ample bosom.

"Did you get a chance to check out the drowning angle?"

"Would you like to see the rest of the hive, Max?"

Marcia cupped her impressive jugs and offered them toward Max. Stark jumped between them again.

"OK, kids. I think I'll just take these files and head out"

"There is a significant drowning angle, Stark. I checked up on the names you had on the list you sent me and the cause of death in all cases was drowning."

"Thanks, Marcia. I do have to go now. I'm meeting Jazz in five minutes. Why don't you two kids stay here in case something pops up?"

"I think something's popping up now, Max. Should we go back to your place to get to the bottom of it?"

Max and Marcia walked the few blocks to his room at the Dancing Bare Inn. After a few hands of canasta with Yogi and Boo Boo, and having emptied the contents of the mini-bar, Marcia got up from her knees and wiped the corner of her mouth with her sleeve. She whispered softly.

"Wow. I've never done that before."

"Holy shit. That was a first for me too. You were fantastic. You sure seemed to know what you were doing."

"No. I've done *that* before. I meant with my left hand."

"Oh. Well, I see. I've never reacted like that before."

"You mean asking me to marry you and yelling out the Pope's name?"

"No. I've done that before. I meant the yodelling."

Chapter Thirty-Four

Kootenay Lake – 1898

Captain Lars gingerly lifted his head and looked around the room. He was lying on a lower bunk in a small log cabin. The log walls were chinked with mortar to keep out the cold wind. His head began to swim and he returned to his former fully prone position. He drifted off to sleep and awoke to a gentle female hand lifting his head up to help his lips reach the rim of the glass of water that was offered. He took a sip of water and lay back down, exhausted by the effort. A face appeared—short black hair, angular features, sun-weathered skin, bright blue eyes. He held the gaze of a woman he had not seen for several years. Gunpowder Gertie, the Pirate Queen of the Kootenays. Lars had met her five years earlier, before she was Gunpowder Gertie, before she was a pirate and even before she was a woman.

When Lars awoke the next morning, Gunpowder Gertie was nowhere in sight and he was sure he had only imagined her while he was delirious. Gunpowder Gertie had been born Gertrude Wallace, after her mother, who had died during her birth. Her father never got over it, never remarried and had raised Gertie alone. He was a craftsman who built small skiffs and dories for local fishermen. Gertie spent her formative years in Kaslo, living above a marine supply store and spending all of her free time on the docks and boats moored in the harbour. At the age of twelve she had built a fishing dory in her father's shop. By the time she was fourteen she was helping him build a small schooner. When her father died during a cholera outbreak, she had no means of support and lacked the skills a woman would need to gain employment as a domestic servant or seamstress. She had decided that if she couldn't find work as a woman, she would find work as a man. Her small flat-chested frame fit into her late father's clothes like a glove. Disguised as a man, Gertie soon found work on a sternwheeler as a deckhand.

When Lars first met Gertie, she was the second mate on SS *Alberta* and Gertie was Gordie, fireman's helper and general labourer. Lars took the slight young lad under his wing, being struck somewhat by the keen look of wonder in his bright blue eyes. As time went by the two became fast friends, surprising given the age difference. Lars enjoyed mentoring the young man, who was smart, keen, quick-witted and unsettlingly attractive. Six months later, alone on the upper deck under a canopy of stars, Lars and Gordie witnessed a meteor shower. As they lay beside each other on the wooden deck staring up at the falling stars, Lars could no longer resist the strange urge he had to kiss his shipmate. As their lips touched, Lars felt electricity and a stirring in his loins. Gordie kissed him passionately but softly at the same time. Lars gave in to the new feelings, never having been attracted to a man before. He felt Gordie unbutton his trousers and reach in to fondle his hardness. He did not resist when Gordie's lips made the journey south down Lars body and engulfed his manhood. Lars had not felt anything so intense in his entire life and began singing all the choruses of the *Pirates of Penzance*. When a crewmate scrambled onto the deck to check out the commotion, Lars had to fake a heart attack to avoid being discovered. While Lars was lying in sick bay at the medical clinic in Kaslo, the crew mate who had witnessed their adventure had threatened to report it if Gordie did not submit to sexual favours. Gordie had refused to be blackmailed, and was beaten severely and blackballed in the local shipping community instead. Unable to work on any ship as a man, Gordie had become Gertie again, refurbished her late father's schooner and began raiding vessels on the open water. Gunpowder Gertie, the Pirate Queen of the Kootenays, was born.

A few hours later, when his shoulder was feeling stronger, Captain Lars left the cabin and snuck aboard the caboose of a freight train that had stopped near Hidden Creek to replenish its water. There he found some provisions stashed in a cupboard and a two-day-old newspaper. As he began walking back down the tracks, he heard a familiar bark and turned to see a mangy black dog running toward him, furiously wagging his tail. Lars was glad Tank had survived the sinking and had located him. In the safety of the shack he reviewed the paper and read about the tragedy. Of the thirty-one people on board, only twenty-two had survived. Seven of the crew, including the captain and first mate, and two passengers were lost. Eight bodies were recovered, but the body of the captain was presumed to be four hundred feet down with the broken ship. Lars was sorry to read the names of the victims: the first mate Luke, the replacement fireman Caleb, deckhands Yuri and Yori Jasper, Lucky Jim the barman, young Billy the cabin boy and the two unnamed Italian passengers.

Chapter Thirty-Five

Stark dashed out the door and ran down the block to the restaurant. The Blueberry Blowfish sat between the One Eye Open Optician's Office and the Nervous Sheep Clothing Outlet that occupied the ground floor behind the Foreign Legion. Stark loved the Monday-night meetings in mandatory *Lawrence of Arabia* outfits. The Légion Étrangère had bought a vacant Royal Canadian Legion hall that had fallen on hard times. The membership of the Royal Canadian Legion had dropped to the point where the Legion had become financially insolvent as a charitable organization and social club. Henderson Cairo had stepped in to take over the building's lease and form a branch of the Légion Étrangère, since he had been on its board of directors in Marseilles. Having the only recruitment office of the Foreign Legion in Canada provided Nelson with a number of unique economic opportunities, and the Légion Étrangère had successfully recruited many of Nelson's broken-hearted. Stark himself had considered enlisting when he returned from Japan.

Stark arrived at the Blueberry Blowfish just as Zuzu was making her way down the alley behind the Legion building, stopping to hug the street people as she passed. She was beginning to fit in. She and Stark took a booth in the back by the oversized aquarium. Due to religious beliefs, the vegetarian owners had replaced the live fish with paper ones, made by local pre-schoolers. The menu contained no animal products other than a large selection of free-range, deep-fried insects. Stark thought it had something to do with Zen or with the price of carrots, cucumbers and locusts compared to halibut, scallops and grain-fed beef. Zuzu ordered the salad of the day, which turned out to be a rude arrangement of eggplant, carrot sticks and garbanzo beans, while Stark had the Jungle Surprise, which turned out to be a rude arrangement of grasshoppers and mealworms. Stark noticed the glow on Zuzu's cheeks and commented on how wonderful she looked in the mountains. Zuzu blushed and kissed Stark softly on the lips. Once they had choked down the meal, they shared a large flask of hot sake, filling only each other's cups, as was the custom. Stark took the opportunity to engage Zuzu in their favourite deductive reasoning game, Riddle Me This. He leaned closer to Zuzu and spoke softly.

"North. The man. Riddle me this."

Zuzu glanced at the table closest to the bar. She studied the couple that had just arrived, the man holding the chair for his companion. They wore matching curling jackets and identical khaki slacks. After a moment or two, Zuzu whispered to Stark.

"Dribbler. Left-handed. No sense of direction. Dyslexic. Binge drinker."

Stark commended Zuzu on her improved skills, noting the small stain on the fly of the man's khaki pants, the hand pouring the wine, the forehead bruise, the upside-down pen in the pocket protector and the speed with which he drained his wine glass. Stark filled in Zuzu on his brother Max and the story that Rufus had told him. He explained how it tied into his childhood at the orphanage and outlined his untested theory of how the recent murder and the death of Max's father could be connected. They decided to pass on the cheese-less cheesecake for dessert and headed back to the office to review the letters. On their way out of the restaurant, Stark spotted the Hulk across the street, wrapped in bandages, leaning against a lamppost and pretending to read a newspaper that he held upside down. Stark told Zuzu to run as the big man lumbered across the street after them, surprisingly fast considering the crutch. Once around the corner, Stark pulled Zuzu into the alcove entrance to the Grated Groundhog, a small health-food store that sold only dehydrated meat products from free-range critters and large rodents.

Stark waited for the Hulk to round the bend and then leapt out to confront him on the sidewalk. The Hulk threw a cannon ball–sized fist at Stark's face but met only thin air as Stark redirected the blow high, dropped to one knee, turned and drove both fists straight out from the shoulders in the classic Wu-style tai chi posture "Gorilla Drives One Home," connecting the full force of the front fist with the Hulk's family jewels. As he went down in a heap, Stark advised him to breathe slowly and to pick up a bag of ice on the way home.

Safely back at the office, Stark explained to Zuzu what he and Max had discovered—that Max's letter had arrived in Boulder, Colorado, on a Friday, slipped discreetly under the front door of 513 Elm Street. It bore the address of Mr. S. Nakid at the Baker Street address and a return address of Cuba. Inside the envelope was a slip of paper and a smaller letter, with water stains that had yellowed with age, bearing a stamp depicting a blurry group of bearded soldiers firing rifles in the air and a postmark from Cayo Largo, Cuba. The letter, addressed to a Mr. Jugo Nakid at 1616 Comrade Lane in Cayo Largo, was stamped with a large red "Return to Sender" across the address and appeared to have been steamed open. Stark's letter, addressed to S. Nakid at Suite 4B, 221 Baker Street, included a hand-written note that read "We need to talk." The letter inside had been sent to Jorge Nakid at the same Cuban address and had the same return stamp. Stark opened his letter in front of Zuzu and spread the letter out on the desk. The content was startling:

To whom it may concern,

I would like to beg your forgiveness. I am the man responsible for the sinking of SS *City of Ainsworth* on November 29, 1898. Against better judgement I struck out into a terrible storm and took the lives of eight men. I will regret my decision for the rest of my life. Your ancestors were among the dead. Buried with each of them was an object of great value. As the rightful heir you are entitled to it. Should you have trouble finding your ancestor's remains, a meeting of the descendants will be arranged at the city wharf three weeks after the delivery of these letters.

Captain Lars von Trapp

Chapter Thirty-Six

Zuzu arrived at the yoga studio at ten to seven. The place appeared empty. She walked back down two flights and reread the sign for the Dirty Dog Yoga Studio. She climbed back up two flights and found the same room empty. At five after seven, as Zuzu was preparing to leave, footsteps sounded on the stairs. Namaste Sante Fe rounded the corner in a turquoise form-fitting lululemon outfit. She gave Zuzu a big smile, a big kiss and a bigger hug, before explaining the whole Kootenay-time thing, which meant that one had to add about twenty minutes to any posted time for any event that happened in Nelson. The yoga studio filled up quickly and Namaste led them through a strenuous *vinyasa* yoga workout that included some poses that strained even Zuzu's impressive arsenal. At the end of the hour, covered in sweat, Zuzu lined up to get a goodbye hug from Namaste, who whispered an invitation to Zuzu to meet the next day for lunch. Zuzu couldn't tell if the attraction was based on her own need for friendship or on something else. Namaste's sensual cherry-red lips slowly moved toward Zuzu's before brushing by her cheek at the last minute to make soft contact with her earlobe as Namaste whispered into her ear.

"You need to relax. Let the magic happen. You are not in the now. There is not enough blue in your aura. I have a solution. Please follow me."

Nelson was turning into one long therapy session. Namaste took Zuzu's hand and led her through a door marked "Private" to a beautiful, small studio, lined floor to ceiling with zebrawood panels. Namaste motioned toward the room with her hand before turning to leave. Zuzu felt imbued with the positive ions in the fresh-tasting air. She had visited many yoga studios in Canada and Japan but none had the good vibes of Namaste's private studio.

As Zuzu stepped forward, the heat in the room hit her full on like a Finnish sauna, much like it had in the hot *moksha* yoga classes she had taught at Bent Over Yoga. One corner of the room bubbled with a waterfall trickling down over the pebble-covered wall. Zuzu noticed that she was not alone in the room. A woman sat in the lotus position in front of the waterfall with her back to the room. The woman chanted softly and wore nothing, beads of sweat making the happy journey from a perfectly toned shoulder to a lovely tanned buttock. Monique Percé stood up, turned to Zuzu and smiled as she held out her hand. Zuzu sighed and took it.

When she left the studio, Zuzu could not wipe the smile from her face. She had discovered more than just where Monique's nickname came from. She felt more relaxed than she had in years. Zuzu decided to grab a coffee before heading back to the Laughing Cow for a shower, and stopped at the Gutsy Goatherd coffee kiosk outside the co-op. She opted for a double-shot red-eye with soy foam and noted how her taste for coffee, and other things, was changing.

Chapter Thirty-Seven

Zuzu sat cross-legged on the leather chesterfield in Stark's office, feeling oddly at ease in Stark's unusual domicile. Stark sat in his chair with his feet up on the desk, hitting a paddleball with deft accuracy. Both were deep in thought. A soft knock came from the outer office door. Zuzu moved to rise but Stark gave her the hand across the throat signal and she stopped. The knock sounded again, a little louder. Zuzu looked toward Stark who shook his head. The knock became pounding and rattled the shot-glass collection on the wall shelf nearest Stark's desk. He leapt to his feet and raced through the office to the waiting room where he dropped to his knees and crawled toward the door on all fours, nose to the ground in the classic Sun-style tai chi posture "Anteater Stalks His Prey." When the pounding paused he again leapt to his feet and ripped the door open, in the classic Yang-style tai chi posture "Rhinoceros Welcomes the In-laws." An elderly man dressed in a blue Canada Post uniform stood at the door, peering sheepishly inside.

"Mr. Nakid? I've come about the letter I delivered here last week. My name is Floyd Thursday. Could I have a moment of your time? I just got off shift. I hope I haven't disturbed you."

Stark stood aside and motioned for him to come in. He noted that the man walked with a hop-like gait, much like Walter Brennan in the film *To Have and Have Not*. Stark expected the dead-bee question at any minute.

Stark introduced Zuzu as Jazz De Janeiro and offered Floyd a drink. He made his way to the former kitchenette, which had recently been converted to a bar, and made them a round of Cosmopolitans. Floyd sat on the sofa beside Jazz and Stark rolled his office chair over to join them. Floyd told Jazz her name sounded familiar and reacted like a twelve-year-old girl at a Justin Bieber concert when he realized that she was a radio personality. He asked for her autograph and then hopped around the room whooping in celebration before collapsing once more onto the well-worn chesterfield. Once he had put the autograph away in his jacket pocket and took another swig of his drink, he seemed to calm down and relax. He brought out a worn envelope that looked like the one Stark had found in the bookcase.

"Mr. Nakid, I have been a stamp collector for over forty years. I got this job at the post office to collect more of them. Because there are so many stamps in circulation, and so many rare stamps no longer in circulation, we focus our collections in terms of age, symbols, events or countries."

Stark hid his hand from Floyd's view and made circular motions with his index finger beside his temple to Zuzu while draining his Cosmopolitan.

"I specialize in collecting pre-war stamps from the Caribbean— mostly from rum-producing countries like Cuba, French Guyana and Trinidad."

Stark covered his yawning mouth with his hand, rubbed his eyes and nodded in agreement. Floyd continued.

"I delivered a letter to this address many years ago that had a very rare pre-Castro stamp on it from Cuba. I delivered another one to your mailbox downstairs last week and I was curious to see if you would be interested in selling it."

Zuzu's ears perked up and she looked intently at Stark, motioning toward Floyd with arched eyebrows, pointing at the letter and silently mouthing, "Holy shit."

"Mr. Thursday, are you telling me that you delivered an old water-stained letter like this one to my mailbox last week?"

Stark plucked the letter from the postman's hand and speed-read the address before dropping it back in Floyd's hand. Stark wheeled his chair back behind his desk, rifled through the bookcase and brought out the letter with the rare stamp on it.

"I am not at liberty to disclose that kind of information, Mr. Nakid. As an employee of Canada Post, an official arm of the federal government, I could be imprisoned for a term of not less than seven years for disclosing personal information."

"Then I suppose you won't be seeing this stamp anytime soon, Mr. Thursday."

Stark held the letter up and brought a lighter out of his desk drawer, which he sparked to life and held just below the stamp on the envelope.

"My God. No. Stop. I'll tell you. Please. Yes, I delivered a second letter with the Cuban stamp. The first one I delivered here thirty years ago. The one I delivered last week was addressed to Mr. S. Nakid at this address. I noticed the broken lock on your mailbox when I delivered today's mail. This old letter was addressed to the estate of a Mrs. Wisconsin and was returned undelivered, as it was thirty years ago."

Floyd was sweating profusely and shaking like a leaf, as if he was tied to a spit over a fire at a cannibal convention. He took a linen handkerchief from his inside pocket and mopped his brow.

"Those letters mean a great deal to me, Mr. Nakid. I've seen them before. I am retiring next week after thirty years of service. I spent my first week with the post office helping to move to the Grey Goose building from the City of Nelson building on the corner opposite the Snoring Elk Hotel. To my surprise, I found a metal box containing a bundle of nine letters in an old mail sack that was stuck behind a desk up in the turret. A note inside the box requested that the bundle of letters be posted after a hundred years—in 1983, or perhaps 1998, as the note was water stained and difficult to read. I slapped on some fresh stamps and mailed them. A few weeks later two of them came back marked "Return to Sender," the Wisconsin letter and the one with the Cuban stamp. I heard that the recipients of the other letters had some sort of reunion a few weeks later on a houseboat that blew up. After that I decided to hang on to the last two letters. I found them again recently and wanted to mail them before I retired. When I put an ad in the local paper looking for information on the former recipients, Minnie Ratzlaff contacted me."

Stark took a pair of scissors out of the drawer and cut the stamp off the letter from the bookcase. He took the Wisconsin letter from Floyd and handed him the Cuban stamp before escorting him to the door. Stark thanked him for his dedication to the mail and carefully explained that should this information be revealed to anyone else, he would see Floyd prosecuted to the full extent of the law. Stark also reached into Floyd's pocket and retrieved the autograph that Zuzu had signed. He wrote "Not less than seven years" on it and stuffed it back in the pocket. Floyd shook and cried his way down the hall to the stairwell.

Stark closed the door and returned to where Zuzu remained sitting, somewhat stunned, on the chesterfield. He picked up the letter from the desk and peered at it with a magnifying glass. He handed both to Zuzu.

"Look at the return address on the Wisconsin letter."

The return address, small and smudged, read "Brunhilde Gilker, Suite 4B, 221 Baker Street."

"Spooky."

Zuzu walked over and gave Stark a hug. He walked to the closet and retrieved a large box. He placed it on the floor next to the desk.

"This arrived for you today, Zoo."

Her eyes twinkled as she cut the packing tape with a throwing knife she had pulled from a sheath fastened to Stark's right calf. The box stood about three feet tall and two feet square. She reached in and pulled out a large plush black-and-white penguin, which she hugged.

"Salty Bob."

Zuzu wiped a tear from her eye, crossed the room, stood on her tiptoes and gave Stark a long soft kiss.

"Thank you. You're sweet."

She took Bob with her and walked out of the office, back to the Laughing Cow and enjoyed a good night's sleep.

Chapter Thirty-Eight

The next morning, Stark and Zuzu got off the bus at the closest stop and walked the few hundred yards to the black iron gates of the Dreadlock Mansion. The postman's revelations about Mrs. Ratzlaff and the letter indicated that she was either up to her ears in organized crime like her late husband or she had other masters. On his first visit to meet with the Rat, Stark had noticed that a section of the bookshelf behind his chair had seemed slightly off-kilter. To investigate further, they would need to gain access to the library.

They were dressed as Hassidic Jews in rumpled black suits with white shirts, black-rimmed spectacles, full black beards, ringlet sideburns and *shtreimels*, the large round fur ceremonial hats. The standard ruse of paying respects to the recently departed, who was laid out in the library wake-style, worked like a charm. Since Mrs. Ratzlaff was expected home shortly, the rude butler left them in the library to wait and closed the door behind him. Stark and Zuzu moved past the white cloth-covered table where what appeared to be the pasty corpse of Anton Ratzlaff lay dressed in his favourite plaid suit. Since Stark had witnessed the Rat meet his demise, he knew that after the explosion, the deceased's remains could have been better displayed in a bucket. Stark pushed his finger up Ratzlaff's nose and confirmed that they were staring at a wax figure of the crime kingpin. He surmised that the genuine remains rested in the copper urn at the end of the table. He stopped to grab two straws from the nearby buffet table and placed one in each of Ratzlaff's nostrils. Zuzu chided him for being disrespectful to the dead but chuckled nonetheless. They moved to the corner and quickly combed the bookshelf behind the oversized green leather armchair, hoping to discover anything out of place or out of the ordinary.

Stark grabbed a leather-bound copy of Dashiell Hammett's *The Glass Key* off the shelf, jumped back and spoke.

"Hello. This could be the ticket."

Expecting the bookcase to slide open to reveal a secret passage, Stark seemed disappointed when nothing happened. Zuzu walked over to the large green chair and felt around on the side below the left armrest. She pressed a button and the bookcase slid open. Stark gasped.

"Show-off."

They descended a set of concrete stairs together and except for the addition of a bed beside the fireplace, found themselves in a mini-version of the library above. Both the king-sized bed with rumpled sheets and the small fire in the limestone hearth were still smouldering. Stark approached the bed and threw back the covers to examine the sheets and found stains showing obvious activity. He took out a Q-tip and swabbed the still-damp area in the centre before dropping the Q-tip in a baggy and leaning in to swipe the sheets with his hand. Zuzu winced.

"Ugh."

"Don't be such a baby, Zoo. The act took place within the past several hours. Watson can determine the parties involved with an analysis of this DNA swab.

Zuzu walked around Stark, knelt down and reached under the bed. She held up a pair of black panties with the letter *M* embroidered on the crotch and then knelt down and fished around under the bed again. She stood up and held out a pair of purple hospital scrubs.

"That may not be necessary."

Stark remembered the secret compartment in the Awesome apartment and felt around the edge of the headboard until his finger slipped into a notch. The panel above the bed slid back to reveal a map of the area, stuck with coloured pins marking various locations. A list of dozens of names was pinned to the map, most of which were crossed off in red ink. He noticed the names of Simon and Simone Nakid, as well as Soon Fong and Su Ling Bolder. Stark took a photo of the map with his phone before hearing a noise coming from up the staircase. Stark and Zuzu rushed back up to the main library, closed the bookshelf passageway and grabbed a quick plate of food and a shot of Jack Daniels before Minnie Ratzlaff entered the room. They crossed the room and met her at the door, mumbling their condolences to her as they crossed themselves, said, "Shalom," and fled out the door. Minnie appeared confused as she watched them leave, since her late husband was not Jewish. She thought about running after them when she noticed the two straws protruding from her late husband's wax nostrils. She walked over to the phone and dialled a number. A familiar voice came on the line.

"Jesus McMurphy."

Chapter Thirty-Nine

Zuzu awoke in a strange room. Her head spun as she struggled to rise but she was alarmed to find herself strapped to a gurney. Just breathe, she thought. Recalling her moksha yoga training from when she had obtained certification as a hot yoga instructor the previous summer, Zuzu relaxed and breathed deeply. Each session began and ended with *savasana*—corpse pose, not unlike the pose she found herself in on the gurney. Zuzu performed the eighty-twenty breathing method, taking in a full breath and then violently exhaling twenty percent of it through her nose. She repeated the process several times, snorting loudly like Rocky Mountain bighorn sheep preparing to lock horns in battle. The process cleared the cobwebs and let her enter the zone and enhance her senses to help take stock of her surroundings. Were it not for the confines of the gurney she would have moved through *utkatasana*—awkward pose, Stark's favourite: knees bent, arms straight above the head, hands clasped in the classic diving-board position—and then into *gurudasana*—eagle pose: one leg bent with the other wrapped around it, arms bent and entwined, palms flat with thumbs pressed against the third eye, resembling a praying child who needs to pee. Ordinarily she would have also been sweating like a young calf moose, with the temperature in the studio cranked up to somewhere in the ninety-five to one hundred and five degree range.

Zuzu could feel the sweat bead on her skin as she focused intently on the other thirty-six postures of moksha yoga, although she was able to perform only one. Only after completing the workout in her mind's eye did she realize it really was about a hundred degrees in the room. She was in some sort of greenhouse, with opaque glass windows and flowering plants on the shelves below them. She recognized several varieties of orchid, her favourite flower, which may have explained the heat. The opaque glass roof stood ten feet high while the greenhouse itself seemed to be about twelve feet wide and thirty feet long. The gurney, standard hospital issue, held crisp white sheets above a thin mattress. Three large bands strapped her to the gurney, each one six or eight inches wide. Naked below the sheet, she did not feel uncomfortable given the heat in the room. She recalled a scene in the film *Young Frankenstein* where the monster was strapped to a gurney with wide metal bands. She could see her clothes piled on a workbench near the entrance to the greenhouse.

Zuzu tried to remember how she had wound up strapped to a gurney in a greenhouse but she could only recall shadowy bits and pieces of the previous night. The pounding headache and metallic taste in her mouth returned with each attempt to remember what had happened. The feeling seemed vaguely familiar. She remembered waking up and feeling similar only once, with the headaches and metallic taste in her mouth. Of course, that was ten years ago, when she had woken up in bed with . . .

The door to the greenhouse burst open. She gasped.

"Jesus McMurphy."

Chapter Forty

Jesus McMurphy was Stark's best friend when they were boys growing up together at the Sisters of the Precious Brood Orphanage. McMurphy arrived at the age of ten when his parents and brother were killed in an automobile crash after his father lost control of their station wagon on the highway heading down into Nelson and the car plunged into the swiftly moving waters of Cottonwood Creek. Jesus had removed his seatbelt and was reaching behind the rear seat to retrieve the Nintendo player that his brother Moses had thrown when the car overturned. Jesus was thrown through the window onto the riverbank. The others were unable to free themselves from their seatbelts. The brakes had been tampered with but the investigation failed to turn up a suspect and authorities failed to locate any living relatives. Chief Inspector Francois Davide, a young constable at the time, delivered McMurphy to the orphanage a few hours after the incident.

McMurphy had become fast friends with Stark and they were inseparable from the day he arrived. He was the antithesis of Stark. While Stark was tall and lean, McMurphy was short and stocky. Stark had a mischievous twinkle in his eyes while McMurphy had a darker side. They had remained close friends until they left the orphanage after graduating from high school. They had followed different paths— McMurphy bolting the day after graduation to Gonzaga University a few hours south of the border in Spokane, Washington, where he would go on to medical school and become a pathologist. Stark had stayed behind for a year, working as a grounds keeper at the orphanage to stay close to the gravely ill Sister Moonbeam. On her last day Stark had sat with her and read out loud *James and the Giant Peach*, the book she had read to him when he was a toddler. Stark had left Nelson after the funeral, going to Vancouver to work as a front desk clerk in the Waldorf Hotel, until the siren song of the Kootenays caught his ear once more. Stark had returned home to Nelson to enroll in a new school for detectives, the Vallican Hole School, where he found what Sister Moonbeam had referred to as "his mojo."

Stark and McMurphy kept in touch but did not often visit each other. They had their infamous falling-out when Stark visited Coeur d'Alene, Idaho, for spring break. They both set their sights on the same girl they had met in the Operating Room, a rooftop lounge located on the main drag above the Wells Fargo bank, popular with the college crowd. McMurphy was smooth as a snake, while Stark was more of an awkward turtle. Stark had spoken to Zuzu first, had made her laugh and had discovered they had a lot in common. Instead of supporting Stark in his awkward attempt at romance, McMurphy had taken it as a challenge. When Stark returned to the table with a round of drinks, he was surprised to see McMurphy leave the club with Zuzu, who seemed to be weaving unsteadily. Stark had summoned all of Master Ho's lessons in emotional control in order to not run after them. When he ran into Zuzu at a coffee shop the next morning, she was crying from getting too drunk and misjudging her date's intentions, and Stark was furious. He found McMurphy at the hotel and told him exactly where he could go and the options for getting there. McMurphy told Stark flat out that he would have to choose between their friendship and "the little slut." Stark sprang at McMurphy and feinted with a straight punch before spinning clockwise to deliver a vicious back fist, in the classic Yang-style tai chi posture "Dragon Snaps like Rice Cracker." Stark left McMurphy on the floor, told him to go pound sand up his ass and never spoke to him again.

Chapter Forty-One

Jesus McMurphy was dressed in burgundy hospital scrubs, not only because he had just come off a night shift but also because he enjoyed the freedom of not wearing anything beneath the loose-fitting pants. His co-workers were initially horrified by his commando style of dress but gradually found it less unsettling than the arrogant man who wore it. McMurphy walked straight over to the gurney and cinched up the straps, whistling as he did so. He put the surgical mask over his mouth and nose and spoke through it.

"Welcome to my nightmare, Ms. von Trapp. Your convenient visit to Nelson has saved me the trouble of having to locate you again. I hope you enjoyed our little nightcap last night—I know I did."

He winked and adjusted his junk through the loose-fitting scrub pants. Zuzu glared at him.

"You sick bastard, McMurphy. I know you drugged me and fucked me, just like you did ten years ago on the night we first met. You evil prick. Stark was right about you all along. I'll enjoy seeing him kick your ass."

"Don't tell me you didn't enjoy it, Zuzu. You may not remember what we did last night but you were awake and a willing participant. You cheap sluts are all alike. Your friend Stark is an idiot. He can't save you now, Zuzu. No one can. Let's get down to business. Where is the diary of Captain Lars von Trapp?"

"What diary? Captain who? What the fuck, McMurphy? Why did

you drug me like that? You're a doctor, for fuck's sake. You could have your choice of lonely, horny nurses, doctors, clerks, switchboard operators, candy stripers. The Ladies Hospital Auxiliary is like an old cougar convention. This town is full of free spirits who don't even seem to rank gender as a priority. Why the drugs?"

"The drug I gave you ten years ago was just a prototype. My father, an amateur chemist, developed a potion to help my mother sleep that was akin to a roofie. My father died when I was very young and I did not find out about his hobby until I left the orphanage, came of age and inherited the family estate. I took a greater interest in his hobby when I discovered his secret laboratory. He had invented a new sleep aid, a combination of LSD and what would be considered ecstasy today, although the clinical trials proved it to be a failure. In my youth I found that his invention, when slipped to a companion, provided the latitude to dispense with first-date traditions. I became a practicing pathologist in order to explore my father's hobby and over the years I have refined the formula into a mind-control truth serum that your art collecting friends in the yakuza find fascinating. I call it McJesus Juice. I was in the process of selling the juice to them when you and Stark visited the yakuza in Japan. I just gave you a mouse's dose of the juice last night. Stark was given a larger dose during his interrogation with the Takumi-Gumi clan. It is an effective truth serum, but I have much larger ambitions. Larger repeated doses have a much-enhanced effect, resulting in a much larger increase in the libido and blind obedience to suggestions, a large decrease of inhibitions and a complete loss of memory. Does the term 'sex slave' mean anything to you? The yakuza has big plans to use my formula to increase its hold on Japan's burgeoning sex-trade tourism industry. As for the diary, your great-grandfather stole something from my great-grandfather. A thousand pounds of gold. I need the funds to take my product to the next level—global marketing. My sources tell me that you have recently received the diary. Don't make me ask you again."

Stark had remained still as long as he could in the corner of the greenhouse. He had disguised himself as Audrey, the man-eating plant from the Broadway musical production of *Little Shop of Horrors*. He had found the costume in the prop room of the Alley Cat Theatre. Considering that he stood at least four feet taller than any plant in the greenhouse and sported a Venus flytrap headpiece the size of a basketball, it seemed surprising that he had remained undetected. When McMurphy asked Zuzu the question again and advanced toward the gurney with a turkey baster–sized syringe, Stark bolted into action. Stepping gingerly out of the large clay pot, Stark remained undetected until he caught a leaf on the edge of a planter, knocked it over and fell face first toward the floor.

McMurphy, startled by the loud crash, turned to face Stark and held the syringe before him like a knife. Stark avoided colliding with the floor by executing a shoulder roll in the classic Yang-style tai chi posture "Ape Slips on Banana" before springing to his green fabric-covered feet on the opposite side of Zuzu's gurney. Trying desperately to see out of the eye holes of the large Venus flytrap headpiece he wore, he held the green pods covering his hands up beside his ears before hurtling a pod at McMurphy's outstretched hand. The pod flew with deadly accuracy, knocking the syringe to the floor. Stark took the split-second opportunity to vault over the gurney, narrowly brushed Zuzu's neck with an unruly tendril and drove the heel of his other pod into McMurphy's startled face. Jesus collapsed in a heap on the floor and Stark wasted no time unstrapping Zuzu from the gurney. As he helped her stand up, she stood on her tippy-toes, fiercely hugged his green stocking-clad body and kissed him full on the flytrap, dropping the sheet she wore to the floor in the process.

"I love that outfit, Zuzu. You should wear it more often."

As Zuzu tied up the sheet toga-style, the door of the greenhouse burst open to admit the Hulk, as well as No-Neck from Stark's interrogation in Japan. In a split second Stark had removed the Venus flytrap headpiece and hurtled it at the intruders. He grabbed Zuzu's hand and bolted for the door to the adjacent greenhouse. As they entered the second greenhouse, Stark and Zuzu skidded to a stop and stood stunned by the sight before them. Six more gurneys stood before them. Four held captives in the same state as Stark had found Zuzu. Stark and Zuzu stood with their mouths gaping. Before them lay the strapped-down, sheet-covered, naked forms of Namaste, Monique, Marcia and Holmes. At the end of the room, a Japanese woman in a lab coat and surgical mask turned toward them, lowered the mask, smiled and nodded toward Stark. He recognized the face and gasped.

"Miko-san."

As Stark and Zuzu stood motionless, taking in the scene before them, No-Neck came through the door and gripped his oversized hands around the back of each of their necks and squeezed. Blackness prevailed.

Chapter Forty-Two

As Stark and Zuzu collapsed onto the concrete floor, three black-clad figures dropped to the ground from their observation posts high up on the branches of the black walnut trees that surrounded the greenhouse. Lakeside Park had been the jewel of Nelson since long before the construction of the big orange bridge in the mid-fifties. A sandy beach the length of a football field welcomed visitors at the east end of the park, nearest the orange bridge, while several playing fields encompassed the western end. A restored 1906 streetcar made the journey several times a day along the tracks from the bridge to the Thirsty Trout Lakeside Hotel during the busy summer tourist season. Between the beach and the playing fields, next to the streetcar repair shop, sat several greenhouses.

The three black-clad figures silently made their way toward the end of the greenhouse where Stark had discovered Zuzu being held prisoner. A lone figure stood nervously behind a willow tree some twenty yards away. As the three figures approached the man warily, he watched them blend in with their surroundings to the point of disappearing completely. When he stepped out from behind the tree to take baffled glances around the park, they sprang to their feet less than two feet in front of his face. He noticed that two wore black ninja attire while the third was dressed in a monk's hooded black robe. Brother Mo removed the hood while Master Ho lifted his balaclava and addressed the other ninja.

"Moneypenny. Recon the greenhouse and report back."

Brother Mo knelt down to tie up his black roman sandals while Moneypenny covered the ground to the greenhouse in seconds before disappearing inside. Master Ho turned to face the lone figure by the tree.

"Watson. I got your message and established surveillance here about twenty minutes ago. How did you discover the whereabouts of Holmes, Knee-High and the others? I did not even know they were missing."

Watson reached into his pocket and brought out a pink iPhone. He showed the map with a blinking red dot on the screen to Master Ho.

"Holmes was summoned to an emergency meeting of the Nelson Historical Society in the Hoarse Hound Room at the Snoring Elk Hotel. Nothing unusual there. Holmes is on the board of directors and refers to it as the Nelson Hysterical Society since all of the meetings are considered an emergency. It must have been a set-up. The locator beacon began blinking on the phone in her office as soon as I returned from dropping her off. That's when I sent you the message. I had to gas up Betsy on the way. I double-parked on Second Street and rushed down here."

Master Ho, used to Watson's rambling nature from his stint at the Vallican Hole, began to lose his patience.

"You must stay here in case we encounter problems inside. You will need to contact Chief Inspector Davide and get some backup should we not return in short order. Do not, under any circumstances, attempt a rescue on your own. From what we could hear from our treetop perch, some sort of truth serum or poison may be involved. We may need you to develop an antidote."

Moneypenny returned with a large syringe in her hand, holding it out to Watson.

"The syringe lay on the floor in the first greenhouse. A man wearing burgundy hospital scrubs lay unconscious beside it. I could see several others held captive in the next greenhouse. The captors appeared to be preparing them for injections."

Watson took the large syringe, held it up for inspection and nodded.

"This is a Hamilton gastight syringe, model 1825, if I am not mistaken. It can be used with a needle to inject a liquid or without to inject a gas. I shall return to our Baker Street rooms and analyze what's left in the syringe. Holmes maintains a small laboratory in the master-suite walk-in closet to test her latest formulas on some of the slower neighbourhood pets. She presented a monograph on truth serum antidotes to the National Police Chiefs' convention in Vancouver last summer. Oddly enough it has a local connection. Holmes discovered that combining a dab of Buckley's Mixture, the famously awful-tasting Canadian cough syrup, with a dollop of Ryckman's Kootenay Cure for Rheumatism, manufactured in Nelson in the late eighteen hundreds, resulted in an antidote for everything from swimmer's itch to the black plague. I shall dash home to the lab, brew up a batch and bring it back pronto. I pray they do not harm Holmes. She is my north, my south, my east—"

Master Ho moved quickly to cover Watson's mouth with a gloved hand.

"We get the picture, Doctor. If you could hurry along, we may yet save the captives."

Watson scurried up the path and across the train tracks to Second Street, saw no trace of the double parked vehicle, and called a cab to retrieve Betsy from the impound lot.

Chapter Forty-Three

McMurphy regained consciousness, awkwardly pulled himself to his feet and stumbled into the second greenhouse. Stark and Zuzu had been strapped naked to gurneys and covered with sheets like the others. McMurphy staggered over to Stark and struck him a vicious blow across the face.

"I should have killed you ten years ago, Nakid. I won't make the same mistake twice. In the meantime, I believe you will make an interesting test subject. Miko-san, begin the injections."

Stark shook his head to recover from the blow. He glanced down the room to watch Miko-san inject a struggling Marcia in the thigh with a large needleless syringe. She immediately went limp. McMurphy spoke again.

"The serum need only be injected into muscle tissue to be effective. I modified a needleless syringe that uses a blast of air pressure to penetrate the skin and deliver the goods to the muscle layer of the thigh. No need for qualified medical practitioners to administer the dose. Ingenious, don't you think?"

Stark raised his head off the gurney.

"Ingenious or insane? Psychic or psychotic? Too close to call. Miko-san is your assistant?"

"Ah, yes. Miko-san. You have some history with her, Stark. She became the first test subject for the McJesus Juice in Japan and has been my companion, although you might use the term slave, ever since. I used Miko-san to develop my patent-pending McSlave mind-control program. You would be surprised what a little sleep deprivation and aversion therapy can do when the McJesus Juice removes inhibitions and enhances the pleasure centres of the brain. She was under the influence of the juice and already a McSlave when you first met her. I arranged to have the yakuza demand you sleep with her."

Zuzu raised her head off the gurney, her eyes burning with rage.

"Is that the slut you fucked in Japan, Stark?"

"A gentleman never speaks of such things, Zoo. I can assure you it was strictly a business transaction. I took no pleasure in it whatsoever. Other than the first go, possibly the second."

Miko-san giggled and squeezed Stark's sheet-covered package as she made her way up the room. She worked quickly, injecting Namaste, Holmes and Monique before returning to the workbench to get two more syringes. She returned to fire a dose into the thigh of Zuzu and finally Stark, the only one to scream like a girl before passing out. McMurphy motioned for No-Neck to follow him and strode to the exit, turning to hand Miko-san a box of assorted marital aids at the doorway.

"They should be coming around in a few minutes. You may begin the McSlave training. I have a meeting with Mr. Moto."

Chapter Forty-Four

McMurphy arrived late for the meeting, slipping in through the alley entrance at the Blushing Beaver. The driver escorted him up the stairs to the VIP booth overlooking the stage. A muscular henchman dressed entirely in black snarled at him as he entered, stepping aside to reveal Mr. Moto seated alone at the far end of the plush velvet booth. Mr. Moto turned his glance from the stage to McMurphy.

"I do not enjoy being kept waiting."

"Please accept my apology, Moto-san. I was detained by a minor complication but the situation is now in hand."

"You have disappointed us, Mr. McMurphy. You promised to deliver a functional serum to our organization some months ago. We cannot accept delays to our plans. I trust you are ready to complete our transaction in short order. I am heading back to Kobe tomorrow afternoon."

"Again, I apologize, Moto-san. The serum is very close to completion but remains unstable. I believe I have corrected the flaw in the formula by adding an equal measure of the popular local drug ecstasy and maple syrup. The final testing should be complete tonight."

"Deliver the serum in the morning or we will look elsewhere for a supplier. Inspector Francois Davide has been asking awkward questions regarding our relationship and is beginning to suspect we may have Sergeant Harry Stuttgart under our influence. The Takumi-

Gumi always covers its tracks. Do not disappoint us again."

Mr. Moto snapped his fingers and the henchman approached the booth to escort McMurphy to the door.

Chapter Forty-Five

Master Ho, Brother Mo and Moneypenny returned to perch in the trees as they waited for Watson to return with the antidote. The trio relished the opportunity for fieldwork. Stealth and stakeouts were part of the curriculum at the Vallican Hole but teaching staff was not permitted to go out in the field, other than to monitor the progress of students. The trio practiced the silent-ninja communication system developed at the Hole, which was an adapted form of Gestuno sign language—the international form of communication for the deaf that was used at the first Deaflympics in Paris in 1924 and every four years since. Brother Mo remained a novice at the practice and continually slurred his words, much to Master Ho's chagrin. Brother Mo also had a naturally occurring twitch in his left hand due to some impact-inflicted nerve damage, which resulted in his beginning almost every other word with the letter *C*. Master Ho demonstrated the correct signing of the phrase that had brought Moneypenny to tears when Brother Mo had tried to compliment her on her reconnaissance skills and an impressive hunt. They heard Watson crash through the bushes below them and dropped to the ground to join him at the base of the walnut tree. He unzipped a compartment on his fanny pack and retrieved two syringes. Master Ho smiled and Brother Mo began to sign toward Watson at rapid-fire speed. Watson gasped.

"Good Lord, man. That sounds nasty."

Master Ho grabbed the syringes from Watson and ran toward the greenhouse with Moneypenny in close pursuit. Both froze in their tracks when they burst through the door into the second greenhouse. They stared in shock at the sight before them. Holmes, Monique, Namaste, Marcia, Zuzu and Stark were spread out on a tatami mat in the centre of the greenhouse. They were all naked, covered in what smelled like coconut oil and writhing together as if in a perverted version of *Twister*. Miko-san manipulated the numerous marital aids at various locations in the twirling mass. The McJesus Juice had kicked in and intensified the pleasure centres of the brain. All five seemed to reach a tremendous orgasm simultaneously before collapsing in a naked heap on the mat.

Master Ho seemed a little embarrassed by the whole scene while Moneypenny seemed a little jealous. They quickly moved toward the panting orgasmic group with the antidote syringes. Watson entered the greenhouse just before the second coming and wondered how on earth Holmes would manage to wipe the smile from her face. As Master Ho administered a dose to Stark, the front door of the greenhouse burst open. Stark looked up through bleary eyes.

"Jesus McMurphy."

McMurphy surveyed the room quickly and decided to cut his losses. He called out to Zuzu, who had not yet been given the antidote, to join him. Forced to obey his commands, she ran toward McMurphy, once again fashioning the sheet covering her sweaty form into a crude toga. McMurphy grabbed Zuzu's wrist and backed out the door, motioning with a hand across the throat motion to No-Neck and the Hulk to take care of the others. As No-Neck pointed what looked like an Uzi toward the group, Master Ho and Moneypenny flew into action, diving toward the walls with one hand outstretched in the classic Sun-style tai chi posture "Baboon Grabs a Cold One," while reaching with the other hand to grab and deploy the Dim Mak throwing stars they each had at the ready. The throwing star hit No-Neck at the junction of the lung and the heart meridians, halfway between the nipple and the armpit, before he could pull the trigger. The effect was striking. The Dim Mak throwing stars had raised blunt ends on the star points in order to deliver a concentrated force to a thumbtack-sized pressure point. No-Neck froze as the strike caused a temporary paralysis that would last up to twenty minutes before realistic but false stroke symptoms appeared. Moneypenny's target was the junction of the kidney and pericardial meridians located inside the thigh just below the Hulk's testicles. The throwing star hit the target at the precise moment the Hulk levelled his machine pistol at the crowd. Once again the effect of the throwing star was instantaneous, and caused him to drop his weapon and lose control of his bladder as well as all sense of balance as he collapsed on the floor.

As Stark bolted toward the exit to chase McMurphy and Zuzu, he began to feel the antidote kick in. His erection subsided and the effects of the McJesus serum began to fade. He raced naked out of the greenhouse toward the beach, pulling on the only clothing available—a red Danskin leotard he found hanging on a hook by the door. To clear his mind he moved through the Fu-style *chi gong* power-stretching exercise "Four Postures of the Wind." First, *ha feng* (west breeze): running forward on tippy toes, hands stretched fully up, fingers spread to touch the sky. Second, *dong feng* (east gale): leaping up and forward, arms out and back, fingers spread, as if trying to break the plane of an invisible finish line with the nose. Third, *gundong feng* (rolling wind): diving forward horizontally, tucking the head into a forward roll, then springing to the feet. Fourth, *tai feng* (typhoon): leaping skyward and spinning, arms stretched high above the head, fingers spread, hands waving. A group of onlookers near the boat ramp appeared stunned to observe the tall man in the red leotard having some sort of mental breakdown. Stark repeated the process four times and wound up near the water's edge, feeling the damp sand squish between his toes.

The exertion left Stark panting and sweating, taking huge gulps of the cool lakeside air into his grateful lungs. He saw McMurphy at the edge of the lake, bundling a dazed Zuzu into the rear seat of a tandem kayak. McMurphy noticed Stark running down the beach toward him and pushed the kayak off the shore and into the lake. Stark stepped into the water in hot pursuit, until he came within ten feet of the slender boat. All of his senses screamed in unison as the glacier-fed water hit his lower thighs, causing him to bounce back onto the shore at twice the speed of his entry into the lake. Stark realized his chances of surviving a prolonged battle with McMurphy in the frigid water were slim. Glancing around the beach, he saw only two upturned canoes, both with large holes bashed in their hulls. McMurphy enjoyed Stark's frustration and held the kayak in place, paddling gently against the downstream current, satisfied to maintain the thirty-foot space between the kayak and the shore.

Stark raced frantically down the beach, past the old rowing-club boathouse, and skidded to a halt as he suddenly remembered what was stored inside. He dashed to the west end of the boathouse and broke the lock off the double doors with a hammer fist. McMurphy had lost patience with Stark's frantic beach run and begun to focus on paddling down the lake with a woozy Zuzu in the seat behind him. He glanced back at the beach in time to see Stark emerge from the boathouse with a large, clear plastic ball, about seven feet in diameter, which he started rolling down the beach toward the lake.

Stark had remembered the balls as soon as he saw the old boathouse. When he had been president of the rowing club, he had decided to import several water-walking balls, which had been the latest summer fad in Japan. The fundraising plan had failed—it had been a total disaster from the start. The giant, clear, inflatable plastic spheres could be climbed into to walk across water, but were designed for use under close supervision in swimming pools and were not suited to the open water or strong currents of Kootenay Lake. No fatalities had ensued but the club had only avoided a lawsuit by agreeing to destroy the balls and by impeaching its president.

After his impeachment, Stark hadn't been able to bring himself to destroy all of the water-walking balls and locked one away in the old boathouse. He enjoyed the sensation of walking on water, although maintaining balance proved difficult inside the big plastic balls. Stark found he could manoeuvre the ball competently by utilizing the skills developed with Master Ho's hamster-wheel training. During his days at the Vallican Hole School, when a student arrived late for class, did not pay attention or could not demonstrate a requested tai chi posture, the student would be relegated to the hamster wheel. The hamster wheel, a human-sized version of the rodent-cage exercise device, had been built from an old paddlewheeler frame by Master Ho. Since Stark was habitually late for class and had a penchant for daydreaming, he had spent a lot of time in the wheel. Stark would forget to press his palms and nose flat on the window when performing the classic Wu-style tai chi posture "Leopard Makes Silly Face" and Master Ho would shout, "Knee-High. Hamster wheel," and Stark would spend the rest of the day running inside the big squirrel cage. Stark would forget to bring enough gum for the entire class and Master Ho would shout, "Knee-High. Hamster wheel," and Stark would pass the rest of the day running on the large rodent device.

Stark left memory lane and let the ball roll down the beach. He ran after it and timed his dive perfectly to hit the vertical black line on the ball as it rose toward him. The black line opened up for his slithering form, then closed up just before the ball rolled into the lake. McMurphy had a lead of about fifty feet, and was madly paddling the kayak toward the Thirsty Trout Lakeside Hotel. Stark kept his breathing steady and focused on running tall in order to maintain his balance. A small cluster of Japanese tourists were standing at the end of the city pier beside the hotel, snapping photos of the chase. Stark waved and smiled at the group as he passed, wondering what they thought of the man in the red leotard in the big plastic bubble who was running down the lake. He began to slowly gain on the kayak but had only closed the gap to twenty-five feet by the time they passed the hotel dock. McMurphy seemed to be heading toward the boathouse wharf a few hundred yards down the lake. Stark could see a hooded black form race up toward the end of the boathouse wharf. As he grew closer he recognized Brother Mo flashing steel as he moved into the Wu-style tai chi broadsword posture "Magic Dragon Puffs Smoke."

McMurphy noticed Brother Mo and redirected the kayak toward Bonnington Falls. Stark began to tire inside the plastic ball but knew he must catch up to Zuzu before they reached the treacherous one-hundred-foot drop over the falls. Stark increased his pace and had closed the gap to ten feet by the time the falls were in sight. McMurphy, paddling wildly, worked his way toward the flat rock outcrops that lined the southern edge of the river. When they were within ten feet of the falls, feeling the current strengthen and pull at the kayak, McMurphy stood up. He threw the paddle in the water and jumped to the safety of the shore, causing the kayak to lurch back into the river toward the falls. He turned and yelled back as he ran.

"Sayonara, Zuzu."

Zuzu seemed to regain her senses and screamed as she neared the edge of the falls. She thought she heard Stark's voice over the sound of the waterfall.

"Sit up, Zoo. Sit up."

Zuzu rose higher in her seat, straining to hear Stark's voice. Out of the mist she saw a large plastic ball roll toward her on the water, and inside it, a man in a red leotard. Stark had timed his approach to the split second. As the vertical slit in the ball came over his head, he dove forward, causing the ball to roll over the back seat of the kayak and suck Zuzu into the opening. As he gasped for breath, hugging Zuzu fiercely and looking into her glazed green eyes, Stark felt the ball roll over the edge of the falls.

Chapter Forty-Six

Once Captain Lars felt up to it, he returned to the beach with Tank and floated the crate that had saved his life behind the waterfall and into the cave. He remembered the cave from boyhood prospecting expeditions with his father. The blow from the oar to the side of his head seemed to have cured his episodic blindness—his vision remained clear and crisp, although the mangy hound remained at his side, often tugging at his sleeve to steer him clear of objects in the dark cave. Once he had the crate secured, half-submerged but resting on the sand behind the waterfall at the mouth of the cave, he could confirm his suspicions as to why the crate had not sunk in the storm. He lit a torch and pried off the top of the crate with a piece of flat iron that he had found near the tracks. Much to his surprise, Lars found the crate to be filled with glass balls. From his younger days working on coastal freighters, he recognized the colourful balls used by Japanese seiners to float the big nets. The blue glass orbs routinely came off the nets and drifted across the sea to end up on some west coast beach.

Lars assumed the glass balls were for the Japanese garden at the new hotel in Idaho. Something about the crates still didn't quite add up. Captain Lars had watched them load the crates at Pilot Bay. The weight had almost snapped the hoist, adding to their problems in the storm. With two cords of wood on the back of the bow and the large heavy crates on the front, the waterline had run dangerously high to be heading into the heavy swells of a major blow.

Lars kept coming back to the crates. Glass floats are not heavy. A crate full of glass floats would not weigh more than a few hundred pounds. The one full of iron eagles would have been very heavy and would have sunk to the bottom of the lake. Based on how both were loaded onto the sternwheeler, the crates should have weighed a few thousand pounds. The difference seemed curious.

Lars spent the next few hours unloading the glass balls, placing them carefully on the floor of the cave. The balls were made of thick blue or green glass but varied from the size of an orange to a grapefruit. Tank wanted to use one for a game of fetch but was unable to pick up the slippery glass orb with his mouth. When Lars got about halfway through the crate he discovered two shelves that were fortified and braced on all sides to keep them sturdily in place in the centre of the crate. Each shelf held a row of black oblong statues no taller than one of Lucky Jim's wooden legs. Lucky Jim had begun his career as a seaman but had lost a leg below the knee to a shark off Vancouver Island—at which point he had become a beekeeper and lost the other leg to a hungry bear that had attacked his hives. Opting for a safer career, he had decided to become a bartender. One shelf held five of the statues, the other, six. The statues were painted black and resembled portly penguins. They were heavy. Lars estimated each one weighed at least a hundred pounds. As he finished stacking the heavy birds in a corner of the cave, Lars noticed the mark on the bottom of one penguin's foot. A name was scratched into the surface: "Luke."

Lars had worked with Luke on several occasions over the past few years, usually on short trips around the lake on one of the smaller boats. He kept to himself a lot and always seemed a little edgy and nervous. When Lars had posted the *Ainsworth* voyage to Bonner's Ferry, with stops in Kaslo and Pilot Bay, Luke had signed on as first mate. Luke had seemed particularly excited and mentioned the bonus for the speedy delivery of the cargo waiting on the wharf in Pilot Bay.

Luke seemed to relish the poorer weather, working as much as he could in the harsh winter months.

Lars knew little about Luke. Word had it that he spent most of the year living hermit-like in a trapper's cabin near Cape Horn. When the winter winds began to blow and slow the sternwheelers on the west arm of the lake, Luke would work at the smelter. Luke knew his way around a ship, having served as fireman, porter and second mate a few times—mostly as a last minute fill-in for a no-show or an injured crewmember. Luke had enjoyed the hard physical work on the boats and the lack of supervision. He had seemed to have a dark cloud over him most of the time and Lars found it odd that he had never heard Luke laugh.

Thinking about him now, in a cave filled with glass balls and heavy black birds, Lars remembered the letter that Luke had given him to post at Pilot Bay. Lars had left it in the inside pocket of his jacket that was hanging on the back of a chair in the beach shack. He secured the crate again, made his way out of the cave through the waterfall in the fading light and hiked the few miles south along the tracks to the shack.

Lars got a fire started in the small woodstove and lit the oil lamp on the workbench. He found the letter in his jacket and brought it closer to the stove to dry. Luckily it was written in pencil. Inked text would have been lost to smudges and running. Lars opened the envelope, addressed to a Mrs. Agnes Wisconsin of Boswell, and took out the still damp page. He laid both on the table near the stove.

After eating some hobo stew he had prepared from the supplies scavenged from the train, the letter felt dry enough to read. He brought it closer to the lamp to help read the small but neat handwriting.

Dear Mrs. Wisconsin:

My name is Luke St. James and I was a friend of your boys, Sven and Ole, may they rest in peace. Not a day goes by that I do not replay the tragedy that took place six years ago at Cape Horn. I was with them on the day they died. We went to search for some lost cows up on

Pilot Point Peninsula and rowed over to the Tipi Camp. Before we could mount a search for the cows, Ole found a large gold boulder covered with moss. We decided to take the rock across the bay and divide up our fortune.

When we tried to get the boulder into the boat, disaster struck. The rock, far heavier than we imagined, broke the rope we were using to lower it. The last thing I saw as I waited in the boat with Sven was Ole flying over the edge of the bluff, the rope caught around his foot. The heavy boulder hit Sven, smashing him through the deck of the boat. I was thrown clear and never saw a sign of either Sven or Ole again. I am sorry that I have been too much of a coward all these years to fess up to what happened. I no longer want anything to do with the gold. It has brought nothing but misery. I am trading the gold for passage to the Far East to a man who wants to build a new railroad. As Ole used to say, shit happens and it floats. Go figure.

Toodles,

Luke St. James

Lars felt stunned at what Luke had written. He had heard a version of the gold boulder story in one of the waterfront bars down the lake. The story was not out of the question, since a massive silver boulder had been found north of Kaslo some years back. If Luke had found the big gold rock it might explain the heavy birds in the crate—perhaps Luke had smelted the gold into the eagle statue moulds for the new hotel in Bonner's Ferry. A half tonne of gold would be worth a fortune —about three hundred thousand dollars. It would also explain the urgency with which they needed to reach their destination on the night of the storm, as well as the bonus money. Lars collapsed on the cot and quickly fell asleep.

Captain Lars awoke an hour later, refreshed from the short nap, having dreamt a solution to his problems. He knew he could never make things right for the pain and suffering he had caused with his decision to continue the voyage through the gale. The result had been eight lives cut short: the first mate Luke St. James, the young fireman

Caleb Mogadishu, the brothers Yuri and Yori Jasper, the barman Lucky Jim Germaine, the cabin boy Billy LaRue and two Italian passengers.

Captain Lars took Tank for a walk along the tracks to flesh out his plan before scurrying back down inside the cave. Lars carefully placed the ten birds back in their nest in the crate and replaced all of the fishing floats. He had overheard the brakeman of the train at Hidden Creek tell a passenger, while the train was refreshing its water tanks, that eight coffins were laid out on the government wharf across the lake in Kuskanook waiting for transport. Under the cover of night, Lars floated the big crate across the lake and dragged it onto the sandy shore beneath the wharf. He made the journey up onto the wooden deck eight times to place a heavy black bird in each coffin, timing his trips to coincide with the guard's rounds off the wharf. When he had finished, each coffin weighed a hundred pounds more than it had when he started. Lars waited until the coast was clear before creeping up to the small guard shack at the end of the wharf to copy the shipping manifest for the coffins. The last two birds had to wait for the next evening, when Lars found an unsecured skiff and rowed the twenty miles to Gray Creek. Lars found the tombstones of Sven and Ole Wisconsin on the north edge of the Gray Creek cemetery. He felt lucky to find a shovel near a freshly dug grave. He dug up the two coffins and added a black bird to each. The bodies of Sven and Ole had decayed into a stinking green mass that the black birds sunk right into. Lars wondered what his mother would think if she knew he had just added grave robber to his list of accomplishments.

Captain Lars made his way back down the lake to Kuskanook and floated the big crate back across the lake and safely into its berth in the cave behind the waterfall at Hidden Creek. He had accomplished the first part of his plan, but the heavy work had taken a toll on his injured shoulder. Lars knew the letter from Luke would never reach Mrs. Wisconsin, the Wicked Witch of the East Shore, whom he had shoved into the lake in a rage. He pledged to right the wrongs of his fatal decision to strike out into the storm.

The next morning Captain Lars woke up early and started the long trek by handcar along the tracks to Nelson, carrying a heavy pack, with his dog at his side. He returned to the cave near midnight, exhausted and delirious from having worked the handcar thirty miles in each direction. In a daze he repacked several of the glass balls in the crate and paddled it out into the middle of the lake to let it drift off on its own, then swam back to shore. His shoulder throbbed as he felt the cold seep through to his bones. He swam through the waterfall and collapsed onto the beach inside the cave.

Captain Lars dreamt about leaving Kootenay Lake with Gertie and starting a new life in Europe—perhaps even in Salzburg. Haunting apparitions of the eight lost men swooped into view before the scene changed and he swam through the waterfall and out into the lake. A sailboat flying the familiar skull and crossbones approached. He saw his wife Mildred on deck—another apparition, rattling a sabre in his direction. Tears filled his eyes as he spotted the impressive figure of Gunpowder Gertie on the foredeck in full pirate regalia, beckoning to him.

Chapter Forty-Seven

Stark and Zuzu left the office once the effects of the McJesus Juice had finally worn off. Stark had given her the antidote as soon as Chief Inspector Davide drove them home from the foot of Bonnington Falls, where their plastic bubble had beached itself after the one-hundred-foot plunge. The plastic globe had acted much like a beach ball dropped from a vast height would. The crew of power linemen working near the beach had gasped as they witnessed the plunge and the resultant bounce, and Stark and Zuzu rolled onto the beach before them much like Glenda the Good Witch appearing to the Munchkins in *The Wizard of Oz.*

With Zuzu still suffering the effects of the serum, they spent a night of intermittent debauchery, with Stark committing unspeakable acts at her command. Stark, driven by love, blindly pleasured her even though his dose of serum had worn off hours before. They exited the building somewhat sore and exhausted at ten in the morning, holding hands as they walked along Baker up to Ward, pausing briefly at the Wino Rhino for two espressos and two biscotti to go. They continued down Ward toward Vernon, stopping for a moment's silence at the exact spot where a poorly tuned piano had met its maker only a week before.

At the corner of Ward and Vernon, opposite the Snoring Elk Hotel, stood the infamous Nelson courthouse, built in 1909 and designed by France Ratzlaff himself, the patriarch of the Ratzlaff empire. The impressive stone structure, a fine example of Beaux Arts Chateau–style architecture, would have looked at home in a small French village in the Pyrenees. Great swaths of green ivy made the three-storey climb up the silver-grey–hued marble block walls from the plush lawn to the edge of the black slate roof. Stark had once attempted to climb up the thick mass of ivy in order to illegally obtain some documents from a third-floor law library but lost his footing and fell thirty feet to the ground. Were it not for the foam-rubber black-widow spider costume he had been wearing, he may not have survived.

On Stark's insistence, they were disguised as Tyrolean mountain guides. Both wore black leather lederhosen but while Stark had complemented his with a yellow shirt, green felt hat and false moustache, Zuzu had paired hers with thigh-high white stockings, braided pigtails and a tight white barmaid blouse. Both made sure to add a lot of "*ja*," "*danke*" and "*schiesse*" to their speech, and seemed to be blending in well with the crowd of tourists waiting for the courthouse tour. Zuzu had a passable Swiss—or German—accent, while Stark sounded more like a Swedish chef than a Berliner. They managed to slip away from the group on the third floor and made their way undetected to the locked room that housed the museum archives. Stark took only seconds to pick the lock and silently closed the door behind them. Zuzu swiftly located the box they were looking for.

The wooden box had a sliding lid and stood about a foot high, ten inches wide and two feet long. The end of the box read "Archeological Society of British Columbia—Kootenay Lake Deep Water Dive—June 2011." Inside the box was a collection of small items recovered from the wreck of SS *City of Ainsworth*, including a pickle jar, a whisky bottle, a sextant, a compass and a silver cigarette case. A logbook was also inside, water damaged with a splayed spine, as if it had been dropped in a bathtub and then dried in the sun. Stark tasted one of the pickles and quickly spat it out, inspecting the hundred-year-old jar for an expiration date. Zuzu took photos of the last ten pages in the logbook with her iPhone. The small logbook held the ship's manifest, which was the record of freight and passengers carried from port to port on each voyage. The pages documented the weight of cargo and the number and names of passengers, as well as names of the crew for each shift. The last few pages in the book were the only ones of interest. They finished their task swiftly and made their way back downstairs in time to join up with their group for a final tour of the judge's chambers and a beer in the jury room. No one seemed to have missed the two strangely dressed alpine tourists.

The judge's chambers had not changed much during the past century except for the odd dusting. The walnut panelling bore black-and-white photographs of former judges, politicians, and historic Nelson events. Stark recognized a photo of the *Ainsworth* leaving the city wharf, strategically taken so that the crew's backs were to the crowd as they lined up on the deck and peed overboard. Stark noted the brass plate marked "Bon Voyage—November 29, 1898" and wanted to take a closer look at the photo, but he needed a diversion to distract the crowd of tourists sipping their beers. He whispered something to Zuzu and she slowly backed toward the photo, steering a couple behind her closer to the wall. She turned quickly toward the paunchy middle-aged man and slapped him across the face, pulling the top of her blouse up as she did so.

"Keep your hands to yourself, sir. These puppies are spoken for."

The man's wife swatted him across the skull, causing him to careen into the wall and knock the photo of the *Ainsworth* to the floor. As Zuzu knelt to remove the photo from the broken frame Stark helped the man to his feet and herded the couple back into the crowd. Stark spoke to the group in broken Swedish.

"Notting to see her, fawks."

The Tyroleans made a quick exit out the door.

Chapter Forty-Eight

Bud at the front desk of the Laughing Cow handed Zuzu a package and a handful of letters and messages. He asked her to sign for the package and complimented her on the latest *Jazzercise* show. She took the bundle to her room, sat down on the bed and read them. Most of the letters were of the fan mail variety, from listeners who professed their love for her or the show and offered to give her a big hug when they saw her. The package looked different. Inside a FedEx envelope about twice the size of a standard letter sat an old, wrinkled brown-paper parcel and a letter. The parcel address read "Von Trapp Family Seiners," General Delivery, Nelson, British Columbia. The letter came from the law firm of Whacked and Waystead, of Kettle Falls, Washington, and was addressed to Zuzu "Jazz" von Trapp. Zuzu did not know of any relatives she had in the Kootenays, although she did know there was a branch of her family tree that had broken off.

The letter informed her that with the recent passing of a Mrs. Cindy Louhoo of Napa Valley, California, who had been found at the bottom of a wine vat, Zuzu had become the last surviving relative of a Captain Lars von Trapp. The enclosed package contained his private journal. The letter was signed Jason Waystead, LLB, and affixed with the company seal. Mr. Waystead had listened to the radio show and learned of her true identity from a call to the station. Zuzu gingerly unwrapped the brown paper parcel and found a black leather-bound notebook about four inches by eight inches in size. She opened it to the last pages and noted that the last two entries were not written in English. Zuzu recalled her father Christoph standing before the blackboard in the den, slapping a riding crop against the words written in chalk. She was reluctantly grateful that he had insisted she learn to read and write Swiss-German, her grandfather's language. It had made the study of Japanese in university much easier and it enabled her to read the entries in the journal.

Captain's log—November 30, 1898—The birds are sleeping with the angels where they will lie for the next one hundred years until the memory of this tragedy has faded. If I were to reveal all now, I would most certainly be hanged and my family ruined. I am exhausted from travelling to town and back on the handcar I found on a track siding. I sought out Brunhilde Gilker, the postmaster's wife, an acquaintance I knew I could trust. She secured a box at the bank and will arrange for the letter to be sent when a century has passed. I have kept none of the cursed birds for myself. I gave one to Brunhilde but didn't tell her what it was made of. The map will be safe in the bank vault. The key is with the words I write. I am leaving this cursed land to live a simple life away from the water. Mildred and George will be better off without me and without my shame. When Gertie returns we shall flee to a new life in Europe.

Zuzu flipped to the last entry, written in the same Swiss-German but by a different hand.

Gertie's log—June, 1923—My darling Lars. Isn't it funny how life turns out. Twenty-five years have passed since I last saw you. I found your old logbook among Mildred's belongings. She died of influenza a month ago. We have lived near Salzburg since I left you in that cabin on Kootenay Lake. After our time together on SS *Alberta*, when I got caught with a mouthful and beaten senseless, I realized that we could never be together. Quite by accident, I began an affair with the nurse who tended to me in the hospital. By an odd coincidence she turned out to be your wife Mildred. When I found you on the beach and nursed you in my cabin, I didn't know how I would choose between you and Mildred. When I got back to the cabin your infected shoulder looked bad and you were ranting about black birds, letters and keys. I left you in the cabin to get help from Mildred. When we returned to the cabin you were gone. We followed your footprints along the beach to a cave behind a waterfall. Before we entered the cave I was preparing to say goodbye to Mildred. Fate intervened when we found you had succumbed to your injuries. We took your logbook and left you there with a mangy black dog that would not leave your side. I dressed in some of your old clothes and fled to Europe with Mildred and young George. For the past twenty-five years I have lived as Lars von Trapp, raising your son near Salzburg. You would be proud of George. He has followed in your footsteps and is a Captain in the Austrian Navy. He married a countess and they have several children. Not the sharpest knife in the drawer—he never discovered his father was a woman. Go figure.

As Zuzu read her family history, somewhat dazed, she ran her finger down along the inside margin, the book's gutter, and felt something prick her fingertip. She brought the wounded digit up to the soothing confines of her mouth. She took a closer look along the book's gutter and noticed a thin piece of metal poking out along the edge of the binding. It took her nearly an hour to dismantle the spine and remove the cover of the Captain's logbook without damaging it. Inside the spine, where the pages were bound together, she found a hollowed-out space that hid a thin, old key of some sort. The key looked about as long and wide as a flattened cigarette with a few notches cut out near the end. It appeared to be made of brass and had "MBH #18" engraved on it. Zuzu jumped up, grabbed the book, the key and her coat before hurrying out the door and scurrying up Baker Street to Stark's office.

Stark answered the door dressed in full Arab gear—a flowing white robe and roman sandals, with a red *keffiyeh* head scarf. Stark had just returned from the annual general meeting of the T. E. Lawrence Society at the Foreign Legion. The AGM always included a viewing of the original *Lawrence of Arabia* film, which, next to *Casablanca*, was his favourite. Stark rummaged through the bookshelves and came up with a textbook from his locksmith class at the Hole, and quickly determined that the key belonged to an old bank safety-deposit box. At Stark's insistence, they trod upstairs to seek the assistance of Holmes and Watson, whom they found settled into cozy chairs in the drawing room before the fire, each with a glass of brandy in hand.

Like Zuzu, Holmes and Watson didn't flinch at Stark's unusual attire, as disguise was more the norm than the exception for them. Zuzu asked Holmes if she had any idea what the markings on the key meant. Holmes placed her glass on the mantle, picked up a magnifying glass the size of a frying pan from the desk and began pacing back and forth across the room, examining the key. Satisfied, she placed the frying pan back on the desk and turned to face Zuzu.

"Have you any idea, my dear girl, what a boom town Nelson was on the eve of the twentieth century? By 1898, the first anniversary of its incorporation, Nelson had eight fine hotels, dozens of bars and its own hydroelectric plant. It is common knowledge that the first branch of the Royal Bank of Canada in British Columbia opened here in 1898. What most people don't realize is that the original location was next door to its present location at the corner of Baker and Stanley. In 1898 the bank was located in the building that currently houses Lonely Lizard Jewellers and Flaming Ferret Insurance. The Royal Bank name came into effect in 1901 but in those days it was known as the Merchant Bank of Halifax—the 'MBH' on the key."

Watson turned from the fire to face the group.

"You weren't always such a local-history buff, Holmes."

"'My salad days, when I was green in judgement, cold in blood'— *Antony and Cleopatra*, act one, scene five. In fact, Watson, some years ago I wrote a monograph for the Hysterical Society on secret passages and old bank vaults hidden below city streets. Safety issues prevented them from embarking on what would have been a disastrous tourism campaign. When the Royal Bank moved to their current location, they left the old subterranean vault in place. From what I recall, it was sealed up a decade later with the old safety-deposit boxes intact. If we could get inside, we may find the box that the key fits. The subterranean vault sits on the west side of the building, located below the basement of Flaming Ferret Insurance."

Chapter Forty-Nine

The gang of four returned at midnight, dressed in the costumes closest to burglar outfits that they could find in the Alley Cat Theatre prop room. The black suits with ruffled white shirts, large black bow ties, fake black beards and black stove-pipe hats were left over from a locally produced musical entitled *Four Abe Lincolns in a Volkswagen,* which understandably had closed after opening night. As they were making their way down Baker Street to Lonely Lizard Jewellers, a Nelson City Police squad car passed them and shone a spotlight on them. They tipped their hats in unison and the officer waved and drove on. Just another Saturday night in Nelson. They made their way to the alley and the rear of the building. Max, near exhaustion from a marathon lovemaking session with Marcia, was waiting patiently behind a dumpster, dressed in black slacks, a black turtleneck and a black toque. Stark commented on his lack of imagination, while Holmes picked the lock at the alley entrance to Flaming Ferret Insurance.

Once safely inside the building, Stark took out the security cameras with Silly String, while Holmes rewired the silent alarm system to send rude email messages to Chief Inspector Francois Davide on the half hour. The unlikely band of brothers and sisters made their way down to the basement lunchroom and laid out the blueprints on the table. Watson put the kettle on for tea and began rummaging through the cupboards for a snack while Stark brought out a tape measure, conferred with Zuzu and then drew a large letter X on the floor under the table. He stood up and turned to Max.

"Did you manage to find all the supplies on the list I sent you? Any trouble getting the fireworks? We understand that your father worked as a mercenary and a freelance explosives expert."

Max handed a small black backpack to Stark, who handed it to Holmes.

"Who told you that? Rufus? My dad was a fireworks salesman. He even volunteered for the American Foundation for the Blind and travelled across the country teaching the blind how to safely set off fireworks in their own homes without freaking out the guide dogs."

Holmes removed the twenty-five roman candles and bound them together with duct tape, pulling out all the fuses except the one in the middle, which she poked full of holes before tying all the fuses end to end. She placed the bundle on top of the X and turned to Max.

"Did you know, Max, that the active explosive ingredient in a roman candle is similar to a half stick of dynamite? If one multiplies the effect and redirects the energy from a propelling force to an inhibiting force, the explosive result is akin to military-grade C-4 explosives. 'By the pricking of my thumbs, something wicked this way comes'—*MacBeth*, act four, scene one. Perhaps we should all leave the room for a moment."

Holmes lit the fuse as they rushed en mass to hide behind the stairwell door. Stark counted down from ten and had reached six when Watson stood up and grabbed the door handle. Zuzu tackled him, knocking Watson to the floor. He grunted.

"I beg your pardon, young lady, I thought the kettle whistled."

The explosion was deafening. Luckily the steel stairwell door had no window and held fast when the hinges were blown loose. Zuzu and Watson stepped back from the door and let it fall. The smoke began to clear, revealing a lunchroom in need of renovation and a large hole in the concrete basement floor. They could hear fire truck and police sirens racing to the Lonely Lizard next door. Holmes had told them not to worry as Nelson's finest would not find anything awry and would not come looking in the Flaming Ferret. She was right—the noise faded and life outside returned to normal. Zuzu and Stark were lowered by climbing ropes to the floor of the abandoned bank vault. The headlamps they wore illuminated the rusting rows of metal boxes that lined the east and west walls. Zuzu found it first. It was located at hip height midway along the wall. As Stark aimed his headlamp on box number eighteen, Zuzu sprayed the key with some graphite lubricant and slid it into the lock. After some gentle wiggling, the key turned in the lock and the door swung open. Zuzu reached in and pulled out a worn envelope. They signalled to Max and Watson to haul them up.

Chapter Fifty

After breaking into the bank vault, Stark sent Master Ho, Brother Mo, and Moneypenny to meet with Max to help locate some of the sites identified on the map they had found in the vault. Zuzu had already translated the Swiss-German notations on the map, which was similar to the note in the Captain's logbook. In total there were seven sites on Kootenay Lake and one on Slocan Lake identified on the map, including Crawford Bay, Gray Creek, Kaslo, Riondel, Boswell, Argenta, Nelson and New Denver. Moneypenny located the sites on Google Earth and printed maps and directions to all the locations. The group dispersed to the four winds to reconnoitre the areas in question.

Holmes, Watson, Zuzu and Stark focused on the evidence before them including the letters from Cuba, the Captain's logbook and the *Ainsworth*'s manifest from the archives, which described the location of the vessel when it had floundered and the cargo, crew and passengers it carried. As Stark suspected, the photo of the *Ainsworth* taken from the judge's chambers held a clue. An inscription written on the back of the photo read "Thanks, Brunhilde" and was signed "Captain Lars." Odd that a dead man could inscribe a photo that had been taken the morning of his supposed demise. The recent murders were all linked to the descendants of the *Ainsworth* incident. Holmes had determined that if they could find Captain Lars's cave, more answers would be revealed. She sat at her desk, pipe between her lips, as her hands alternated between a glass of scotch, the pipe and a laptop keyboard. In moments she had calculated bearings and distance from the point where the ship floundered to where the Captain may have drifted, and quickly determined their destination.

With Zuzu riding with Holmes in the backseat and Stark sitting up front with Watson, the ancient Land Rover boarded the Osprey ferry for the ten o'clock sailing from Balfour to Kootenay Bay on the east shore. The forty-minute crossing remained the longest free ferry passage in British Columbia. Holmes and Zuzu chatted non-stop about matters of the heart and all things girly. Holmes told Zuzu about meeting Watson in college and chided herself for not making a move when she had the chance, afraid to commit to a man she was not physically attracted to but who seemed to get her on a soulful level. She explained how they had gone their separate ways but met up every other year in Edinburgh to slake their thirst for Conan Doyle. Holmes also told her how she had met Rufus and what a charming man he was.

"He was not my soulmate, though. Deep down he knew it too. We drifted apart a little more each year—he had his law practice while I had my post at the university. After ten years of drifting we found ourselves on separate ice floes heading out to sea. The opportunity to teach at the Vallican Hole seemed like a life preserver thrown to us both. I never thought I would find my soulmate but Watson proved me wrong. I remain good friends with Rufus to this day. Watson and I have even gone skiing with Rufus and his new wife in Boulder. 'We that are true lovers run into strange capers'—*As You Like It*, act two, scene four. Life is short, my dear—do not let our boy slip away from you again."

They parked at the Gray Creek Store and made their way toward the rental kiosk at the side of the building. They were somewhat dismayed to find only one tandem kayak and two stand-up paddle boards left to rent. Holmes and Watson called dibs on the kayak. Fortunately the lake was dead calm as they left the dock and ventured out into the open water. Holmes pointed with a paddle to the right, to Pilot Point and the Tipi Camp off in the distance across the bay.

"That is where it all began, my boy. Luke and the Wisconsin

brothers found the boulder over there and started the wheel in motion. The *Ainsworth* floundered in the bay just there. Nine men lost. Well, perhaps only eight."

The kayak struggled to keep up with Stark and Zuzu on the paddle boards. While neither had experience with the stand-up paddle board craze both took to it like bears to honey. Stark motioned to Zuzu to slow down and let the kayak catch up. Holmes shouted at Watson.

"Watson. Heave-ho. We don't have all day to get to Next Creek. Feather the blades, jay stroke. It's all in the rhythm."

"There are two paddles, Holmes. You could help."

"Pshaw, Watson. Everyone knows the front seat is for the navigator. Put your back into it, man. It's good for the core muscles. According to these GPS coordinates we need to head south by southwest."

An hour of encouragement from Holmes and an hour of grumbling and complaining from Watson brought them within eyesight of the small waterfall at Midge Creek. Holmes continued to berate Watson, pointing repeatedly with the paddle and motioning to manoeuvre along the shoreline in front of the waterfall. She reached into her pack and brought out a black box about the size of a box of crackers, which she pointed at the waterfall.

"Have you ever seen one of these, Stark? I borrowed it from Inspector Davide when he carelessly left it unguarded in his squad car. It is a heat-sensing unit once used to find marijuana grow-ops before they became commonplace. I was told that they also had a helicopter-mounted unit that beeped when it passed over a building that had an unusual heat envelope. They had to shut the thing off when they flew over the Slocan Valley. The noise was deafening."

They passed by three more creeks with waterfalls before nearing the small sand beach beside Hidden Creek. At each waterfall Holmes would yell at Watson to keep the boat steady while she brought out the box of crackers, adjusted a few dials and motioned to move on.

Stark and Zuzu made landfall on the small sand beach beside the creek. Watson barely manoeuvred the kayak onto the beach, gasping and sweating as if he had run a marathon. Holmes made yet another "tsk-tsk" sound.

"What is the matter with you, Watson. You really should exercise more often. You don't see me huffing and puffing like a madman."

Watson struggled out of the kayak and collapsed in a heap on the shore. Zuzu appeared concerned but Stark assured her that Watson would be just fine after a little rest. Holmes stepped over him, dropping her backpack on the sand. She took out a map and checked the coordinates on the GPS unit. Satisfied, she returned to the pack, brought out the box of crackers and pointed it at the waterfall.

Watson managed to sit up and took the water bottle Holmes offered. He gulped it down like a man lost in the desert for months. She patted his hand, kissed him gently and thanked him for his Herculean efforts. The beet-red-ness had faded slightly from his cheeks and he seemed to have recovered the use of his legs. Holmes turned back to Zuzu and Stark as she turned a dial on the box of crackers.

"As I suspected, the heat envelope of this waterfall is unusual because, unlike the others, there is a cave behind it. If I am not mistaken, we will find human remains inside."

Holmes began disrobing and dropping items of clothing on the beach. The group followed suit and soon they stood on the beach in their underwear. Zuzu commented on the lovely black bra-and-panty set that Holmes wore. Holmes prepared to remove the bra to show Zuzu the comfy lining when Watson, who had prepared for the journey by wearing a Speedo under his trousers, harrumphed loudly. Holmes thought the better of it, diving instead into the cold lake and swimming toward the waterfall. Watson's obvious arousal at the underwear parade faded quickly as he hit the glacier-fed lake. Zuzu followed and Stark brought up the rear, dragging a floating pack wrapped in a black plastic garbage bag behind him. The waterfall was about twenty-feet wide, with the cave behind it similar in height and twice as deep. The cave had most likely been carved out of the rock wall prior to the opening of the Bluebell mine up the lake in Riondel. Similar small caves and test shafts were located up and down the lake as a testament to the number of miners searching for the motherlode in the late eighteen hundreds. Directly behind the waterfall enough light shone through to make out the basics—further back it was pitch black. Stark waded out of the lake and onto the short sand beach strewn with blue glass fishing-net floats. He quickly unwrapped the pack and handed out headlamps, bunny slippers and jogging suits made out of space blankets. Holmes had crawled through the four-feet-wide opening at the end of the cave and shouted for the rest to follow. Once through the portal, a cavern of similar dimensions to the main cave opened up. Zuzu wandered to the end of the cavern, following the scratches on the rock wall. She recognized some of the First Nations pictographs from an art history class. Near the end of the cavern the scratches changed. A ship flying the Jolly Roger, a penguin and ten coffin shapes were scratched into the rock wall. Zuzu was making her way down the wall, tracing the markings, when she tripped on something and fell awkwardly forward. Stark sensed the movement and sprang to her side just in time to catch her before she hit the rock floor. Holmes and Watson came over and shone their headlamps on the base of the wall to see what Zuzu had tripped over. Faded fabric and gleaming bones greeted them. A smaller animal skeleton lay beside the human one. Holmes crouched down near the larger skeleton before standing up and holding a finger toward Watson.

"Maggot!"

Watson pointed back toward her, before responding.

"Piss-ant!"

"I beg your pardon, Watson?"

Watson pointed again, past Holmes to the cave wall behind.

"Piss-ant! There, on the wall—they have a nasty bite. Steer clear."

Holmes placed the maggot in an empty pill bottle and gestured toward the skeleton.

"Looks like you found your great-grandfather. Zuzu, meet Captain Lars von Trapp."

Chapter Fifty-One

Once safely ensconced in the comfy confines of 221 Baker Street they reviewed the pencil rubbings Zuzu had made from the etchings on the cave walls. Holmes paced madly back and forth in front of the fire as she called up each member of the second unit who were at their posts at the map sites. She held the cell phone in one hand and signed in Gestuno with the other toward Zuzu, who stood near the liquor cabinet. Zuzu did not know Gestuno but recognized the gesture as the universal sign for "pour me a stiff one."

"Yes, Max, I realize you are standing in the middle of a graveyard in Kaslo. As I suspected, the map sites are all cemeteries, as per the coffin scratches on the walls of the cave. You need to locate the two graves of the Jasper brothers, Yuri and Yori. Do you have a flashlight and shovel on you?"

Zuzu handed Holmes a snifter filled with brandy, which she quickly drained. Animated yelling could be heard from the cell phone.

"That's too bad, Max. Perhaps you could take the licence plate off the car and use that. I believe Watson used one to dig me out of a tight spot in the "Battle of the Bulge" case. You must retrieve a portly black penguin from each of the coffins. It could be a little nasty inside. Do you have any Handi Wipes? Also, try not to raise the suspicions of the local constabulary. The mission is not yet legally sanctioned."

Watson and Holmes made calls to Master Ho, Brother Mo and Moneypenny. They were tasked to retrieve the birds from the graves of

Lucky Jim, Caleb, Billy, Luke and the Wisconsin brothers. Zuzu had found the website Daisypusher.com, through a link from the Nelson Hysterical Society website, that identified grave locations in every small cemetery in Canada.

Moneypenny had retrieved a Maltese penguin from the grave of Lucky Jim Germaine in a small cemetery on the shores of Slocan Lake in New Denver. Once she had secured the bird in the trunk of her car, she returned to replace the sod and clean up the grave. She noticed that a small area in the rear of the cemetery was cordoned off with a low lattice fence and traditional Japanese gate. When she moved closer, she saw a cluster of a few dozen graves that had tombstones inscribed in Japanese characters. The cemetery was home to members of the Japanese community who had been interned in the area during the Second World War. Moneypenny spent a few hours clearing away overgrown brush and weeding around the graves. When she finished, the small graveyard had the look of respect it deserved. As she turned to her car, a man she recognized as the yakuza leader Takumi Moto came up to her, bowed and spoke in Japanese.

"You have honoured my ancestors by honouring their graves. My name is Takumi Moto and I was born here while my family was the guest of the government during the war. I live in Kobe now but I return here to pay my respects whenever I am in the country on business. If there is ever anything I can do for you do not hesitate to ask."

The man offered Moneypenny a business card, which he proffered toward her with both hands. She took it, thanked him and bowed to show her respect, before climbing into her car and heading back down the highway toward Nelson.

Chapter Fifty-Two

The pauper's cemetery at St. Sebastion's Church, marked on the map, contained the remains of the two Italians, who were later identified as the Cubans Jugo and Jorge Nakid. Since the letters sent to Cuba had come back unopened, Stark was given the task of travelling there to find his ancestors. Zuzu stayed at the office to man the phones while Holmes and Watson dashed off to meet Pastor Vlad at St. Sebastion's Church. Stark hurried down to the Grinning Gopher and found Yeti and Dmitri, the Melting Glacier Air pilots, fully engaged in their favourite pastime, *tigr prikhodit*, the famous Russian drinking game where a player yells, "Tiger is coming," and the other players have to hide under the table and down shots of vodka until someone yells, "Tiger is gone." Stark ordered eight cups of coffee for them and chartered their plane for the long flight to Cayo Largo, arriving early the next morning.

After travelling to the village and mingling with the locals as a coffee salesman, Stark gained directions to the small country church he was seeking and took a bus back to the village a short time later. As Stark stepped off the bus into the bright Cayo Largo sun, he was struck not only by the incredible natural beauty of the island paradise but also by an elderly gentleman on an orange moped. He regained consciousness some hours later to find himself strapped to a gurney in a hospital corridor. He noticed that he was not the only overflow patient in the emergency ward of the small hospital, as there were two other gurneys further along the corridor. One of them held a comatose Cuban man who was hooked up to several IV lines and who may have been the oldest person Stark had ever seen. The other gurney held a portly flushed-faced man, dressed in red-plaid shorts and a matching plaid cap, who was yelling at no one in particular.

"For the love of God, does anyone here speak English? Why am I strapped to this thing? Where are my golf clubs?"

Stark propped himself up on his elbows, with only a mild amount of nausea, and waved at the yelling man.

"Dude. Chill. I can answer all your questions. I speak English. I don't know about the rest of your golf clubs but that looks like a sand wedge skewering your left thigh. The caddies in Cuba can be a bit sensitive about comments regarding the virtue of their mothers. I'm guessing that is why you are strapped to the gurney. Enjoying your vacation so far?"

Stark lay back down and promptly blacked out. He awoke with a start, leaving an odd dream in which he was an altar boy serving snifters of four-hundred-year-old cognac to some elderly men in tall pointy hats in the Sistine Chapel. Glancing around, he found himself lying in the sort of bed one might find in a condemned hospital or a really sketchy hotel room. The sickly sweet smell of disinfectant led him to believe he lay in the former rather than the latter. The fact that he wore only a short pale-green gown that tied up at the back was the clincher, as was the well-endowed dark-haired young thing in the clinical-looking white dress and hat who winked at him slyly as she pulled the thermometer from his ass. He asked her in Spanish why they didn't use one of those fancy new thermometers that go in the ear. She squeezed his scrotum lightly and winked at him.

"Where's the fun in that?"

She used her phone to snap a quick photo of Stark's genitalia "for an art project" before making a note on his chart and exiting hastily out the door as a doctor in purple scrubs entered. He appeared to be under thirty and Cuban, and was missing an eye, if the large black pirate patch was any indication. He smiled broadly at Stark while perusing the chart and spoke in English.

"Glad to see you are back amongst the living, Mr. Valdez. My name is Doctor Trudeau Sanchez. We were a little worried you might not survive both the accident and the lunch menu."

"Please call me Juan. Forgive me, doctor. I have no memory of what you describe, although I do remember something about an orange moped."

"You were run over in the street while stepping off a bus after visiting the San Miguel de Cortez cemetery. The small cemetery is located behind a church in my old neighbourhood and is not exactly a tourist magnet, Mr. Valdez."

"Juan. I insist."

"Do not for a minute think we do not know your real name, Mr. Valdez. We Cubans are not a naive people. Officials from the mainland are on their way to our little island as we speak. When you are well enough to be released you will be interrogated, not in a kind way, by customs officials at the airport. Might I ask you the real purpose of your visit to Cayo Largo? What is your interest in the cemetery?"

"Did you say that your first name is Trudeau?"

"My friends call me Tru, but yes, that is correct. If you are from Canada, Juan, you may know that Cayo Largo has played a special role in fostering a friendship between our two countries. I was born on January 27th, 1976, the day that our fearless leader, Fidel Castro, met with your fearless leader, Pierre Trudeau, here on Cayo Largo to go fishing as part of a short state visit. In tribute to your prime minister, who had spent a week in Cuba in 1948 toiling in the sugar-cane fields, El Jefe ordered that all boys born on that day be named Trudeau. I was the lucky one in my family. My brother Humperdink was born the day that El Jefe's favourite singer visited Cuba."

"Dr. Sanchez, if I may be frank, I have come to Cayo Largo to find information about two men who died in 1898 when a sternwheeler sank in a storm on Kootenay Lake, near my home in Nelson, British

Columbia. Their names were not recorded as victims of the disaster that took nine lives. They were listed on the memorial as 'two Italians.' They were buried in St. Sebastion's Church Cemetery in Nelson. Their names were Jugo and Jorge Nakid. I asked around and was told I might find answers at the San Miguel de Cortez Cemetery, where I found their tombstones."

"Jugo and Jorge. That sounds so Italian. An easy mistake to make. The cigars and rum didn't give them away? Jorge Nakid was my great-grandfather—Jugo, his brother. The graves you saw were empty. They were for ceremonial purposes only. They did not return home from their years in Canada."

Stark turned to face Dr. Sanchez and placed both hands on his shoulders.

"I know the whereabouts of Jugo and Jorge, doctor. If it's all right with you, I would like to bring them home."

Chapter Fifty-Three

Holmes and Watson met Vicar Vladimir Vladivostok in the church manse, the vicar's living quarters. Vladimir told Holmes to follow him to the sanctity of the confessional. When she tried to open the door to the confessional booth she found it locked. Vladimir motioned that Holmes should enter the Vicar's side and handed her a boxy black pillbox hat. She closed the booth door behind her, placed the hat on her head and sat down on the bench. She heard a muffled rustling through the lattice curtain. A voice spoke.

"Father, forgive me."

"There, there, my child. Vicar Vladivostok is just outside. My name is Holmes Barcelona and I've come to help you."

Holmes pressed her face close to the lattice screen and peered at the person on the other side. She recognized her from a photo in the *Nelson Daily Crow*.

"Sanctuary, Miss Eldorado? Do not be alarmed. My colleagues and I are in the process of finding those responsible for the attempt on your life that resulted in your mother's death. We believe some unsavoury underworld figures are responsible for a number of recent suspicious deaths."

"Please help me, Ms. Barcelona. I have been in hiding in this church since the piano accident. Vicar Vladivostok has been more than kind but did not allow me to attend the funeral."

She burst into tears, tugging on Holmes's heartstrings.

"Please accept my condolences, my dear. It would be far too dangerous for you to appear in public until the matter has been resolved. 'As flies to wanton boys are we to the gods, they kill us for their sport'—*King Lear*, act four, scene one. Once the coast is clear, I will send a message to Vicar Vladivostok and you may leave the grounds. When this is all over I should like to speak to you about a part-time teaching position at the Vallican Hole School. We have been considering adding pole dancing to our curriculum for some time. Go with God, my child."

Vicar Vladivostok took Holmes and Watson into the basement of the church manse where they found a dozen plain wooden coffins lined up neatly at the far end of the room. A stack of rotten wood boards lay in a heap in the corner, remnants of older coffins. The Vicar motioned with an outspread arm to the coffins.

"We were forced to move the old cemetery to make room for the new wing. Many of our flock believe we have desecrated these graves."

Holmes approached the two coffins marked "Italians—November 1898," lifted the lids and peered inside. Both contained gleaming skeletons in scraps of clothing. In addition to the skeletons, each coffin held a portly black penguin. Holmes motioned to Watson to retrieve the heavy birds, which he did with much grumbling, loading each on a handcart before making the journey outside to deposit them on Betsy's back seat. Holmes asked Vicar Vlad to prepare the two coffins for transport and thanked him for his help, promising him a large donation for the congregation when the dust settled. Watson was leaning on Betsy's bumper and appeared to be in cardiac arrest when she exited the building.

"Watson, have you loaded the birds? Good Lord, man, you look as though you have just emerged from an iron lung. You really need to hit the gym once in a while. Shall we return to our lodgings?"

In the meantime, Moneypenny had decided to call in her marker with Moto-san. She dialled him up and explained the urgency in locating Jesus McMurphy and having him attend a meeting set up by Stark and Holmes. Moto-san sounded only too happy to have a chance to be rid of McMurphy, his disrespectful attitude and faulty formulas, without having to resort to gunplay. He told Moneypenny that he would ensure McMurphy would be at the meeting. They agreed to meet at the cemetery and to go out for tea the next time he was in the country.

Chapter Fifty-Four

Holmes brought everyone together for a meeting in the lounge at the Foreign Legion. The large room was inspired by Rick's Café Américain from the film *Casablanca*, complete with white tablecloths, Moroccan accents and a piano player in the corner belting out a mix of Hoagy Carmichael and Cole Porter songs. By the time Stark and Zuzu arrived, everyone else had finished a round of introductory hugs and were taking seats at several tables facing the dance floor. Stark thought the life-size, bronze "slave girl" sculpture of a bare-breasted woman carrying a tall water vessel on her shoulder that stood in the corner of the room looked vaguely familiar. Eight black portly penguin statues were lined up along the oak bar in the front of the room. Holmes and Watson had brought along Cooper, a Baker Street Irregular. The Director of the Vallican Hole was in attendance, as well as Master Ho and Brother Mo. Max and Marcia were there, as well as Awesome Eldorado, who arrived with a police escort, and Jesus McMurphy, who was delivered to the meeting hogtied inside a mail sack by a muscular fellow dressed entirely in black. Also in attendance were Geronimo Germaine, the son of the late mayor, Minnie Ratzlaff, Lonesome Bill LaRue, Sergeant Harry Stuttgart, Inspector Franco San Francisco and Chief Inspector Francois Davide. Once all were seated semi-comfortably with drinks ordered, Holmes stood up and began pacing on the hardwood dance floor.

"I gathered you all here today because you all share a common sliver of time. Six degrees of separation. Whether you know it or not, you are all connected to each other and to something that happened on Kootenay Lake over one hundred years ago. I shall relate the tale to you all. Please do not interrupt me with foolish questions. Some of you will know some of this story already. Bear with me. None of you knows the whole story."

Holmes reached into her inside jacket pocket and produced a silver flask, uncorked it and relieved it of half its contents before slipping it into another pocket.

"I first became aware of the tragic events of a stormy Tuesday night in late November of 1898 several days ago. SS *City of Ainsworth*, a steam-powered paddlewheeler, went down in heavy swells. This sinking was brought about by overweight cargo, the incompetence of a junior crew and by the ill-fated decision of one man, Captain Lars von Trapp. Through the magic of snail mail, where a letter can embark upon a voyage around the world for well under a dollar or remain in a sack behind a desk for eighty-five years, the mystery of that vessel's fate has been revealed. It is among the most baffling cases I have ever encountered in the remote wilderness that is British Columbia. I beg your pardon. I'm as parched as a lake trout in a frying pan. Cooper, if you please."

The young actor improvised his mime skills, seeming to pull a cold can of Harvest Moon Hemp Ale out of the ass of Chief Inspector Davide, much to Davide's chagrin. Master Ho bristled at the mime movements, dropping into a low horse stance with the left hand raised chest high, right hand raised above the head, palms down, fingers spread and hand waving in the classic Sun-style tai chi posture "Praying Mantis Hails a Cab." Cooper quickly clasped his hands together and bowed toward Master Ho, which seemed to settle him, before firing the beer at Holmes, who caught it with an outstretched hand, popped the top and drained half of it in one long pull.

"Nine men failed to return to shore when the ship went down in the storm—seven crew members and two Italian railroad workers. The seven crew included Captain Lars and his first mate, Luke. Eight bodies were recovered. The discovery of the ship's logbook shed some light on Luke's connection to the freight on the overloaded ship. Several years prior to the voyage, Luke and the Wisconsin brothers had found a heavy gold boulder at Cape Horn, off Pilot Point, on the east shore of Kootenay Lake. The boulder was almost pure gold and weighed about a half tonne. The Wisconsin brothers drowned in an attempt to move the boulder into a boat for transport. Luke was left with two dead friends and a fortune in gold. He spent the next six years executing a plan to break the boulder into more manageable chunks and find somewhere to sell it. Working in a smelter at Pilot Bay, Luke poured the molten gold into eagle moulds that had been prepared for a new hotel in Idaho. Luke gave them a coat of molten lead and painted them black, which made them look more like portly penguins than eagles. The gold was aboard SS *City of Ainsworth*, on its way to the new hotel, when the storm capsized the vessel."

Holmes paused to drain the rest of the beer from the can before tossing the empty toward the waiter, who caught it deftly and continued filling the large Middle Eastern water pipes that were the centrepiece of each table. Holmes patted Watson lightly on the shoulder as she paced by him and continued.

"You may be asking yourselves how you could possibly be connected to this historic event. As you may not know, the Vallican Hole School of Stealth, Detection and Hard Knocks keeps extensive DNA records of all of its students and staff, gathered under the guise of a diabetes test during the entrance-week physical. Thanks to the networking skills of Henderson Cairo, the school's database is connected to the Nelson City Police records library as well as the Canadian Security Intelligence Service DNA registry and its Interpol counterpart. Sir Arthur Conan Doyle sent a number of his early detective novels as a gift for the inauguration of Nelson's first chief of police in 1897. In a twist of fate, the books were assumed to be scientific journals and the Nelson City Police followed the described procedures, saving bloodstained evidence from every accident and homicide victim in the area. When the Vallican Hole School opened, we were able to catalogue and digitize the police records library's DNA database, with the assistance and cooperation of Chief Inspector Francois Davide. By performing some extensive queries of the database, I made some astonishing connections to the people in this room."

Holmes paused for effect, retrieved the silver flask and toasted the group before continuing.

"The man in command of the *Ainsworth* on that stormy night in 1898 was Captain Lars von Trapp, the great-grandfather of Zuzu von Trapp, or Jazz de Janeiro, as she is better known on the local airwaves. Even though he succumbed to his injuries within a week of the sinking, Captain Lars's young son was spirited away to Europe and continued the bloodline that led to Zuzu."

An audible gasp sounded from almost everyone present. Jack MacLeod looked stunned as he stared at Jazz.

"Luke St. James was also a father the night he died in the storm, although he was unaware of the bun in the oven. The great-grandchild of Luke St. James is—"

Stark leapt to his feet and spoke.

"Chief Inspector Francois Davide."

"Incorrect, my boy. You have not been paying attention. As Master Ho has said on many occasions, 'There are no strange coincidences, only strange incidents.' Would you care to try again?"

"Jesus McMurphy."

Seven sharp gasps, one belch and a fart were heard throughout the room. Watson appeared red-faced but reacted quickly by whirling around and glaring at Jack MacLeod, who would have none of it and flipped him the bird. Holmes continued.

"Correct. Caleb Mogadishu, the replacement fireman, and young Billy, the cabin boy, were both too young to have any offspring, although they are distantly related to Brother Mo and Lonesome Bill LaRue, respectively. The Jasper brothers were related to Awesome Eldorado while the great-grandson of Lucky Jim, the barman, is Geronimo Germaine. That leaves the two Italians. Although on the manifest they were listed as Italian railroad workers, they were not actually Italian. They did come to Canada on a freighter full of olive oil to work on the railroad, but they were in fact Cubans. They were brothers Jugo and Jorge, whose last name was Nakid. I'm saving the big one for last. Jugo Nakid was the great-grandfather of Max Bolder. I'm sorry to tell you this, Stark, but you and Max are not brothers by blood. Max's birth parents were Stark's adoptive parents. Your mother Simone thought she was barren and adopted you, before discovering a year later that she was pregnant with Max. Life is a long, strange trip, and it often unfolds in ironic ways. Stark's adoptive mother gave birth to Max, yet he was the one raised in an adoptive family by Soon Fong and Su Ling. Stark was the adopted son and yet he was raised by his birth mother, Sister Moonbeam at the Sisters of the Precious Brood Orphanage. She joined the order after her family forced her to give up the baby and to stop seeing the father, who left Nelson for Vancouver and became a radio personality. Is that not so, Jack MacLeod? After Simon and Simone were killed on the houseboat, Stark returned to the orphanage and Sister Moonbeam."

Jack began to weep openly, stealing quick glances at Stark across the room.

"There are villains in this tale as well, aside from the Captain, who made the decision to continue the voyage into the storm, and Luke, who arranged to transport the secret cargo. A man named Charles Dreadlock, a prominent railroad tycoon, had contracted with Luke to take the gold in exchange for passage to the Far East aboard one of Dreadlock's freighters. Dreadlock wanted the gold to help finance the expansion of his empire. He had in turn commissioned a young architect named France Ratzlaff to design and build the finest waterfront hotel in the Dominion of Canada."

Holmes walked back to the table where Watson sat, two coconut shells with straws and tiny umbrellas before him. Holmes picked one up, took a long sip and returned with it to the dance floor.

"Cuban Missile Crisis. Good choice, Watson. Where was I? France Ratzlaff did not design and build the hotel for Charles Dreadlock, in part due to the events that followed the sinking of the *Ainsworth*. Charles had been counting on the gold to shore up his faltering fortune and allow him to build his Grand Funk Railway into an empire to rival Charles Foster Kane's. When the boat sank with the gold aboard, Dreadlock became something of a recluse, holing up in his mansion up the lake. Anton Ratzlaff's grandfather went back to designing and building government buildings like the Nelson courthouse, but became bitter at the loss of his chance to become the most famous architect in the Commonwealth."

Holmes paused, walked over to Stark and Zuzu's table and took the water pipe hose from Stark's hand, puffed madly for a bit, removed the chopsticks that held her hair in a Chinese bun and left one on the table before lightly caressing Watson's shoulder and returning to pace on the dance floor.

"Zuzu von Trapp received the private journal of Captain Lars, rightfully sent to her as his great-granddaughter. With the help of the journal, the chain of events following the sinking of the *Ainsworth* became a little clearer. Captain Lars put a portion of the gold in each of the coffins of his victims. He made an arrangement to have letters sent to their descendants once a century had passed. You are the descendants of those victims of Captain Lars. Because of this connection you have all been in grave danger of late. Chief Inspector Francois Davide can attest to the danger and the recent spate of murders in our normally quiet town."

The Chief Inspector nodded and made a gunshot-to-the-side-of-the-head gesture. Holmes motioned to Cooper, who this time appeared to pull a beer from Marcia's cleavage before firing it to Holmes. The miming proved too much for Master Ho, who pounced upon young

Cooper and instantly had him on the floor. Zuzu rushed over and lead Master Ho back to his seat with the help of a cup of jasmine tea.

"Years after Charles Dreadlock became a recluse he heard rumours of the gold boulder's discovery and some mysterious letters. His banker had had an affair with the postmistress and Charles used blackmail to obtain a copy of a letter and the mailing list. He summoned France Ratzlaff and entered into an arrangement to recover the letters, extract their clues and eliminate the intended recipients. Ratzlaff began his well-documented slide into insanity and became a ready partner. With the fortune in his sights, Charles Dreadlock sailed to England to fulfill his dream of creating the greatest transportation and hotel empire in the world. He met with the owners of the White Star Line in London, and they agreed to join forces once he had secured his expansion capital. Unfortunately, Charles Dreadlock chose to return home on the maiden voyage of RMS *Titanic*. He did not set foot on dry land again. When France Ratzlaff heard the news of his associate's demise, he sped up his slide into madness. He left town and spent his final years tormenting his wife and young son with his demented ramblings. Decades later, after his father's demise, his son returned to Nelson, taking up residence in the house Charles Dreadlock had owned and assuming the guardianship of Dreadlock's orphaned grandson. He made a fortune running boatloads of rum across the border during prohibition and built up a criminal empire, which his son Anton took over after his death. He kept young Damian Dreadlock out of the criminal limelight, but encouraged his dark tendencies and the mad plan to kill off the descendants of the *Ainsworth* disaster in the hopes of finding the gold, which had risen in value to close to twenty million dollars."

Holmes abruptly stopped her monologue and walked around the room slapping the heads of those nodding off in the audience.

"The killings, beginning with a few boating accidents and leading up to the houseboat explosion, and more recently, the golf cart explosion and bathtub and piano murders, were all deaths involving drowning. If anyone had managed to link them, they would be looking for someone seeking revenge for the sinking of a paddlewheeler a century before. If they had discovered the group of descendants, they would not have been looking outside it for the murderer. In fact, the logic is correct. It does no good to eliminate members of a group if you will not be left to claim the prize at the end. Chief Inspector Davide, you may now arrest the person responsible for at least twenty murders over the past forty years: Mr. Damian Dreadlock. You will find, Chief Inspector, that Mr. Dreadlock is the real kingpin behind the Ratzlaff criminal organization. He ordered the killings of Simon and Simone Nakid and ten others on a houseboat on Kootenay Lake in 1983, continuing the work of his mentor. You might also take into custody their accomplice amongst this group of descendants—"

Stark leapt to his feet.

"Jesus McMurphy."

"Correct. A quest for world domination, and a general lack of insight, resulted in the evil partnership between Damian Dreadlock and Jesus McMurphy."

Chief Inspector Davide stood up and slapped the cuffs on the table just as the windows facing Baker Street imploded and three figures carrying Uzis and dressed in SWAT-team fatigues swung into the room on ropes from a waiting helicopter. The leader ripped the mask from his face and Damian Dreadlock addressed the room.

"I'll take those blackened fowl, ladies and gents. I have waited a long time to regain the rightful legacy of my grandfather. Mr. McMurphy was kind enough to let us in on the location of your little gathering."

Stark calculated the combat options available and found that without the help of automatic rifles or attack dogs, the odds were stacked against the good guys. As he surveyed the room he thought he noticed that the bronze statue was carrying the water vessel on her other shoulder. When he looked again it was back where it belonged. Holmes interrupted Dreadlock.

"The odds may be stacked against us, Mr. Dreadlock, but we have the law on our side. 'Asses are made to bear and so are you'—*Taming of the Shrew*, act two, scene one. It reminds me of 'The Case of the Twice-Pierced Rack.' If you surrender now, we could assure you of a prison sentence of no more than four consecutive life terms. Inspector Davide has only to raise his hand to signal a squad of police officers to pounce."

Damian Dreadlock turned his Uzi toward Inspector Davide and shot him once in each bicep. The inspector glared at Holmes and crumpled to the ground clutching both wounds. When Stark and Watson heard Holmes convey the "Twice-Pierced Rack" secret code, they moved quickly to unscrew the chopsticks Holmes had left on the table, remove the poison dart from inside and insert it into the end of a water pipe hose. As Inspector Davide crumpled to the floor both Stark and Watson blew hard into the water pipe hoses and simultaneously fired darts into the necks of Dreadlock's henchmen. They both collapsed in a heap. Master Ho used the diversion to launch a throwing star at Dreadlock, hitting him inside the left elbow, which momentarily paralyzed his hands and caused his Uzi to clatter to the floor. Sergeant Harry Stuttgart stepped out in front of the statue and levelled his sidearm at Stark. In a blur of bronze paint, the bare-breasted statue came alive and threw the water vessel against the wall, grabbing the two short bokken from inside as it shattered. Moneypenny utilized Musashi's whirling-wind technique to hit Sergeant Harry six times in two seconds, causing a severe head wound, two broken elbows and a collapsed lung before he crumpled to the floor. Stark nodded thanks and handed her a Foreign Legion robe to cover up.

McMurphy and Dreadlock backed up toward the window, hoping to grab a rope and escape. McMurphy grabbed the first rope and was beginning his ascent out the window to the chopper when another of Master Ho's throwing stars severed the rope. He fell heavily onto the floor and was quickly pounced on by Brother Mo. Dreadlock had backed his way onto the small balcony outside the window and reached for the rope when Stark grabbed a penguin off the bar, fired it toward him basketball-style and yelled.

"Don't forget your legacy, Dread-Head."

Damian Dreadlock turned and instinctively reached to grab the black bird. He did not expect the one-hundred-pound weight or the force of the throw. The impact sent him hurtling backward as he hit the railing and sailed over it, making a lasting impression on the sidewalk below.

Jesus shook off Brother Mo, knocked Cooper to the floor and made a mad dash for the door. Master Ho pounced on him in a flash, with one knee raised and a tiger-claw grip on the throat and crotch in the classic Chen-style tai chi posture "Weasel Hits the High Notes." Paramedics arrived in short order to take Chief Inspector Davide to the hospital as Inspector Franco San Francisco frog-marched McMurphy to the squad car.

Chapter Fifty-Five

Max stopped by Stark's office before heading down to the train station. He had completed his quest. Now that Jesus McMurphy was safely behind bars, he could go back to Anaconda. He had called his friend Freddy and received an offer to join the Surf and Turf team. Marcia and her girls, as she called them, had agreed to go with him, but only on the condition that she could land a position with the *Anaconda Standard* newspaper and that Max work on his hugging skills. He got a big hug from Stark and a promise that he would venture south for a visit in the spring.

On his way out, Max held the hallway door open for a client who was on his way in. As the man stepped around Max and into Stark's office, he stubbed his toe on the portly black penguin propping the door open. Hopping around the room in pain, the client turned to Stark and glared.

Stark glanced down at the bird then gazed off into the distance. He thought of the gathering at the Foreign Legion the previous night. After the police had taken away Jesus McMurphy, the prison medics had taken away Sergeant Harry Stuttgart and the coroner had taken away Damian Dreadlock, Holmes had handed out the birds to their rightful owners—Awesome Eldorado, Friar Horace Mogadishu, Geronimo Germaine and Lonesome Bill LaRue. The Wisconsin brothers' birds were donated to the Sisters of the Precious Brood Orphanage. Two more of the birds would soon embark on a long journey. The bird holding the door open, recently delivered from the Fussy Packrat, was worth about two million and change—not a bad return for a five-dollar investment. The client hopping around the room stopped, rubbed his foot and swore under his breath.

"Son of a bitch. I think I broke my foot. What the hell is that?"

Stark placed his hand on his chin and answered thoughtfully.

"'Such stuff as dreams are made on'—*The Tempest*, act four, scene one."

Chapter Fifty-Six

Zuzu carried her suitcase up the four flights to Stark's office. She wasn't totally sure if she would be leaving or unpacking. She rapped softly on the door, twice. Inside the room, Stark made the subtle shift from dead asleep to fully awake, his cat-like reflexes responding instantly to the soft rapping at the door. He leapt from his comfy perch on the leather chesterfield, where he had spent a blissful dream-filled six hours, once he had lost consciousness while watching a *China Beach* marathon on the fifty-inch flat-screen television that sat riveted to his waiting-room wall.

Catching his foot in the blanket, Stark fell forward and instinctively rolled into a ball, hands over the genitals, in the classic Wu-style tai chi posture "Aardvark Takes One for the Team." Disregarding his own safety he tossed the blanket clear and lunged for the door. Grasping the handle in a Vulcan death grip, he ripped the door inward and leapt back with the right knee held high and arms spread wide, as if wrestling with a chest of drawers, in the classic Chen-style tai chi posture "White Crane Needs a Hug." His actions coincided with Zuzu's impatience as she stepped forward to pound more noisily on the door. As the door flew inward, Zuzu fell forward into the room and was caught reflexively by a large, naked, white crane looking for a hug.

She decided to unpack.

Chapter Fifty-Seven

The journey was relatively painless. They left Nelson at six in the morning, driving the ancient aluminum Land Rover they had borrowed from Holmes and Watson. Stark had planned the route with the same level of intricate detail that filled the rest of his life, which meant that when they were filling Betsy up with gas at the Petro-Canada and Zuzu asked which route they were taking, he decided to utilize the Douglas Adams navigational method of following the car ahead of him. The spur-of-the-moment route decision resulted in a very scenic twelve-hour journey instead of what should have been an eight-hour drive. The fact that Stark had to stop at every landmark and lookout for a group photo did not help shorten the journey. They arrived in Calgary forty-eight minutes before the Montreal flight departed and three minutes before the check-in deadline. They arrived in Montreal at midnight and spent an uncomfortable five hours on a padded bench near the twenty-four-hour Cava Java coffee bar. Check-in for the flight to Cuba came at five in the morning, with another two hours to wait inside the security enclosure before their flight departed. Stark slept for most of the four-hour flight to their destination, an island fifty miles south-southwest of Cuba in the middle of the Caribbean Sea known as Cayo Largo.

After a cursory passport check and five-minute bus ride they checked into their room and headed down to the beach in front of the hotel. They found two empty lounge chairs under the shade of a *palapa* some fifty feet on the west side of the Scandinavian section of the beach, which was marked by a sign that read "Finnish Nudity." After disrobing, they noticed Holmes and Watson, sitting three palapas to the west, raising their glasses toward Zuzu. Holmes had each of her toenails and fingernails painted alternately blue and green. Watson was managing to keep his arousal in check with a well-placed magazine. Next to them were Henderson Cairo and Moneypenny Constantinople, who gave Stark the "I'm watching you" sign. Namaste and Miko-san waved from their chairs on the far side of Holmes and Watson. One palapa to the left of Stark and Zuzu sat Marcia and Max, who bore exhausted grins.

After laying out the beach towels on the chairs and settling in, Zuzu gazed at the gorgeous turquoise water and powdery white-sand beach. A few hundred yards toward the hotel, a cloud of dust rose near the entrance to the beach. When the dust settled, two military jeeps and a black stretch limousine with four diplomatic Cuban flags on it skidded to a halt on the sand. Doors flew open and an elderly bearded man emerged delicately from the rear seat. The elderly man, dressed in military fatigues, commanded attention even as he stepped gingerly toward them on the beach. A younger aide sporting a pirate eye patch and dressed in green hospital scrubs and two soldiers with automatic weapons escorted the elderly man. Stark turned to Zuzu and shrugged.

"I told you not to bring that maple syrup in your suitcase, Zoo. These customs people do not fool around."

The military party made an abrupt stop at the Finnish nudity sign and began to disrobe. Zuzu turned to Stark.

"Does the old guy have a leather jacket on under his fatigues?"

"I think that's his skin. He must have been out in the sun for the past hundred years or so. Try not to stare."

The official brigade, wearing only hats and smiles, walked directly to a spot ten feet in front of Stark and Zuzu. The two soldiers saluted the old man, shouldered their automatic weapons and spun around to face the sea. Zuzu observed the sight before her and let out a low whistle. The elderly bearded gentleman in the green military hat snapped his fingers, causing the pirate aide to dash down the beach and bring back a chair, which he placed between Stark and Max. El Jefe gazed intently from Stark to Max and held out his hand. Stark shook it.

"Hola. You are the Nakid brothers?"

"Hola. Yes, I am Stark and this is Max. It is a profound honour to meet you, sir."

"I hope you don't mind if I sit down. My brother Raúl did not want me to make the journey here at all. I wanted to come and meet the Nakid brothers. I wanted to thank you for bringing home to Cuba the remains of your ancestors and for the generous donation of gold toward an orphanage in their name here on Cayo Largo."

Max wore the same look as when Rufus had told him his family history. An elbow in the ribs from Marcia brought him back to the moment. None of them would have even believed that El Jefe was still alive, never mind sitting here on the beach with them. The aide, whom Stark recognized as Doctor Sanchez, handed cigars to El Jefe, Stark and Max, and handed cigarillos to Zuzu and Marcia. Tall iced glasses of Cuba Libre followed. The old man lit the three cigars, took a long pull of his drink and continued.

"I wanted to meet you in appreciation for what your ancestors have done for me. When I was a younger man, I met here in Cayo Largo with your prime minister. Truly a fine man, educated, thoughtful, hard-working and dedicated to his people. We had much in common and became fast friends. I still can't believe I outlived him. I attended his funeral in Montreal to pay my respects. You may be aware that we met here in 1976. We fished during the day and talked long into the night. What you may not be aware of is an assassination attempt by Meyer Lansky, the American mobster who abandoned his Havana casinos when I came to power. Javier Nakid saved both our lives when he pushed us off the boat into the open sea. He said something about a bomb and the next thing we knew we were in the water. The boat exploded and he vanished. When he first pushed us off the boat I considered having him flayed alive, but when the boat exploded I was most grateful. He was a brave patriot, the father of Doctor Sanchez here, who was born about the same time his father met his maker. I believe Doctor Sanchez is your cousin."

Doctor Sanchez refilled their glasses, avoiding any eye contact, since nude beaches were only for tourists and were strictly against Cuban morals. He nodded meekly toward Stark and Max, then relit El Jefe's cigar.

"We swam to shore and were whisked away by special-forces personnel. The lovely Mrs. Prime Minister was so startled by the explosion while tanning on the beach that she couldn't find her top. She took it all in stride—might have been all the mojitos. She was quite a looker. I don't mind telling you that a recurring three-way fantasy involving the two of them has kept me rigid for thirty-seven years, as you can see."

Zuzu tried not to look but couldn't resist. She winced at what resembled a wrinkled Cohiba Robusto and turned to face him.

"That's such a lovely story."

Max looked dumbfounded.

"Sweet."

Stark wiped a tear from his eye.

"That's very touching, El Jefe. I am glad to bring the remains of Jugo and Jorge Nakid back to Cuba and to return the gold that was buried with them after they perished in a storm on Kootenay Lake."

They hugged goodbye and Stark was pretty sure El Jefe squeezed his ass, but he let it pass and waved to Doctor Sanchez as the Cubans retrieved their clothes.

After the old man had left, Zuzu looked around the beach at their fellow undressed patrons. She reached over and gave Stark's leg a squeeze. He squeezed back, stood up and gestured with his hands outstretched.

"My people."

Zuzu looked out over the rest of the group who had ventured, splashing and laughing like children, into the blue-green waves. She turned to Stark.

"I can't believe I'm on a beach in Cuba and I'm naked with you."

Stark pulled Zuzu up from her chair and hugged her tightly. He kissed her neck and whispered in her ear.

"I'm naked without you."

Acknowledgements

Writing a work of fiction is not as easy as it looks. It's not like you can just make this stuff up. Without the encouragement and support of loved ones and an extensive wine cellar, this book would not have been possible. I owe a debt of gratitude to Ian Shaw and Deux Voiliers Publishing for providing the opportunity to join a talented team of collaborative writers, editors, graphic artists, readers and others. Thanks to my fellow DVP authors Nicole Chardenet for editing support and advice and Gerry Fostaty for proofreading. I would like to heap thanks upon my insightful copy-editor Katherine Ovens for the amazing job she did pointing out the errors of my ways. Thanks to Ivan Kesic for the cover image. Finally, thanks to my fellow residents of Nelson, BC for the inspiration, the coffee, and the hugs.

About Sean McGinnis

Sean McGinnis grew up in the libraries of the west coast, fed a steady diet of classic detective and comic mystery fiction. He remains a herbivore and an avid reader. Stark Nakid is his first novel. He works as a public servant and is considered a manservant at home. When relieved of his duties he enjoys skiing, running, hockey, and tai chi. He shares an appreciation for the absurd with his two sons and he lives with his soulmate in Nelson, British Columbia.

About Deux Voiliers Publishing

Organized as a writers-plus collective, Deux Voiliers Publishing is a new generation publisher. We focus on high quality works of fiction by emerging Canadian writers. The art of creating new works of fiction is our driving force.

We are proud to have published *Stark Nakid* by Sean McGinnis.

Other Works of Fiction published by Deux Voiliers Publishing

Soldier, Lily, Peace and Pearls by Con Cú (Literary Fiction 2012)

Kirk's Landing by Mike Young (Crime/Adventure 2014)

Sumer Lovin' by Nicole Chardenet (Humour/Fantasy 2013)

Last of the Ninth by Stephen Lorne Bennett (Historical Fiction 2012)

Marching to Byzantium by Brendan Ray (Historical Fiction 2012)

Tales of Other Worlds by Chris Turner (Fantasy/Science Fiction 2012)

Romulus by Fernand Hibbert and translated by Matthew Robertshaw (Historical Fiction/English Translation 2014)

Bidong by Paul Duong (Literary Fiction 2012)

Zaidie and Ferdele by Carol Katz (Illustrated Children's Fiction 2012)

Palawan Story by Caroline Vu (Literary Fiction 2014)

Cycling to Asylum by Su J. Sokol (Speculative Fiction 2014)

Stage Business by Gerry Fostaty (Crime Fiction 2014)

Twisted Reasons by Geza Tatrallyay (Thriller 2014)

Please visit our website for ordering information
www.deuxvoilierspublishing.com

www.ingramcontent.com/pod-product-compliance
Lightning Source LLC
Chambersburg PA
CBHW051304210726
48287CB00002B/666